SIGHTLINES

Pat Pack

SIGHTLINES

Leona Theis

COTEAU BOOKS
TWENTY-FIVE YEARS

This is a work of fiction. Names, characters, places, and incidents either are the product of the author's imagination or are used fictitiously. Any resemblance to actual persons, living or dead, is coincidental.

Edited by Edna Alford.

Cover image, "Seated Woman" by Helen J. Vaughn/Superstock. Reproduced by permission.

Cover and book design by Duncan Campbell.

Printed and bound in Canada at Houghton-Boston Lithographers, Saskatoon, Saskatchewan, Canada.

McCourt Fiction Series #16.

Canadian Cataloguing in Publication Data

Theis, Leona, 1955–
Sightlines
ISBN 1-55050-160-7

I. Title.

PS8589.H4517 S54 2000   C813'.6   C00–920035-5
PR9199.3.T4445 S54 2000

COTEAU BOOKS
401-2206 Dewdney Ave.
Regina, Saskatchewan
Canada   S4R 1H3

AVAILABLE IN THE US FROM
General Distribution Services
4500 Witmer Industrial Estates
Niagara Falls, NY, 14305-1386

The publisher gratefully acknowledges the financial assistance of the Saskatchewan Arts Board, the Canada Council for the Arts, the Government of Canada through the Book Publishing Industry Development Program (BPIDP), and the City of Regina Arts Commission, for its publishing program.

for Murray and Michael

and in memory of
Phyllis Elizabeth Lane Theis

CONTENTS

POWERS OF SIGHT

We built small blazes at first. Built them for the smell of fire nibbling at straw, for the thrill of the sudden flare. And for the drama of the miniature world we imagined down in the grass burning up. The fires were tragic for the tiny people who lived there. Now they must run from their minute homes and travel for a day to set up camp four feet away in a fresh forest of unscorched grass.

Lorie and Pen and I did our fire experiments in Peterson's pasture, which wasn't far from our own street. The middle of the field was in full view from our picture window, but we went in by a side path and stayed behind the poplar bluff where we'd be out of sight. The only house that bordered directly on the pasture belonged to dim-sighted old Mr. Peterson. People said he sat and watched his new TV most of the day, his chair pulled right up close to the screen so he could see the shadows and light that went with the sound.

1

We went to the pasture often. Lorie was the one doing the honours, usually. Building a low stook out of dry grass, striking a wooden match from the box she'd swiped from her mother's kitchen, glancing over her shoulder toward town when the stook caught fire. The three of us stomping the fire out once the straw bundle had burned completely. Wiping our canvas running shoes on the thick quack grass in the ditch, trying to scrape the disobedient smell of hot rubber off the soles.

The day we had a blaze we couldn't stomp out we ran out of the pasture the roundabout way and picked up the path that took us back into town behind the school. A block from home Lorie said, "Wait. Slow down. Act like we just came from climbing trees over by the school." Lorie was the boss, which was fine with Pen and me. We forced ourselves down to a casual pace, kept it up all the way to where Lorie's house faced ours across the gravel street. We split up, Lorie to her place, Pen and I to ours.

Mom was in the kitchen making cookies. She'd spilled flour in thin trails on the countertop and there was a small white mound of it on the floor, but her dress, which she hadn't bothered to cover with an apron, was still clean and fresh and blue.

Pen and I said hello and went straight to the living room. We were allowed to play there as long as we were careful not to disturb the fabric and dressmaking patterns and the dummy that was always partly clothed; also on the condition that we put our things away immediately if someone Mom was sewing for dropped by. Pen took out the Betsy McCall cut-outs she hadn't played with for over a year and I picked up my sketchbook and started to

2

draw. A pencil in my hand calmed me down, made me feel I had control over some small thing, whatever else was going on. I was drawing horses that summer. Most girls my age were doing the same, if they could draw at all. We did it by formula, a set of straight lines and curves and triangles put together in a known way. A full, round jawbone, a wavy mane rolling along the neck like a waterfall. The consensus was that my drawings were better than average. I knew how to lay shadows in just the right places and erase out highlights to show where light played on the hide and the mane.

Mom came into the living room with her Pyrex bowl and her sticky wooden spoon held carefully away from her bodice, and stood there talking about Grandma's recipe for gumdrop gems. She looked out the picture window and her back went suddenly broomstick straight. "Is that smoke in Peterson's pasture?" She set her bowl in the armchair and twirled the crank on the phone, still looking out the window.

"Nettie," she said when the operator came on. "Fire in Peterson's pasture!" Not two seconds later, the siren on top of the telephone office uptown began to blare. The same siren gave a short signal every weekday at twelve noon, but I'd heard the long wail that signaled a fire only twice before. Once when Marty Sonter got mad at the principal for giving him the strap in front of all the grade eights and he started a fire in the boys' basement at school for revenge. And again the night Gerwing's house caught fire, over at the edge of town where it lit the sky. The next day every girl in grade three gave one of her own dresses to Sarah Gerwing because her clothes had burned up.

The volunteer firemen rushed past our house, in cars and trucks, on foot, down to Peterson's pasture. Paul Tredwell from the hardware, who ran right up to Mr. Peterson's door and yanked it open; Norman Shepherd and two crewmen from the railway station; Ginger Mack in his overalls. Mr. Nichol from the grocery store, driving the old truck with the red-painted plywood box that held the tank and the hose. We'd given them all something to get excited about on a hot afternoon, expanded the thrill to someone beyond ourselves. Judging from the number of people who came running out to see, they were happy to be let in on it, even though the blaze was under control within minutes.

THE SUMMER OF THE PASTURE FIRE was also the summer they put up the fancy new street lights in Flat Hill, the summer we started looking over our shoulders, Pen and Lorie and I. Looking for the electric eye, the mysterious gadget that kept watch so it knew when to turn the lights on at just the right shade of twilight. If it could see when the dark arrived, what else could it see?

Mom was the one who told us about the eye in the first place, the evening she came home from the special meeting. She went to every public gathering the council organized, went because Dad had been on council until his death two years before and because the town overlooked a year's back taxes on the house. And because Ginger Mack, the carpenter with hair the colour of brown sugar, was a council member.

Town council was busy bringing progress to town.

4

Flat Hill in the sixties was at a stage other towns had passed through in the fifties. Water and sewer had been brand new just two years ago. Our city cousins laughed at the fact that our phone numbers had only two digits and you still had to go through the operator for a connection. The new street lights were billed as very modern – notably more advanced than the ones down the road in Ripley, the mayor said – so modern they merited their own public event. Mom came home from the street light meeting and spoke as though she'd heard of a new kind of enchantment. The way she said 'electric eye' and raised her thick, dark eyebrows, made me think of how she called the long tube on the vacuum cleaner 'the wand' and waved it as if it could grant three wishes.

That was the way she looked at things. Fairy tales and magic hidden inside who knows what. When we were small, we used to listen on Friday mornings to a lady who read stories on the radio. We had a counter-top radio with a hard green moulded plastic casing. It suffered a bump or two from time to time – it seemed to get in the way of baking and bread making. One serious crash took a back corner off the casing and left some inner workings of the radio exposed. Now you could see into a tiny space inside, small as Dad's thumb, where a light bulb no bigger than a pea was mounted on the wall. You could imagine you were looking into a miniature room. *That room is where the story lady sits to read*, Mom said. I rolled my eyes at Pen behind her back, but then I craned my neck to look, trying to imagine what size of book the story lady would read from.

"Mom – ?" Pen asked. "Mom, does the electric eye see when Bertie Weeks holds his cat upside down by the tail?"

"No, Penny. It doesn't."

"Mom?" (me this time). "Does it see when the junior high girls go into the United Church to smoke?"

"No, Kate."

I was twelve and Pen was eleven. We knew the eye didn't see anything, really. We kept on with our questions, though, because Mom kept on answering. And because she shook her head slightly and looked surprised to hear we had thoughts in our heads that she hadn't put there.

At first I imagined the electric eye to be an awkward contraption that pointed a thick lens directly ahead. It looked something like the complicated, rust-coloured projector Mrs. Kovach asked one of the grade eight boys to thread whenever we watched films at school. Gradually, my image of the eye grew legs and walked about town, watching. Its head, rounded out like a globe, acquired the ability to swivel; its one metallic eyelid stayed open not just at dusk to mark when darkness fell, but all day and all night. I drew pictures of it, black and white, comic-book style. The legs I dreamed up for the eye were shiny stainless steel, modeled after the telescoping golf ball retriever Uncle Philip received for Christmas the year before. Under the tree, the retriever was two feet of ribbon-wrapped mystery, but once unbound and extended, it reached across the room.

We wondered, Pen and Lorie and I, if the leggy, unblinking eye followed us, tracked along behind us, on the days we borrowed bikes and pedaled six miles down the blacktop to Horseshoe Lake. (*We'll stay in town, we promise. We'll stay off the highway. Of course.*) Or did it have more important things to look for? Was it busy watching the Sawatsky boys with their BB guns, as they shot at the sign that marked the turnoff into town from the highway? (They liked the noise. Ping. Ping-ping.) Mr. Morrison, driving by, had got in the way of a ricochet once and got a nice crack in his right rear window. He gave them hell all right and everyone went on about what could've happened. But in the end nobody could stop the boys and, anyway, the grownups did it too, every year when hunting season started.

"MOM? MOM, DOES THE EYE SEE BAD GUYS?" Pen asked one day.

"No. What bad guys?" Mom said. She was at the stove, stirring a pot of soup.

"You know.... Robbers. Murderers. People who set buildings on fire."

"Arsonists, you mean," Mom said. She tasted the soup. "We don't have arsonists in Flat Hill. No murderers either. No robbers, for that matter." She spooned in salt from the jar on the cupboard, spilled a few grains, flicked a pinch of it over her left shoulder. "Keep the devil away. The bad guys too."

We believed in the electric eye the way we believed in other impossibilities; the way we believed if we walked over the grave of the small boy with the small name in the cemetery (Jon Roy, 1922-1926) a hand would reach up through turf that had settled over forty years. Reach up for the foot. We knew there was no hand, but all the same if one of us took a dare and stepped on the grave, she shivered and jumped clear.

THE DAY OF THE FIRE, Pen and I went along with Mom as she followed the fire truck over to the pasture to have a look. By the time we arrived, there wasn't much to see. Large patches of black where not long before we'd been stamping desperately on the flames, smoke rising around us, Lorie giggling, me laughing too, but feeling my shoulders shrink from the eye's powers of sight.

"It's lucky you spotted it, or it would have been quite the blaze," Ginger told our mother.

"Yes, lucky," she said and smiled and turned to go back to the house. He followed her, and Pen and I came along a few steps behind.

Ginger came in for a visit; he came around to the house almost every Saturday, checked in to see what kind of fixing up he could do. One week a tear in the screen, which Mom could easily have fixed. Once an element on the stove, which she also could have fixed. She was good at those things, just didn't get around to them. Another time it was the banister, because I'd swung back and forth around the newel post so hard and so often that the whole arrangement was wobbly.

After he mended whatever needed mending, Ginger Mack would stand in the kitchen, compliment Mom on the taste of warm cookies or the smell of fresh bread, drink a glass of water or Kool-Aid, make small talk while I counted to see how many seconds before the drip on his bottom lip fell away. I didn't mind his visits. When he smiled at Mom, or at Pen or me, it seemed like he meant it. Once in a while I wondered what Dad would have thought about Ginger coming around, but it hardly mattered because I knew Dad wasn't any place where he could think about anything, he was just gone.

Six people had died from sleeping sickness in Saskatchewan two summers before; my dad was one of them. The first signs showed up when he was at work: headache, stiff neck. They brought him home from the station; his temperature climbed. The next day Mr. Shepherd took him to the hospital in Ripley where things happened that Mom didn't discuss with us. We had ears, though; we heard conversations: swelling inside his head, convulsions, a faraway kind of sleep that wouldn't end. So much depends on chance, Mom said. The weather that year, the water standing in dugouts, the mosquito that happened to bite him being one of the ones that carried the germ. Up until that summer, he'd been known as Lucky Carl, a person good things happened to as a matter of course. The trouble with luck is that it can go bad.

People took their turns coming by to help out in the weeks after he died, treading quietly around our misfortune, cushioning it with food and tea; even doing household chores, unbidden – sweeping our floors, wiping up the bathroom, rearranging the crowded mess in the fridge, things we might have considered private if we'd cared. All of them worried about Mom – you could tell by the quick looks people gave each other, by the way they backed out the door when it was time to leave, their uneasy eyes still on our little triangle of a family. But Mom just kept on going, in spite of her reputation for being fragile as a teacup and about as practical. She had less lift in her limbs at first, but gradually she bounced back. Never stopped humming tunes she heard on the radio, anything that caught in her head and had an easily followed lilt. "Blue Skies," of all things, a tune some people might think was inappropriate for a woman so recently widowed if they'd heard the way she whisper-sang it around the house. Sometimes a hymn, "I Come to the Garden Alone," and sometimes Hank Williams, "I'm So Lonesome I Could Cry." Very quietly.

For the first few months after he died, Dad showed up in my dreams. *Yes*, he would say, *I was dead. But I'm back now*. He'd ask me did I want to drive over to the lake or go to Chan's for an ice cream cone. Later on, he stopped showing up with his invitations. Just gone. I couldn't adopt Grandma Mueller's notion of a separate place, flooded with light, where he walked around healthy as ever, surrounded by other good souls. And Mom, the person on whom I usually depended for magic, had nothing to say on the subject of heaven.

ON SUMMER NIGHTS, Pen and I waited until Mom was asleep, then slipped out the back door and into the dark, waited on the corner for Lorie to join us, and wandered off with her up and down and across the cool, shadowy streets of Flat Hill.

Some nights we walked around to the far side of the church shed where the moonlight shone on the shaggy caragana bushes. In spring we picked and chewed the yellow flowers from the hedge. In early summer we made crude, shrill whistles from the slim seed pods. We sat there, our backs to the west wall of the shed, and made up ridiculous stories about any easy target. Limp-faced Pete Stevenson, the town's best drunk. Scruffy Bing Sonter who, so the rumours said, had jam tins full of money buried in the back yard but wouldn't spend a nickel on his wife and kids. Bent old Billy who lived in a crazy shack at the north edge of Flat Hill and paid his grocery bill with money he collected going door to door selling ornamental butterflies made out of crepe paper and clothespins.

We had other nighttime destinations too. We followed the train tracks to the edge of town and sat cross-legged on the level top of the hill, cracking sunflower seeds between our teeth. We blanketed the grass with empty shells, while the cold hard ground pushed into our sitbones. We left the hill some nights and crossed the expanse of darkened golf course, out of range of the street lights, all the way to the fifth hole where the shack toilets were. Turned the flashlight beam on the verses printed inside: *Here I sit broken hearted. Paid a dime and only farted.*

Funny because it was a city rhyme. Nobody paid to go to the bathroom in Flat Hill.

Traces of parties – butts and beer bottles and cigarette foil – littered the scrubby bush behind the fifth hole toilets. I read these remains as a promise of the high school social life I'd be admitted to one day.

Other nights we climbed one of the maples that bordered the schoolyard and sat on a branch that reached across the fence and out over the sidewalk. We listened as the night changed mundane sounds into something more. Car mufflers on Main Street hit a lower note than they did in the afternoon. The open and shut of the beer parlour door, infrequent and low-key in the daytime, became at night a lively, repeated slap. Trails of dissolving conversations drifted by, from down near the freight train stopped on the tracks, from the hotel uptown, from people in cars pulled even with each other at the turnoff from the highway. Men's voices usually. Women's, occasionally. Shouts. Challenges. Backslaps. Laughter, high and low.

OTHER THINGS happened that summer.

We found a loose board, the three of us, in the big door at one end of the rink and snuck inside the dark building to search under the benches for change that had fallen out of pockets during winter hockey games. I was reaching for a dime crusted with dried mud when Lorie stopped me with a hand on my back: "Did you see that?"

I hadn't. Pen hadn't either. "There was a flash," Lorie said. "Over there – over near the boards on the other side." She told us it must have been sunlight flashing off a knife blade. She pointed to a slice of light that slanted down from a crack high in the vault of the ceiling. She whispered and nodded her head. Someone was over there in the blackness, she swore it, crossed her heart. We stopped breathing, listened. Maybe a Tramp with a Knife. The three of us crept out the way we'd come in, but much more quietly, then ran off on an unsuccessful search for someone to impress with what we'd seen.

WE TIED PEN to the poplar tree in front of the house. The rope we used was the one we'd lifted from Lorie's dad's shop with the idea of making a rope swing. We'd given up when we realized it wasn't strong enough for a swing and used it instead to practise tying hangman's nooses. Then Lorie took the rope, looked at Pen and me, and said what we needed was a real prisoner.

"Come on, you guys!" Pen yelled. "Untie me! Kate! Lorie!" She stamped and struggled and kicked backwards at the tree with the heel of her canvas runner.

When we saw the three youngest Sawatsky brothers coming up the street in their blue Ford, Morgie at the wheel, fifteen years old, driving without a licence and shooting gravel behind the tires, Lorie and I ran around the corner of the house to hide. Left Pen with her hair hanging in her eyes and her shirt all crooked and her new childish breasts forced straight out in front because of the way we'd tied her wrists together behind the trunk. The boys drove past once, burned a U-ball, drove by again, and then they were gone. Pen cried the rest of that afternoon, had to be coaxed to go to school the next day.

I was two jaggedy halves – one part kids' games, the other part half-considered ideas about what would come next. Lorie and Pen and I each had a crush on a different Sawatsky boy. I was just old enough to like boys, which meant only that I wanted them to like me back. I didn't contemplate possibilities beyond that, except to daydream about what Donna Cardiff did when I saw her get into boys' cars and ride off.

Donna was the only girl in our end of town who had a figure already. A high school girl. All the boys liked her. Pen and Lorie and I waited for the day that boys would ask us into their cars. They would hold our hands, gently touch our faces, say nice things to us.

And everything would be a little enchanted, the way it was between Ginger Mack and Mom.

IT RAINED for an entire week in July. The day it stopped we went out to loosen the springs coiled inside our leg muscles from being in the house so long. Everything looked different, the way it does after a rain. The way a picture looks if you use tempera paints instead of pencil crayons. The green trim on Nichols' house was brighter, the dirt roads were blacker. The cracks in the sidewalk had multiplied. They showed up now as a network of dark, wet veins.

Down by the school a man in an old Pontiac like the one my uncle used to have rolled his window down a few inches and called to us. We couldn't hear what he said. We knew he wasn't from Flat Hill.

"Probably looking for directions," Lorie said. We stepped around puddles at the side of the road, walked over to his car. The ground was still muddy, the air rain-damp. Rivulets ran down the steamy car windows, grey hair stuck to the man's forehead in distinct, damp curls, and drops of sweat or water made tracks down his temples and slid into the corners of his wet eyes.

"How'd you girls like to make two bucks?" he said.

"What for?" Lorie asked him.

He said something else I couldn't hear. He rolled his window all the way down and motioned for us to look inside the car. I was behind Lorie; her shoulder blocked my view. Then – whish! – Lorie spun around so her back was to the man in the car. She moved so quickly Pen and I had to jump back.

"Let's get the hell out of here!" she said. We walked off as quickly as we could without running, Pen and I taking our cues from Lorie, until we reached the reassurance of Main Street.

"How come we left so fast?" Pen asked. "What did he say?"

"He said he wanted a piece of tail," she said, looking straight ahead. Then she looked at us and grinned a little. I grinned too, because it was dirty talk, and you always grin at dirty talk. I knew what the expression meant but I had nothing accurate to go on. The naked pictures we found picking through magazines at the junkyard were all of women. The man's part I made up from things Lorie had said and from the way the boys looked in their wet trunks at Horseshoe Lake.

"Had his pecker right in his hand," Lorie said. "We should sic the electric eye on him. Keep a watch on the dirty old bugger."

"Right," I said.

In August, Lorie went off to Winnipeg to visit her cousins and Pen and I were left on our own. We continued to wander, developed our own habits. We made discoveries in the ditches alongside the highway and the grid roads. You can find a lot in the ditch if you keep your eyes on the ground. A singleton work boot, full of dirt and with brittle yellow grass growing out at the ankle; a torn red shirt to make up a crime story about; a crescent wrench, rusted somewhat, which I pocketed and presented later to Mom, who seemed pleased and put it in the junk drawer.

There were bluebells in the ditches and thin, round sedge grass that was special because we could thread the hollow stalks back into themselves to make ankle bracelets. We found purple vetch vines and braided them into crowns and became empresses; we found the fat, jointed reeds that Mom called prairie bamboo, the ones with pointed black tips that you can dip in a bottle of India ink and use for a drawing pen. Until they dry up and fall apart, section by section. Best of all, we found bottles that we gathered in gunny sacks and turned in for two cents apiece, beer bottles to the hotel, pop bottles to the café. Mom called it free money and she let us spend it on pop and jawbreakers.

Pen and I still wandered out after dark. We went to the church shed and just sat, up close to each other, warm in our wool sweaters. Or we climbed to our favourite perch in the maple tree at the school and listened to what there was to hear. As we sat there one night, a group of kids came along down the sidewalk that ran underneath the branch. Older kids, mostly grade nines and tens. Marty Sonter and Brenda Woodrow and some others. Freddie Gunther, who was way older and probably pulled the beer for them. And sophisticated Donna Cardiff.

They laughed and swore and shoved each other roughly off the sidewalk and onto the street.

"Who's got the fuckin' beer?"

"Wait up, I gotta take a leak."

"Don't do it on the flowers at the principal's house."

"Why not? S'good for the snapdragons!"

Pen and I looked at each other, grinned in the dark. We waited until the group was a couple of blocks ahead, then nodded to each other and dropped down, followed the voices out to the golf course and across it in the moonlight.

The group set their six-packs down in the clearing in the bushes near the fifth hole. Pen and I crept up unseen and found a hollow place big enough for two bodies inside a clump of scrub chokecherries. We squatted there in our observation post, screened off from the others. Pen backed up – clink – into four or five beer bottles left from some private party. She picked up two of the empties and dumped a dripping butt out of one, letting out the ash-beer smell. She held the bottles in front of her eyes with their long necks pointing ahead like misshapen binoculars. Through the branches, I could see where Marty Sonter was moving closer to Donna on the grass. The others, six or seven of them maybe, were in a group at the far end of the clearing. I couldn't hear much of what Marty and Donna said. My insides heated up at the thought of being so close to a boy that way.

"All the boys like her," I whispered to Pen. Then I heard Donna talking. I couldn't tell quite what she was saying, but I didn't like the sound of her voice. And then Donna was on her back in a puddle. Right in the mud with Marty on top of her, the two of them thrashing around. Muck coated the hair on the back of her head so it twisted into ropes.

I moved closer for a better look and I said, "Pen, take those bottles off your eyes and watch this." Pen watched and I watched and I could hear Donna because her voice was louder now and she said, *No Marty, I don't want to*, and he said, *How come? It's not like you never did it before*, and she said, *Leave me alone, you pig.*

17

The others stayed at the far end of the clearing and none of them paid any attention to Donna and Marty. Marty said, *Come on, Donna, do me a favour here, come on.* He pushed, fumbled at her pants, fell sideways on his elbow, swore, fumbled at her again.

Pen put those stupid bottles up in front of her eyes again and I said, "Give me one of those," and took it right out of her hand. I raised it and looked for an opening in the branches, thinking I should throw it at Marty Sonter's moving behind. But I didn't and I didn't and still I didn't. Pen said to me, "What are you doing, Kate?" She said it so loud Marty looked straight at the chokecherry bush we were crouched behind. We ran as fast as we could, Pen and I, and we heard him yell, *Hey!* but he never caught up to us and maybe he didn't try very hard.

LORIE CAME BACK from her trip and told us about everything she'd seen in Winnipeg. She said her aunt and uncle drank booze at every meal except breakfast. She said her aunt took her to a store that was four stories high, plus a basement. She said she'd seen a street in downtown Winnipeg where half the women were prostitutes; she knew because she'd heard her aunt say so to her uncle.

Pen and I told Lorie what we'd seen happen between Marty Sonter and Donna Cardiff on the golf course. The last part I changed a little. I said I'd thrown the beer bottle and got Marty right where it counted. I thought it made a better story that way, me actually doing something instead of just watching. Pen didn't let on it wasn't true.

"No kidding." Lorie said.

"No kidding."

Lorie said, "That's nothing." She told us her uncle went to a store in Winnipeg where all they sell is just newspapers and magazines, rows and rows of them. He bought a paper there that said a woman in Montana gave birth to a baby that looks like a monkey and it even has a tail, a little one, and now she's in a coma but the baby is doing fine. There were photographs to prove it. Her uncle was going to mail her the newspaper when he was through with it, Lorie said, so she could take it to school in September for current events day. Then we could look at the pictures for ourselves.

But I was thinking that what you see or don't see isn't such a big deal. We'd thought all summer about that oversized eye stalking through town as if it was some kind of a cop, but it didn't actually *do* anything. Didn't stop us from lighting fires, didn't discourage that guy from pulling his pecker out – if that's what he'd done; didn't rein in Marty Sonter; didn't stop anything, no matter what crossed its sightlines. All it did was look around.

AIR MASSES

It's hot, sweltering. It's been that way for days now, so hot the milk is turning sour, as if even the fridge isn't equal to the challenge. There was a storm last night. A tornado touched down east of the city; it flung buildings apart and pulled up trees and put them through a spin cycle. The temperature in the city dropped fifteen degrees in a single hour after dinner, but this morning the cement patio on the south side of the house was baking again by breakfast time. When Mellie went out to water the flowers this afternoon, she turned the hose on the cement first to wet it down so she wouldn't scorch the soles of her bare feet. Now the city crouches in that still poise it assumes in the heat of a summer afternoon – the kind of heat that could build into another round of thunderstorms and funnel clouds, or then again might just dissolve in a late afternoon breeze.

Mellie's nighttime dreams have multiplied, as they

sometimes do in the heat. She dreamed her old dream of waking up in a department store wearing nothing but a mauve slip; and the other one where she was back in school writing exams for subjects she'd never studied. She dreamed of driving up a hill, a hill that became steeper and steeper as she climbed, the wheels lifting off the road when the grade became finally too abrupt, the car drifting backwards in slow somersaults through still, quiet air.

Paul doesn't seem to understand about dreams of falling. A dream about hills, he told her this morning, doesn't make sense for a girl from the prairies. He must be unaware that it takes almost no effort of imagination to exaggerate a landscape – at night, in the dark, in a dream. And apparently he's forgotten about the hills hidden in the countryside back home. Not the low hummock close to the grain elevators that gave Flat Hill its name – it wasn't much of a hill – but the other ones, the ravines that took you by surprise on country roads; slopes that, instead of rising from the horizon, slid suddenly below it.

Earlier today, Paul picked up the boys from Carol's place and took them out east of the city to see the damage from the tornado. Mellie declined to go along. It isn't that she doesn't like the boys. In fact, she enjoys the time she spends with them. They're good kids, well-mannered for teenagers, rarely bored with themselves. In some ways it's a shame she only sees them on odd weekends.

Just over two years ago, the day Paul got his decree absolute, punctuating the divorce he and Carol had been moving toward for years, he'd said to Mellie,

"We'll have the boys every second weekend, let's buy the three-bedroom we looked at in East Hill, get out of this apartment. Move as soon as we can so they'll have a second home. Have Dad come and stay for a week or so every summer so the boys don't lose touch with their grandpa."

Instant family, Mellie had thought. One divorce didn't seem to make Paul wary of a second marriage. When she'd gone so far as to ask him about that, he'd made a joke of it. "The first time is just practice," he'd said. When Mellie reminded him of the obvious – that this would be the first marriage for *her* and did that make it *her* practice run? – he'd smiled and told her he couldn't think of a single thing she needed practice at.

Today, on his way out to get the boys, he'd stood at the door patting his pockets for his keys and asked if she was sure she didn't want to come along. She'd located his keys on the counter by the coffee maker, tossed them to him and said, "No thanks. Say hi to the kids." She didn't feel any need to join an expedition to see property damage. There's enough of that on the TV news.

This year tornadoes and other fierce winds are a regular occurrence, it seems, and it's still only June. There is no explanation and there are a dozen explanations. People talk about climate change; they talk about volcanoes erupting in the Pacific and skewing the weather patterns; they talk about the end of the millennium or the end of the world. When Mellie was a girl, any wind powerful enough to toss houses around and kill people and animals was rare, wasn't it? Something that happened in books or movies or the

United States. Which was why the one tornado she could remember had created such excitement.

"Remember the tornado in Blake," she'd said to Paul last night.

"You mean when we were kids?"

"Yeah."

"Vaguely," he said. "I never went to see."

MELLIE HARDLY KNEW PAUL when they both lived in Flat Hill. He was older; his family occupied one of the higher rungs on the short social ladder. His father owned the hardware store and the family was well off in the small town way that during the sixties meant they had a few things other people didn't have – the first colour TV in town, a new car every three years, running water from their own well even before the town put in the water lines.

Paul had eventually taken over the hardware business, but that was long after Mellie herself had left town. Some time in the eighties, he'd allied his store with a major chain; it was the only way to keep a business like that going in a small town. The store is still there, out in Flat Hill, but he's hired someone else to run it for him. When Paul saw the chance to move to the city and buy into a flagship store in the same chain, he took it, moved to Saskatoon with Carol and the boys. Mellie's glad Paul has his finger in more than one financial pie; his first family is still in the big house in Lawson Heights and it's surprising how much money kids need for clothing and lessons and sports equipment and even for school, which Mellie thought was supposed to be free.

PAUL SAYS he doesn't recall much about Mellie from back home, says he just remembers a skinny kid and he'd never have recognized her if she hadn't come up to him that night in the Artful Dodger and said, "Aren't you from Flat Hill?" Mellie could do that sort of thing by then, just walk up and say that. She could do it because by then she'd found out that the divisions that kept people apart in her home town were erased by time and – mysteriously – by living in the city. And she could do it because after eighteen years at Stereo Source they'd made her assistant manager that week and she was feeling buoyant.

THERE ARE DAYS when Mellie feels she somehow woke up inside the wrong life. Or the right one. On her day off, after Paul's gone and she's loaded the breakfast dishes into the dishwasher, she sits and reads the paper and drinks coffee from her favourite over-sized mug. Two sugars for her sweet tooth. She feels the house around her. Mellie likes her house so much that sometimes she leaves the newspaper spread on the table and walks through the rooms still carrying her coffee mug. She stares into a Robert Hurley print or sits in the armchair and looks at the piano Paul inherited from his grandmother. Keys reflected in the glossy wood, leafy shapes carved into the front legs. She walks upstairs and makes the bed and watches the light and the wind move through the elm branches that shade the bedroom window. She touches the wall lightly as she passes through the hallway, comes back down to the kitchen and looks out the window at the six kinds of lilies that bloom all at once in the back yard.

Once in a while, on days when Mellie feels particularly safe about the distance between past and present, she'll make some mention to Paul of her mother or father, both dead for years now. Paul says he only remembers a few things about them. Her mother, he can picture on the stage of the town hall singing *Crazy Arms* the night they taped the amateur hour for radio. He remembers Mellie's dad, he says, only as the man who swept the floors at the store for a few years, never caused problems for Paul's dad, and always moved out of the way for customers.

Mellie thinks Paul remembers more than he lets on, but maybe he doesn't. Maybe history isn't terribly important to him. "What about the money in the jam tins?" Mellie asked him once. "You must remember the thing about the jam tins?"

"Jam tins. Jam tins?"

"There was a group of boys who used to make fun of Dad, used to say he had a fortune buried in jam tins in the back yard."

"Maybe I heard that. I don't know. I bet every town has a story like that, some character who's supposed to have a million bucks buried in the yard or under the mattress or stashed away in sacks in the root cellar."

"They believed it though," Mellie said. "They came right into the back yard once and dug holes looking for it."

"You mean they made up a story and then they believed their own story?"

MELLIE SONTER, twelve years old, sat leaning against the brick wall of Flat Hill school, high up on the iron fire escape platform. She'd just finished carving her initials into the soft sand-coloured brick beside the fire door, using a nail someone else had left up there, probably after doing the same thing. She sat forward and looked around. From here, she could see all the way out to the highway if she looked south; if she turned around and looked north, she could see past the grain elevators and the railway tracks and out to the water tower. She heard cars going by on the highway, dull rumbles. She heard sparrows singing in the maple trees that bordered the schoolyard and she heard the empty metal rings on the flagpole ting-tinging with the wind in the purposeless way they did all through July and August when the janitor didn't raise the flag.

Mellie loved to sit here; up here she had a kind of power. Even if someone mean or someone who made her nervous cut though the schoolyard, odds were they wouldn't see her; they'd have no reason to look up. She would call out if she saw someone she wanted to talk to – sometimes she startled people on purpose that way – or she could just keep quiet if she didn't want to be noticed.

As Mellie surveyed the schoolyard and its surroundings, Linda Murphy came out of the house across the street. She was one of the principal's daughters, a girl with bleached skin, pale eyes that were barely blue, limp hair that was a weak shade halfway between brown and grey, a girl so colourless you wanted to pick up a crayon and fill her in. Linda crossed the street to the schoolyard and lay on her stomach on the teeter-totter,

SIGHTLINES

slanted upward, chin propped on her hands, a book in front of her.

Linda had latched on to Mellie this summer, as she had last summer. Summer was Mellie's time of year. She never felt quite at home in the ordered world of the school year – though she did all right with the work; she'd never flunked a single test. But in the summertime she could pick and choose what she did, could do whatever made her feel good. In summer, girls like Linda were more friendly toward her, girls who didn't seem to know what to do with themselves if their time wasn't organized for them by someone else. Linda came looking for Mellie sometimes in the summer. She let Mellie make decisions about where they should go, what they should do for fun. She even let Mellie boss her around a little.

"Hey, Linda," Mellie shouted. "Look where I am." Linda looked up, her hand shading her eyes so Mellie could hardly see her face.

"Come on up."

Linda left her book and came puffing up the fire escape. Her steps shook the platform slightly and the soles of her runners made a dull ringing sound against the iron stairs.

"Sixteen, seventeen, eighteen," Linda said, counting the stairs the way they did. She sat down on the platform facing Mellie.

"You hear about the tornado?" Linda asked.

Mellie looked at her.

"At Blake," Linda said. "People are driving over there to see what it did. Everyone's meeting at three o'clock at the parking lot by the train station. Anyone with extra room in their car and anyone who needs a ride."

"You going?"

"Yeah," Linda said. "Dad's taking us."

"Can I go with you?"

"Won't be room. Sorry."

"Oh."

"Well, my aunt and uncle are coming with us too." Linda said.

"Oh."

MELLIE CAUGHT A RIDE in the last car leaving the parking lot that afternoon. All the others had pulled away when she walked up to Mr. Gunther, who was standing by his red Dodge with the driver's door already open, and asked him if he had room for her.

"Your mom and dad say you could go?" Mr. Gunther asked her.

"Yeah, they said I could go."

"Because I'm not taking anyone if their parents don't know where they are." He looked down at her. "Get in if you're getting in," he said. "Not much room left."

Mellie took a breath and climbed into the last free spot, in the back seat beside Ox Kovach. Ox was in her class at school, but he was older; he'd been held back twice. He was usually mean to Mellie if her older brother Marty wasn't within earshot, but he couldn't bother her here, not with five other people in the car besides themselves. It was half an hour south to Blake on a dusty grid road and all the windows were down to fight the heat. Mellie's hair whipped her cheeks. A few miles into the trip, the road banked around a slough. The angle of the car as it rounded the curve pressed Ox's weight toward Mellie. As the car straightened again, the motion slid his body back to where it should be and slackened the pressure of his thigh on hers, but right away again he pressed his thick leg against her thin one and kept it there. It was nothing she could call him on; the car was crowded, Ox took up a lot of space, and there were bumps and sways to contend with. She moved herself closer to the door and he used the next bump in the road as an excuse to follow.

When they finally arrived in Blake, she opened the door and hardly waited for the car to stop properly before she scrambled out. Ox was close behind. He leaned down in her direction, spoke quietly so no one else could make out the words, "Smelly Mellie, if I marry you, can we dig up all the money your old man has buried in the back yard?"

She stepped away from him. She knew how to handle this; she was used to saying *as if I care*, over and over inside her head until she just about meant it. Ox walked off in one direction and Mellie went another. People wandered in ones and twos among the torn-apart houses and trailers, people from Flat Hill and people she didn't know, from other towns. The tornado had touched down right at the edge of town and a farmyard had taken part of the hit. Mellie saw a grain auger that was bent back on itself like a giant hairpin. She headed over to what used to be a house. The ragged wood smelled wet from the rain that had come with the tornado.

"Just look at this house," a woman beside her said to

anyone who'd listen. She seemed almost pleased. She was a slim woman, wearing a print, A-line skirt, picking her way through the mess in a polished pair of flats, as if she were on her way to church. "Reduced to a pile of sticks," she said.

But they weren't sticks at all. They were boards and half-walls, and most of the roof was still intact, as if you could jack it up to its former height if only you had sound walls to go underneath it.

"Look at the devastation," the same woman said to a well-dressed man coming toward her through the remains of a vegetable garden. He wore pants with a crease and a pressed white shirt with a loosened tie. "The potato beetles survived the tornado," he said as if he were in some way proud of their fortitude. The woman tore a scrap of powder blue wallpaper from an exposed wall. "Just look at the devastation," she repeated.

Mellie walked across the road to the remains of a house trailer. A boy who'd been shuffling through nearby piles of rubbish looked up. "That's my house," he said. He must have been about the same age as Mellie, because their eyes were at the same level when she met his look. His hair was dull brown, and parted so that a loose fan of it hung in front of one eye. He pushed his bottom lip out and blew straight up so the hair lifted for a second, then resettled.

Two men stood close to Mellie and the boy, shaking their heads over a toppled pine tree, its roots spread in the air like a many-fingered hand looking for something to grab hold of. "I heard this is all because of the Russians and their nuclear testing," one of them said.

"All the weather patterns are messed up this year and that's what it's from."

"You better believe it," said the other man.

"Look," the boy said to Mellie. He lifted a corner of aluminum and wallboard that used to be a trailer wall. He pointed underneath. "That's my room," he said.

The wind had taken the trailer apart and left it in half a dozen twisted heaps. When Mellie followed the boy's gesture and peered underneath the wall, she saw a yellow, diamond-patterned floor and the corner of what might be a green curtain or bedspread. "Wow," she said. "That's something. You're sure lucky."

"I wasn't in there," he said. "I would've been, but my mom's baby came yesterday. Dad took her to the hospital last night just about an hour before the tornado hit, and I went over to my aunt's house. He pointed to a grey-and-white two storey a few houses away that had no more damage than random patches of missing shingles and a split maple tree in the front yard.

"You shoulda heard the noise," he said. "Like ten trains all at once. My aunt made us go down to the basement and the next minute it was over and done with."

"Yeah?"

"Yeah. That's not all. Come here, I gotta show you something," he said.

Mellie hesitated. She didn't want to lose track of Mr. Gunther, didn't want to miss her ride back. The boy had walked away without looking to see if she was with him, but he hadn't gone far. He stopped near a power pole. Mellie followed. Two men were belted near the top of the pole working with a thick black power line.

"See that wire there," the boy said. "This morning it

was down here on the ground. It was live. Jumping and sparking."

"You mean live like it could electrocute someone?" Mellie said.

He nodded. "I touched it," he said. He nodded again.

"You couldn't have," she said. "You'd be dead."

"I did it."

Mellie could see people moving toward the parked cars. She wanted to get back to Mr. Gunther's car soon enough that she wouldn't end up beside Ox for the half-hour ride back to Flat Hill. She looked at the boy once more and said, "I gotta go. See ya."

"See ya," he said.

At the supper table that night, conversation started and ended with the tornado.

"I heard some people went over to Blake this afternoon," Mellie's father said. "To have a look at what the tornado done. Want to drive over there after supper, Queenie?"

"Sure. Might be a nice ride. You kids should come too. Want to come?"

Marty snorted. Mellie said no thanks, but didn't tell them she'd already seen it.

Their father ignored Marty's snort. "Some people say it's the Russians and their nuclear testing. Messes up the weather."

Marty snorted again, then let the snort grow into a laugh that sounded made up for the benefit of those who could hear it, rather than for his own pleasure.

"Don't laugh," Mellie's father said. "You explain it

then. Tornadoes don't come around too often."

"It's like that blackout a few years ago," Mellie's mother said. "Where the electricity went off all through New York and there, in the States. The TV news said it could be the Russians. They said: Just think what one Russian with a pair of pliers could do. You never know."

Marty ended up going down to Blake with their parents in spite of his pretended disinterest, but Mellie stayed home. "Fine," her mother said. "You can do the dishes then." And she did do the dishes, up to the pots and pans at least. Rather do that than go somewhere with her parents.

She didn't mind being with them as long as it was only family. Her parents left their kids alone for the most part, didn't interfere with what they did unless they got into full-scale trouble. What made Mellie shrink from being seen with her parents in public was her certainty that people could guess at every detail of their lives just by looking at them. Her mother wouldn't have embarrassed her so much if it hadn't been for her teeth. They were hard to look at, an unhealthy and uneven brown, crowded and crooked, with gaps in odd places. Mellie thought there should be a way to cover them up, at least partly, thought her mother should learn to put her hand in front of her mouth. She could have been a country and western singer if she were prettier. She could chord a song on her guitar after she'd only heard it a few times. She liked to sing "Whisperin' Pines" and the one about the wooden Indian who fell in love with an Indian maid, and she was practising "Cryin'." She hardly strained, except for the very highest notes, and if you looked somewhere else, you forgot all about the teeth for the time you were listening.

Mellie's parents rarely went by their ordinary names, Charlie and Sylvia. They had special names for each other. Her father called her mother Queenie, and even Marty used that nickname for her most of the time, though he sometimes said, without appearing to care for her feelings, that it sounded like something you'd call a favourite dog.

Mellie's mother had nicknamed her husband Bing because, she said, he looked a little like Bing Crosby. Mellie had seen Bing Crosby on TV and there was no resemblance. Her mother said it was from when they were all of them a lot younger. Bing wasn't the only name he went by at home. When the kids came along, Queenie had started once in a while calling her husband Pop. The two of them made a joke out of the fact that both her names for him were like imitations of sounds. Bing. Pop. Little noises.

Bing had a weak leg and trouble finding a steady job since the lumberyard let him go when business dropped off two years ago. He looked more like a farm hand than like Bing Crosby. He wore overalls almost every day. His face had a soft, disorganized look to it – cushions under his eyes and shallow, soft tucks in front of his ears and his hair that wouldn't stay where it was meant to. He swept floors for the storekeepers and at Phil Gunther's garage and he drove his half-ton around town delivering groceries for Nichols' Red and White. He was good-natured for the most part, but when he got mad he heated up and his face went red and then he'd explode. Hot as Hawaii when he's mad, Queenie said about Bing. His anger almost always had something to do with the mischief Marty found himself in the middle of from time to time.

Bing called Mellie his pixie girl and gave her bear hugs that squeezed the air out of her lungs. If he spent too long at the beer parlour (which didn't happen often) and came home sick and threw up, he sometimes would wake up his pixie girl to help him wipe the vomit off the floor where he'd overshot the toilet. They had to be very quiet so as not to wake Mellie's mother. Queenie didn't get mad often either, but when Bing went off alone and came home drunk, she'd scream and hit. Her own father had been a drunk, she'd remind them all. A drunken old fart, she'd shout, and then she'd say something about money and she'd go upstairs and push the bedroom door shut as far as it would go before it scraped to a stop at the place where the floorboards slanted.

Mellie's brother Marty had two sides, the side she loved and the side that made her cold and scared. He was mean to her in front of other people and good to her when he thought no one else would catch him at it. He taught her to steal chocolate bars from the Red and White store and let her keep what she smuggled out for herself. She took Oh Henrys mostly. She ate them slowly, made herself notice each bite, because they were only good for as long as they lasted and then there was a letdown.

Guys didn't mess much with Marty. He didn't go to school anymore, but he'd done grade nine in reform school after he'd been caught three times siphoning purple gas from farmers' tanks and selling it out of jerry cans. There'd been some business with a lawyer from Ripley, and a series of arguments between their mom and dad, with Queenie defending Marty, sometimes energetically and sometimes half-heartedly. Mellie wasn't in on the details and that was by choice. Whenever the shouting started, she slipped upstairs to her room. She had a way of making a tent by draping a blanket between the iron bedstead and a square-framed wooden chair that she could clothespin the blanket to. Sitting under the tent got to be one of her favourite pastimes and she even did it once in a while for no reason, when there was no fight to hide from. Marty was sent away for almost a year and Mellie learned to make herself think, *as if I care*, when people talked about him in front of her as though she weren't related.

Marty came home wearing the only real tattoo in Flat Hill. He'd met up with a scratcher in reform school who'd bought a tattoo instrument through the mail. He'd drawn an American eagle – the only pattern he knew – on Marty's left arm. The lines of the picture ran from thick to thin and thick again. Parts of it weren't clear at all. Queenie gave Marty a look of disgust when she saw the tattoo. Bing said it didn't make sense for a Canadian to have a picture of an American eagle on his arm.

"You can't take that thing off, you know," he said. "It'll be there till you die."

"That's right," Marty said. "That's the point."

"What's the eagle supposed to mean?"

Marty snorted. "All it's supposed to mean is that it's mine. Nobody takes it away. Who cares what the picture is? It's my arm and I can put on it what I want."

THE DAY AFTER she went to see the aftermath of the Blake tornado, Mellie saw Linda again at the school-yard.

"I met a boy," she told Linda. "Over in Blake."

"Is he cute?"

"Yeah, he's cute. His trailer got smashed, but nobody was in it. Did you see it, all the walls bent just like they were made out of cardboard?"

Linda shook her head. "I hardly saw anything. Dad wouldn't let us out of the car. We drove around once and went home. What's his name?"

Mellie thought quick, thought of her cousin in Ripley, borrowed his name. "Larry," she said. Mellie knew how to lie without even thinking about it. Linda was paying attention. Mellie felt herself quicken the way she always did when people paid that kind of attention. She went on. "He said there's a sports day in Blake next Saturday and he could meet up with me if I can get there."

"Are you going?" Linda said.

"Maybe."

THE ADVANCE ran a feature on the Blake tornado. There was a photograph of the bent grain auger and one of the boy who'd talked to Mellie. He was helping his father lift an accordioned sheet of metal that had been part of their trailer. The man had a serious look, but the boy wore an almost-grin. His hair hung down in front of one eye. The paper didn't give their names.

Off to one side a few paragraphs were boxed in under the heading, "How the Tornado Happened." The explanation made no reference to Russians or nuclear testing. *To understand a tornado you have to think of air as a massive, moving entity. A tornado results when a complicated pattern of updrafts and downdrafts cause the base of a thun-*

dercloud to rotate. In this case, a cool, moist air mass with easterly winds at ground level collided with another, warmer air mass moving southwest, five to ten thousand feet up in the air. They twirled themselves together with increasing speed and became a tornado.

SOMEONE CAME ONE NIGHT and dug holes in Sonters' back yard. There was no way to know who did it. It might have been Ox and his pals, it might not. Mellie heard her father shouting from the back door in the middle of the night. She heard quick footsteps beat past the house and away down the gravel street. When she went outside the next morning, she saw three big holes in the part of the yard they still called the garden even though no one had planted so much as a carrot or a marigold there in years. Whoever dug the holes had used the spade and the pitchfork that usually leaned against the house underneath the kitchen window and abandoned them in the garden when they ran off. There was another spade, one the diggers must have brought, sticking up out of the dirt, its handle splintering into the air where it had broken off when the clay resisted too strongly.

The biggest hole, at the back of the garden, was almost two feet deep and as wide as an armchair. Mellie spent the next several days enlarging it, digging it deeper, making it square, straightening the sides into solid walls. The dirt below the topsoil layer was mostly clay, which was heavy to dig but behaved well when Mellie slapped the walls into shape with the broken spade or the palms of her hands. Neither her parents nor Marty asked what she was doing.

An assortment of weathered boards had leaned against the side of the house under cover of the caraganas for as long as Mellie could remember. When she started dragging them to the garden and laying them across her hole to make a roof, her dad came out with the hammer and worked the rusty nails out, some of them at least.

"Looks good," he said. "You'll need a step down inside."

She left an opening at one end and set a shallow wooden apple box, also from the pile under the hedge, at the bottom to make climbing in and out manageable. She couldn't stand up inside, but she could sit comfortably. Inside her dirt cave she cut designs on the walls with a stick and carved cubbyholes to keep things in and built clay platforms for candles. When she was inside, the hole smelled comfortably of flame and warm wax.

Mellie never invited friends to her real house, but she brought Linda Murphy over to see her hole in the garden. They hunkered down inside. The girls sat facing each other with their knees up and their backs to the dirt walls. They giggled and talked and Mellie told Linda things that weren't necessarily true. She said her mom and dad were saving up to take her on a trip to Banff to see the bears. She said she was having her periods already, had been for months. She told Linda to get the box of wooden Eddy matches out of the cubbyhole in the wall and she lit a candle.

"You're allowed to have candles in here?" Linda said.

"I don't know. I just have them."

"You could start a fire, you know."

"I did once," Mellie said.

"Really? You really had a *fire?*"

"Burned two of the roof boards before I could put it out. Had to find new ones."

"I don't believe you," Linda said. "How'd you put it out?"

Mellie kept her eyes on the candle she'd just lit, moved it down to a lower platform, sniffed the wooden match in her hand to smell the spent sulphur. "Water from the rain barrel," she said.

"All by yourself?"

"Swear to god," said Mellie.

After Linda went home for supper, Mellie stayed crouched inside her hideaway house and looked out through the opening at the two and a half slumping stories of the real house. If a tornado came and took it apart, they'd have to find another place to live. That would be fine. As for her own little underground space, Mellie made an effort to stormproof it. She got Marty to help her roll four old tires across the yard and arrange them over the roof boards as weights. He even put rocks inside some of them for extra weight. He stopped when the job bored him. Mellie half expected a tornado but summer slipped away with nothing more than one dump of slushy hail in August.

IT WAS A COLD DAY in late November. A Saturday, a day for chores. Dick Heise, the water man from Ripley, came by and lowered four blocks of ice into the nearly empty water barrel in the corner of the kitchen. Mellie's mother gave her the usual job, standing on a chair and stirring the glassy bricks of ice around in the water with a broomstick. Or trying to stir them, that is. It was an awkward task for someone Mellie's size, but Queenie was convinced it made the ice melt faster, and she wanted to wash clothes.

Dick Heise had brought some news with him and hadn't been shy about telling it. "You know they're looking for your boy?" he said to Bing.

"My boy?" Bing said.

"Marty. That's your boy, right?"

"Yes."

"Someone said he's the one tried to sell a hot socket set over in Ripley. Phil Gunther had already phoned to the garages in all the towns around to be on the lookout. Said he missed it first thing this morning."

Bing turned away, walked to the table, picked up his cigarette papers, opened his can of Export and rolled himself a smoke.

"The fellow in the garage would've been suspicious anyway," Dick said. "A teenager walking in with a good socket set like that. As soon as he started asking questions, the boy took off in a big hurry."

Bing stood at the table and smoked. Dick took his ice money from Queenie and left. Bing opened the door of the cupboard beside the fridge. The keys for the hardware and for the Red and White and for the lumberyard were all on their nails, but the keys for Phil Gunther's garage were missing.

The back of his neck reddened and the next second he exploded. "So now, Queenie. You going to stick up for him this time?"

Queenie put her purse away in the drawer, moved along the counter, swept up some crumbs with the side of her hand, put a loaf of bread in the breadbox. She sat down. "Wait and hear what he has to say at least," she said.

Bing sat at the table with his coffee and his cigarette. He watched the door as if he dared Marty to come through it. He sat for a long time. No one said a word. Mellie kept pushing the ice around. She could see rainbows way in the middle of the ice blocks, appearing and disappearing according to how the light fell.

When Marty finally came home, there was no waiting to hear what he had to say for himself. He walked in the door with a cold rush of winter air and a false grin which he lost in the split second before Bing was on him with both fists. Mellie and her mother moved from one corner of the kitchen to the other to keep out of the way. The fight started too quickly for Mellie to make a run for her hideaway upstairs, and once it was on she couldn't make her legs take her out of the room, couldn't stop watching the confusion of moving bodies. Arms and legs, feet and fists and elbows. Landing hard, kicking, rolling free, jumping up. Mellie felt as if two big hands were inside her, squeezing her stomach; blood pumped noisily inside her head. Marty was young and tall and well-muscled. Bing wasn't quite so tall, nor quite so big around the biceps, but he moved as if he knew what he was doing. His weak leg exaggerated the way his body rocked when he circled or moved in. Bing landed a solid punch to Marty's nose. A long, thin swirl of blood shot out and decorated a yellow cupboard door. When Queenie saw the blood, she squatted in the corner and put her head between her knees. Mellie, transfixed, heard their breath grate in and out, smelled their sharp sweat, saw each desperate lunge.

Bing lost the early advantage that the element of surprise had given him. The blow to the nose made Marty switch from ducking and defending to pouncing and thumping. Mellie was betting on Marty and she wasn't sure how she felt about this. He'd have come out on top eventually, no question, if the Mounties hadn't come looking for him about the stolen socket set. They must have heard the commotion when they came to the door because they walked right in without knocking. The two cops were larger than life moving across the kitchen. Brown parkas, bright yellow stripes down the sides of their pants, fur hats with flaps tied in place across the top, the smell of winter on their clothes. One cop was beefy and the other was skinny like a mosquito, even had a pointed nose. The skinny cop grabbed an unresisting Bing by the shoulders and stood between him and his son while the bigger one manoeuvred Marty's hands behind his back. "Marty Sonter?" he said.

The rest of that winter whenever people made remarks about her brother, Mellie was tempted to say he was reading a lot of books in jail and she bet he'd be a lawyer by the time he got out. She didn't say it, though, because there are some things no one will believe.

MARTY DOES ALL RIGHT NOW. He got his Class 1A papers and he drives trucks all over Canada and the US. He's seen a lot of the continent from the cab of a Kenworth. Sends Christmas cards from all over and writes short messages inside that almost make Mellie hear his voice: *Take 'er easy. Watch out for falling rocks and other shit.* He called one Saturday last fall on his mobile phone. He was at the outskirts and Mellie gave him directions for how to find the house. When Paul came in after his golf game and saw Mellie and Marty at the kitchen table, each with a drink and the rye bottle between them, he was as friendly to Marty as he'd be to anyone. "What you up to these days?" he'd said, and poured a rye for himself instead of his usual scotch.

"Same old bullshit," Marty said. He didn't stay for more than the one drink, but he was congenial, even warm. The lower third of the eagle tattoo, all that was visible below his T-shirt sleeve, looked unsurprising, unexceptional. He told Paul and Mellie they had a very nice place; he didn't smoke inside the house and he asked Paul how his boys were doing.

Mellie tells herself she shouldn't be surprised. She's changed too. She no longer carries herself through life on a raft of little lies the way she did when she was a girl, though she still catches herself dressing up the truth a little sometimes. After all, most of what can be said without lying is next door to boring, even when life is good. Especially when life is good.

It's all a negotiation with herself. She keeps the big lies so far-fetched they can only happen inside her head:

I smiled at a man on Second Avenue and he smiled back and the next thing you know we're at an outdoor café and his toe is stroking my heel under the table, as if we're the couple who inspired the pantyhose ad on TV.

I went on an extended trip to Vancouver to look up some old friends, stayed in a big house with five other people who still know what the

good drugs are and where to buy them. No one
in the Vancouver house cared about gross mar-
gins in the hardware business.

They have to stay inside her head, lies like these,
because waking up inside this particular life every morning is something she'd like to keep right on doing.

"How did it all go?" she'd asked Paul that day two years
ago when he came home from the lawyer's office with
his decree.

"It went."

"How's Carol about it?"

"Didn't see her."

That's how the process had looked from the outside,
as if he'd just walked away and whatever tumult surged
through the house over in Lawson Heights hadn't
touched him. And since then no fallout had blown in
from across town, as far as Mellie could see. No long
harangues over the telephone, no shouted recrimina-
tions, just two people moving apart as naturally as
clouds will, leaving an empty blue space in between.

Paul had set the papers on the table that day, opened
two Labatt Ices, handed one to Mellie and moved right
along to talking about buying a new place.

MELLIE TAKES A GINGER ALE out of the fridge, holds
the cold can against her cheek and lets a thin vein of
condensation trickle down her neck. Paul won't be
home for at least another hour, maybe longer, depending
on how captivated the boys are by the wind damage.

She turns on the TV, slumps down on the couch, takes a drink of her ginger ale and feels the bubbles break as they pass down her throat. She shifts on the couch and the leather pulls at her skin where her legs are bare below her shorts.

The TV news says two teenagers from the southern US have been found guilty of manslaughter. They swiped a small-town stop sign and the next morning an accident at that intersection killed two people. It's startling how little a person can get away with. Out behind Pavelik's grain bins a few miles south of Flat Hill, where Mellie used to go to parties when she was in high school, a path led into the bush and stopped in front of a checkerboard dead end sign nailed to a poplar tree. This was where the guys went to take a leak. (The girls went to a different spot, up behind the caragana bushes in what was left of the farmyard, close to the fallen-in basement.) Marty and one of his buddies had put the checkerboard sign up. Mellie wasn't sure which road they'd taken it from, but she never heard of any accidents as a result of it being gone.

There's more tragedy on the news: another tornado, this one in the south of the province, and a funnel cloud sighting in Manitoba but no report that it's touched down yet. What seemed like the event of a lifetime when she was a child has somehow multiplied itself. Are there more distressing disasters out there these days, more failures of luck than there used to be? More things that could do a person damage any minute, any day? Flesh-eating diseases and chemical spills and crazy people with bombs.

It's a discussion she's tried to have with Paul. He says

what most people say – that disasters are nothing new, it's just that the newspapers and the TV people are better at making sure we know about each little thing that goes wrong anywhere. It's a trap to worry about every remote possibility, he says. But then, Paul isn't a worrier. He isn't a worrier and he wouldn't know how much trouble some people have just believing life will hold itself together. How they always have one ear listening for the wind to suck the roof up, tires, rocks, boards and all.

RHINESTONES

1.

Mrs. Monk has been an occasional visitor in Linda's mind for years. Linda tracks her image as if the woman is on a worn reel of film. Sees her as she used to be, watches her open the door of her trailer to shake out a floor mat. Hears her softly clear her throat in the post office so Mrs. Turner will look up and come to the wicket. Watches her trudge along Main Street with her grocery bags, keeping to her own side, turning sideways a little when bulky Mr. Gunther, who owns the Texaco station, walks past. The film is jumpy sometimes, as if parts are missing. Linda fills in the lapses on her own, now that the days are so long, so lacking in diversion, so ready to be embellished. She thinks of a Christian name for Mrs. Monk. She calls her Virginia because it sounds dated and old-fashioned, entirely removed from the here and now. She supplies Virginia with prickly fears and tiny triumphs. Puts her inside her trailer and follows her through the day.

Linda has ample time for such amusements. Her mornings and afternoons belong only to herself these days. Her son Bobby is off living in Regina, perhaps deciding whether he will one day go to university or take something at the tech, perhaps just trusting his next step to whatever rides into his life on its own momentum as he drives his Austin Mini with the pizza sign strapped to the roof up Montague Street, down Elphinstone, up to the north end, back downtown.

Linda's husband Myron comes home for an hour at noon every day. After lunch he lies on the chesterfield for twenty minutes and snuffles his way through whatever he dreams at midday, if he dreams at all. When the stove timer buzzes (he sets it himself), he startles awake, clears his throat, says, "Time to go," and walks back downtown to the Credit Union.

Linda stays home and does what there is to do. Three months ago Betty Nowlan, who runs the fabric shop over in Ripley, said she couldn't keep her on the way business had fallen off. Couldn't afford the help. Sewing has slid out of fashion. People buy their clothing, their draperies, ready-made. Buy their children's Hallowe'en costumes from the drugstore. Vinyl capes. Tinsel tiaras. Pitchforks made of moulded plastic. Women who work outside the home, Betty said, don't buy so much fabric. Linda has gone back to working inside the home, which is fine. She freezes corn, makes tomato sauce, relearns how to bake bread. Turns the mattress, paints the kitchen, the bathroom, the hallway. Manufactures movies inside her head, movies starring some other version of herself, or the girls she

50

went to school with years ago, or the boys she used to date, or people like Mrs. Monk.

2.

VIRGINIA MONK twisted to shield her face against a dust devil and adjusted her load. The wind twirled a loose lock of her hair. She blinked against airborne grit. She could feel her load slipping. She balanced one paper grocery bag on the step of her trailer, propped the other bag on a bony hip, and unlocked the door.

The door swung in too fast and rebounded with a clang off the tin garbage bin inside. Virginia tried to step up, but the door slammed her foot hard against the frame. She gasped and dropped her grocery bag. Clumsy, clumsy, for Pete's sake anyway. Ouch.

Virginia's trailer squatted on stout leveling legs beside its twin at the edge of Flat Hill. Together, they looked like a pair of oversized tin breadboxes. Inside one end of Virginia's trailer, a curtain screened off her bed and belongings. The kitchen where she cooked and served meals for the gravel crew took up the rest of the trailer. The second trailer was the bunkhouse where the men slept.

With her skinny freckled arms braced in the doorway and her injured foot hanging limply, she twisted her neck to make a timid scan. The schoolyard and the nearby vacant lots were empty. No one to spy on her embarrassment. Still, her neck prickled with breaking sweat. Other people took small mishaps like this with a natural ease. Other people didn't spill the groceries in the first place, anyway, did they?

Virginia sat down on the narrow trailer step, slipped a finger inside her shoe to probe for swelling, and gave herself a list of reasons to calm down. One: She had negotiated the leaning alleys of shelves in the Red and White store without knocking anything down. Two: Mr. Nichol had been at the cash register, not Mrs. Nichol – a woman who could talk to anyone about anything, a woman who always had more words to give than Virginia felt equal to receive. Three: Even with the mess at her feet, she would still have some time to herself before she had to start supper for the crew. She bent to gather the cellophane noodle packages and raw carrots fanned out in the cocoa-fine dust. She would have an hour, maybe, an hour to do something just for herself. Make a cup of instant. Get out her violet rhinestone brooch and shine it up. She could even walk down the street and give the brooch to the principal's daughter, Linda. It could be a thank-you present, a present to Linda for not being like the others. But there it was, that prickle at the back of her neck again. She had surprised herself with her own idea. Imagine walking right up and knocking on the door of the teacherage. As if she were just like anyone else.

The effort of setting up in each new town stretched Virginia to the limit. Thank heaven the boss made all the arrangements. He established credit with the general store and the butcher; he arranged for delivery of the gas bottles that fed the cookstove; he secured privileges to draw water from the town well. All this he had accomplished within an hour or two on the day the crew arrived in Flat Hill. Virginia trailed along to be introduced, witnessing these everyday transactions with awe – the boss and the butcher and the grocer making up rules together.

And then Virginia was on her own, left to manufacture relationships with the storekeepers, left to signal her social limits in her own way, to mumble her way out of conversations, to nod and escape. Virginia worried at the details of ordinary encounters. A single sentence could hang for days on the screen in her mind, as loaded with meaning as a frame of dialogue in a silent movie. When Mr. Nichol at the Red and White said, "You look warm," he surely meant he saw where underarm sweat made the violet print on her dress turn dark purple. Unsightly. When Steve at the meat locker plant said, "Windy out there?" she knew her hairnet was unpinned and skewed sideways. Unkempt.

The streets themselves were unsettling, unpredictable. Out there she was as exposed as a gopher on the prairie when the hawks are flying. When the boys rode their bicycles so close to the sidewalk that she could feel the wind they stirred – when they laughed to see her jump clear – she was certain she was their special target, the only one they didn't move aside for. Even the path between her trailer and the back alley was frightening. A few weeks ago someone had taunted her from the bushes when she went to take the garbage out after dark.

Teenagers terrified Virginia. Linda Murphy was the first exception in years. All she had done was lend her a hand at the well one day, but gratitude made Virginia less timid with Linda than she was with other teenagers.

INSIDE THE TRAILER, Virginia pulled her curtain to one side and opened a drawer to find the purple brooch. The space she made sacred to her jewelry was afforded at some cost. She confined her things to a hard-sided suitcase stored underneath her cot, two cramped, built-in drawers, and a wire tacked to the wall where her housedresses hung. Bras and garter belts and slips gone grey from too much washing in hard water were scrambled in a heap at the back of the top drawer, but in the front a careful arrangement of cut-off salt canisters and processed cheese boxes housed Virginia's collection of trinkets like a makeshift exhibit in a small town museum. She had three brooches. She had necklaces too, a silver chain and a string of beads that looked sometimes gold and sometimes green depending on the light. And a bracelet with a tiny chain to hold it together if the clasp came undone; built-in protection against loss.

Virginia rested a hand lightly on the walls of her cardboard treasure chest. Once she had seen a time-lapse photo – in *Life* magazine? – of cars moving along a road at night leaving white streaks that marked where their headlights had been. Virginia pictured her trailer moving along the spider-leg lines of a road map while her tin and brass and rhinestones laid down a fine, flashing thread of light that linked the towns she passed through every summer. As if she could join all the geographical stops together like beads and make something more of them.

She set her violet brooch on the counter and put the kettle on. There was plenty of water for her coffee today. Not like the day a couple of weeks ago when she'd had to make a trip to the town well and ended up floundering in the mud. That was where Linda came in.

Virginia had known the drinking water tank was low

that other day when she put the porridge on for the crew at ten past six that morning. She had known, but she couldn't bring herself to ask one of the men to start the truck early and drive over to fill the tank. She could make the water last until evening if she were careful. The porridge used twelve cups of water. Virginia made a little less coffee than usual, but no one complained. She allowed herself the habitual cup of instant after lunch, but nothing more to drink.

That afternoon she'd washed the carrots and potatoes together in the same basin and spilled out the scrub water in the slop pit behind the trailer. There was just enough left in the tank to cook with. She hauled out the big pot from the cupboard beneath the window, chopped the potatoes into it, and pumped the pot half-full, emptying the reservoir. There was enough water in the teakettle to make do for the carrots. She sliced the carrots, slid them along the hollow in the cutting board into their pot, and lifted the teakettle. Slippery fingers or simple clumsiness made her drop the kettle. It landed on its side and water slid out of the spout and across the floor, following a slight pitch in the trailer. There the last of it went and there wasn't enough in the potato pot to rob for the carrots.

She would have to go to the well, would have to manage encounters with whoever might be out at that time of day – children running out to the store for bread, milk, little bricks of ice cream; teenagers delivering the newspapers that came to the post office on the afternoon truck. The men from the crew were due soon and she at least had to have things on the stove by the time they got there. She just had time to walk the three blocks to the well and back and get things going again before they drove up. She turned off the propane under the potatoes, grabbed both water pails, and set off. Two pails meant better balance; no need to look ridiculous with one free hand flapping in mid-air to counterbalance a full pail.

The public tap rose from a bore at one end of a vacant lot near the town office. To save time, Virginia took the overgrown path that cut diagonally across the lot. Calf-high wild clover and tufted purple thistles lifted the hem of her dress. When she reached the tap and turned around, she'd seen Linda Murphy heading up the same path.

3.

LINDA MURPHY was a thirteen-year-old with a mundane burden: she was a good girl. More than that, people had labeled her a good girl, and they acknowledged the label in all sorts of ways. She came to mind when someone thought a girl should look in on old Mrs. Elliot who lived alone. People thought of Linda when the teacher for the beginners' Sunday school class was sick. The school teachers depended on her too. Mrs. Novalski engineered the class election so Linda ended up treasurer of the Room Four Red Cross Society. All the Murphy kids were well-behaved and everyone knew it. Expected it. Robert Murphy was school principal and Elizabeth Murphy was a teller at the Credit Union. They ran a household marked by respect for elders, no bad debts, and a precise measure of kindness to people less fortunate than themselves.

Linda's parents didn't exactly have a set of rules for how to choose friends – at least not one they set out in words – but she knew the system all right. The system drew a line, for instance, between Wendy Kirk and Mellie Sonter, even though both lived in down-at-heel houses and wore clothes that had previous owners. A girl should be nice to Mellie in a democratic sort of way, should never leave her out of a skating party if everyone else was invited; mustn't mention the fact that her older brother had been sent to reform school. But Linda knew her parents didn't approve of her spending too much time with Mellie. Wendy, on the other hand, had the okay.

As near as Linda could figure, it came down to a certain standard that Wendy's mother maintained and Mellie's mother didn't. Wendy's mother had her girls send away for books-by-mail from the provincial library; Mellie's mother let her read romance comics. Wendy's mother watched Front Page Challenge; Mellie's mother listened to country and western music on the radio. Added to this reckoning was the question of Mellie's name, which didn't sound quite right somehow. It might have been the unfortunate rhyme, the easy epithet: smelly Mellie.

In fact, Linda's parents had no idea how much time their daughter spent with Mellie. If they had known, they would have said it was time for a talk. Linda resisted her respectable reputation in timid ways. Who wants people to think you're *always* good? Her anonymous signature was scrawled across a series of minor mischiefs which would have shocked the more easily upset residents of Flat Hill.

Like the time she found herself crouched beside Mellie in the bushes behind the church on a summer night after dark, smoking butts Mellie had pilfered from her mother's ashtray. Linda took a puff and tasted the scorched filter. She coughed into her hand. Mellie took the butt and stubbed it in the dirt. "That's the last one," she said.

They were about to crawl out of their hiding place when the door of Mrs. Monk's trailer opened across the way. Mrs. Monk teetered down the steps and picked her way toward the alley with a bag of garbage. The light from the doorway showed up her stick-woman silhouette topped with a ball of fuzzy hair that had been let out of its net for the night. Linda made ready to take off, but Mellie pulled her back down and sang out, "Oooold Mrs. Monkeeeeeeee," in a mocking voice.

Linda crouched in the bushes again. The dust she had stirred rose, fine and dry, and powdered the inside of her nose. She smelled green life as it steamed from a broken leaf. She had no idea how to act. The slightly seedy reputation of a girl like Mellie promised something more adventurous, more deliciously bad than bothering someone from a hole in the bushes. Still, she fired off a laugh, in the spirit of things.

Linda was relieved at Mrs. Monk's understated reaction to their hoots and cackles. The woman set her bag down, skittered back up the path with her head bent and closed the door. She didn't gasp in fear. She didn't try to come after them with a stick. She didn't even trip in the dark.

"Let's get out of here," Linda said. She twisted free of a twig that pulled at the knee of her pants. The pair ran down the block to the school, around to the far side away from the street lights, and sat in the shadows laughing made-up laughs.

4.

IT WAS ONLY A DAY OR TWO after the girls' small mischief that the incident so important to Virginia Monk happened at the town well.

Flat Hill had a new well with an electric pump that was tricky to use without creating a sea of mud. When Virginia arrived, she hung her first pail underneath the spout and lodged the pail's handle against a knob on the pipe. She walked over to flip the toggle switch mounted on a post a few steps away, then dashed back to hold the pail steady before the water started to flow. She knew from experience that if she didn't steady the pail, the stream shooting from the spout would slap the inside wall down hard and water would spray in all directions. She also knew the water would keep running for a second or two after the pump was turned off. She watched the height of the water in the pail to gauge the right moment to run back and flip the switch off again. To fill two pails Virginia had to dash through churned-up mud from the spout to the switch and back again an extra time.

LINDA APPROACHED THE PUMP that day with a pail dangling from each hand. Each pail was half the size of a regular drinking water pail, to match the half-size muscles of her skinny arms. The school board was replacing the makeshift plumbing fixtures in the teacherage with new double sinks and a full-sized tub. The water had been shut off for three days and this was the sixth time Linda had made the fetch-and-carry trip to the town well.

As Linda approached the well, she saw Mrs. Monk's first pail at the edge of the path, safely full. The second pail hung in place on the pipe and Mrs. Monk was in trouble. She had switched the pump on again and was running back to hold the pail steady. Her foot slipped forward in the mud, and she flipped onto her back. Momentum carried her forward leg through so it stuck straight up and swayed like a mast. The skirt of her yellow dress ballooned from her leg like a full sail. The effect was not lost on a trio of boys riding by on their bicycles. The boy in the lead spun sideways and stopped. His back tire raised an arc of dust.

"Hey, she looks like Harvey Thompson's sailboat out on Horseshoe Lake on a windy day." The leg that acted as a mast crashed down almost immediately, but the boys had already begun their chant: "Mrs. Monk-monk-monkey lady, monk-monk-monkey lady."

At the sight of Mrs. Monk's troubles, Linda dragged herself out of her own late afternoon comfort. This must be what her mother had in mind when she talked about Rising to the Occasion. Someone else might have found a way out of the situation, but for one of Elizabeth and Robert's daughters there was no practical path of escape. She walked over to help, relieved that the boys on the street were a few years behind her in school. They couldn't do much damage by telling people Linda Murphy had caught cooties from the monkey lady. She performed a straightforward rescue. A hand up, a dress rearranged, a wipe with tissues that shrank to nuggets after doing half a job. One person to work the switch and one to steady the pails. Linda's manner was matter-of-fact. Speech was brief, comforting, ordinary.

"Thank you, dear."

"That's all right, Mrs. Monk."

"I'm all right now."

"I can help you carry…."

"No, no. No thank you."

By the time things were smoothed out and wiped down, the boys had spun off on their bicycles. Linda wanted to leave the incident behind as effortlessly as they had. The following week when she walked into the Red and White store and saw Mrs. Monk over by the counter, Linda walked right on past the cereal shelf where she was supposed to pick up a box of Shredded Wheat. She slipped into the back aisle, prepared to wait among laundry detergents and floor waxes until she had the store to herself. She stared at a soap box and listened as rubber-soled footsteps threaded their way up and down the alleys between the shelves. The steps closed in. Mrs. Monk turned into the last aisle at the opposite end from Linda. The aging floor creaked even under the slight step of Mrs. Monk.

The woman's whispered "Hello" was barely audible.

"Hello, Mrs. Monk," Linda answered. She made a special effort to repress the polite smile she had grown up with. It wouldn't do to be too friendly. She didn't look Mrs. Monk in the face; instead, she looked down at the tin and glass brooch that held Mrs. Monk's dress together over the soft, pale skin of her chest. An opening gaped between the brooch and the top button of the dress. Mrs. Monk didn't say anything further, didn't move. Linda turned away and studied the detergents again. She lifted a plastic bag of blue soap granules. The bag had a huge yellow star with the word IMPROVED! printed across it in red. Linda imagined the star exploding and blue soap granules falling down the front of Mrs. Monk's dress. The soap explosion became a storm that created a cover of blue snow and gave Linda a chance to run out of the store in the confusion.

But no explosion of blue snow came to save her. Linda stayed riveted to the floor beside Mrs. Monk, who finally found her tongue, after a fashion. It was hard for Linda to make out her words exactly; there was too much breath and too little voice coming out. Something about how clumsy she was to fall down, how foolish she felt in front of those boys, how kind Linda was…. Mrs. Monk dusted the caps of a row of liquid detergent bottles with a jerky, repeated motion as she spoke. Linda watched the pencil-thin index finger with its ridged nail as it moved in small circles over one blue plastic lid after another. She could hear Mr. Nichol at the front of the store rummaging in the potato bin, slicing cheese at the block, piling Mrs. Monk's carrots onto the scale. She wished he would finish and call Mrs. Monk to the front. What if someone from Linda's class walked in and saw her? People make mental notes of things like that; they file them away to bother you with later.

Linda wanted to say, *What's the big deal? You fell down, you ended up a mess, and some boys laughed at you. It happens. Just forget about it.*

"I have to go. Mom'll be waiting for me."

"Of course. Yes."

Linda headed for the front of the store and slipped out without getting what she came for. She managed to avoid Mrs. Monk for several days. School started up again, but she stayed clear of the end of the schoolyard that bordered the trailers. Most of the time, she didn't even think about Mrs. Monk. Until her sister Bernice said something.

"What's the deal with monkey lady, Lind? She sure takes an interest in you. I saw her watching you from over by her trailer the other day." Bernice leaned across the notebooks open on the kitchen table, almost leering, but not quite, as if she might have something at stake herself. "She a friend of yours?"

Linda dropped her pen beside her open social studies textbook. "Leave me alone about it. She's just weird." She looked at her book again. "I have to read this whole chapter for tomorrow."

"Well, excuse me," Bernice said. She put two extra syllables in "excuse." "Don't get in a stink about it."

A moment later, Bernice looked up from her science book. "Is that a knock at the door?"

Linda kept her head down. "It's that loose end on the eavestrough," she said. "It's been banging in the wind for a week. In case you haven't noticed."

"It's not the eavestrough. There's someone at the door."

"Answer it then, if you're so sure," Linda said.

"I'm a grade niner and my homework's more important than yours. You answer it."

Linda rolled her eyes but got up anyway. "There's nobody there," she said. With her left arm in front of her waist to mimic a butler, she pulled the door open and bowed, all in one motion. "Hello, Mr. Nobody!" she shouted.

Mrs. Monk stood there, framed by the screen window in the outside door, lowering a slack fist that had been raised, ready to knock again. She looked a bit the way Margie Petersen had looked up on the stage on Lit Night when she'd forgotten her lines.

"Oh...uh," Linda said. "Mom and Dad aren't home." She could sense Bernice's stifled laugh behind her, waiting to break out and fill the room.

For an instant Mrs. Monk stayed on the doorstep, shaking only slightly. Then she turned and scurried away. Linda looked over at Bernice. She wanted to say, *I didn't know she was there*, and *What should I do now?* and *I didn't mean to be mean*. What she did say was, "Don't tell Mom and Dad."

"Don't feel bad, Lind," Bernice grinned from her place at the table. Then she quoted Mellie Sonter's favourite saying. "Shit happens."

5.

MRS. MONK left town when the gravel crew moved on but she didn't entirely leave Linda's mind. She showed up at intervals separated by seasons, decades, days.

There was the winter night a few years later when Linda sat in the front seat of a truck beside a boy her parents didn't approve of. She laughed while he spun the steering wheel to make his tires slide figure eights on the ice near the town well. She closed her eyes and leaned this way and that, as if her body could counterbalance the weight of the entire truck as it skated on two wheels. She pictured the acre of mud that surrounded the well in the summertime, pictured Mrs. Monk, her dress askew and her palms painted with mud and her eyes barely under control.

AND THE DAY Linda got married – to a boy her parents *did* approve of – Linda couldn't help but see Mrs. Monk when she looked at Great Aunt Rosemary who sat in the corner at the reception in the town hall wearing that worn mauve dress that didn't seem to have a waist. When Myron's parents came over to be introduced, Aunt Rosemary turned her tin bracelet round and round on her wrist and looked down and away in that embarrassed and embarrassing way of hers.

"Auntie, this is Mr. and Mrs. Shewchuk. Matt and Dorothy Shewchuk."

"Of course. Yes," Aunt Rosemary said toward the baseboard. "Pleased to meet you."

Linda waited for the woman to turn from Mrs. Monk back into Aunt Rosemary before she took Myron's father by the elbow and steered him toward the dance floor.

THEN THERE WAS THE WINTER Linda's mother retired and stayed indoors for three months as if she were afraid of the air itself, just like old Mrs. Monk. Linda dressed her, coaxed her to the kitchen, pinned her hair in place, for Pete's sake, and brought the baby over every day to wait out the winter. *Make yourself some fun, Mom. Buy something you don't need, fry a steak, cheat at solitaire. Turn up the radio at least, and leave it on past the news.* Linda played pat-a-cake with the both of them until March brought Bobby his first tooth and brought her mother a trickle of energy.

AND THE TIME when Bobby was ten and he refused to go to Regina with the school band if Linda came along as a chaperone.

"You're too weird."

Linda checked herself in the mirror that night, leaned in for a close look at her skin and her teeth, backed away to examine herself full-length against the standards a ten-year-old would have for weirdness. Still as skinny as ever, maybe too much so, but she looked healthy all the same. Age had just started to warn her it was on its way; it camped in crescent-shaped pillows under her eyes, in loosening skin at her throat. Hardly unusual. Her hair could stand a new cut, maybe a perm, but the rest was passable. And it wasn't as if she avoided other people, or vice versa. She confirmed her social life to herself, mentally ticked off the list of people she could call friends, tallied up what she thought of as her "extra-curriculars" – judge for the drama festival over in Ripley, Sunday school teacher, president of the rink committee. She was as normal, she decided, as any mother of a ten-year-old. Too normal, maybe, never broke the rules. Normal in every way. Weird would be someone like poor old Mrs. Monk, someone fumbling and fearful and ridiculous.

EVEN NOW, when Linda herself is close to the age Mrs. Monk will always be in her memory, the woman shows up – but then a lot of people show up in Linda's mind. Mellie Sonter, for example. Mellie moved to the city years and years ago and Linda hasn't seen her since, but she directs movies in her mind where Mellie meets outlandish characters in the stereo store. They buy CDs or headphones from her and strike up conversations and take her to parties where all sorts of things go on. Sometimes Linda almost wishes it were herself in the movies. Almost. Linda makes up other moving pictures, some of them featuring Larry, the boy who used to make his truck skate on the ice at the well, the boy her parents disapproved of. Linda is with him sometimes in her homemade movies. In one episode, they found three hundred dollars in an envelope in a cocktail lounge in Regina and instead of turning it in they spent every cent of it that same night. She and Larry laugh a lot in the movies, but they always pretend a little that they don't like each other.

Mrs. Monk comes around more often than the other characters lately. She materialized for Linda just the other day, this time from a pool of water on the kitchen floor. Linda was putting the vegetables on to cook when she slopped a little water out of the pot. Clumsy, clumsy she was these days. She reached for a rag and a pail to wipe up the spill properly and scrub a few other spots at the same time. No reason to hurry. Strict mealtimes aren't important anymore. Linda is attentive to all her responsibilities, but there is only so much demanded of her now that she's unemployed. Her skirt caught under her knee when she knelt to wipe the floor, and a tear at the waistband traveled two inches. She ought to pay more attention to her clothes. The spilled water sparkled violet and blue from the pattern in the flooring. She saw Mrs. Monk standing in the Red and White with a rhinestone brooch holding her dress together. Linda swished her rag and multiplied the brooch into a collection of cheap, precious bangles.

"There you go, Virginia," she said.

HOMEMADE MAPS

Summer in this part of the world is so precious, so distinctly marked off from other seasons, that you can almost see the brackets at either end. Such clear definition makes summers into reference points in children's lives. It had been that way for Jean and now it was that way for her children; the years condensed around the projects of summer.

Last year was the summer of the dump. Her three children, along with various combinations of friends, made trip after trip to the nuisance grounds. Returned with the red wagon rattling behind them, hauling home battered books, maimed toys, orphaned door handles, a pair of old combination-style mailboxes the post office had discarded. This summer the nuisance grounds were history; the new project was digging holes – long, narrow tubes that headed straight down into the earth. They dug with toy shovels, with fingernails, with spoons swiped from the unmatched jumble in the cutlery drawer. Jean had the mother-job of shaking sand from small cuffs and pockets at the end of the day, and she had the hazard of lurching into the children's holes – deep black ankle traps in the garden and the side yard.

"I wish they wouldn't dig up the whole yard," she said to Norman one night as she wound her foot with a tensor bandage. She followed quickly with, "I know I shouldn't complain."

"They're just doing what kids do," Norman said. "You'll have to step around."

Norman's ankles were not at risk. He hadn't set foot in the garden since spring, and his habit was to stop mowing before he got as far as the hillocks of crab grass in the side yard. The same as he stopped washing dishes before he got to the hard scrubbing at the end.

Jean regularly sent the children forth to the garden armed with hoes and cast iron prongs to battle the pigweed and the portulaca. Regularly, the children slipped away from the weeding to finish their holes of the moment. The only buried treasure the earth offered was odd old chips of china, so the children squirreled away their own trinkets, burying them deep at the ends of the earthen sleeves they hollowed out. Jean saw them carry out assorted bits sifted from among the dust curls in the bottom of the toy box – a broken car, a ring from a box of candied popcorn, an arm from a dismembered doll. Sometimes they buried things Jean was certain they wouldn't want to lose; once she saw Susan walk out to the garden with a necklace, a birthday present from her friend Sheila; once, Billy with a set of *Man from* UNCLE bubble gum cards shrouded in a plastic bread bag. And who knew what significant small treasure Cindy, the

70

youngest, stowed away under the dirt and risked losing forever?

Any treasures they failed to recover, though, would be well preserved under the earth, Jean supposed. Down there with their stories locked inside them, some kind of silent record. Something like that glove that had escaped when the astronaut went on his space walk earlier this summer. The newspaper said that when he left the hatch of his spacecraft, a thermal glove followed him out and disappeared. Slipped out and floated away forever. You had to think there was something striking about that, something lasting, a man-made object drifting through space forever.

THE CHILDREN sat at the kitchen table and drew homemade treasure maps, official records to help them dig out what they themselves had buried. According to the children, the rule was that you had to force yourself to wait a few days before you went looking for your treasure. You only cheated yourself, diminished the thrill, if the depression in the ground was too obvious, the place to dig too easily defined by the difference between hard earth and recently disturbed dirt. Their maps took in the whole of the town of Flat Hill. Dotted lines with intermittent arrows that tracked from their own front door, up the street and around the town, past bird's-eye sketches of the school, the church, up to Main Street and past the meat locker plant, the Red and White Store, the Texaco, the Credit Union, around past the post office, back through the alley and into the yard again to stop at the "X" that marked the treasure.

Cindy's maps smelled of wax crayon – she favoured black and green – thick, shaky lines that traced simple routes. Billy set down confident lines, used a pen, no erasing, decorated the page so that it seemed not to matter so much whether or not you found the treasure, because there were other things to be explored: caves in the schoolyard, mountains alongside Main Street, circus tents in the parking lot in front of the train station. Susan drafted no-nonsense, scale drawings, always terminating in a solid, red "X": go to this spot, find something worthwhile.

JEAN HAS UNEARTHED a treasure of her own, though she doesn't know quite what to make of it. She hasn't brought it to the house, but she knows where to find it. She discovered it last summer during what was, for the children, the summer of the nuisance grounds. While they foraged for cast-off objects at the junkyard, Jean had found a cast-off object of a different sort. She'd taken off her apron and left the quiet house one morning after Norman had left for work and the kids had gone off. The sunshine that morning was so bright it made the house seem darker than it should. It was a temptation she often had – and almost always successfully suppressed – to sneak away with no purpose, indulge the urge to idleness. Sometimes a person feels like being in a different place for a while, a place with no washing machine, no garden, no oven, no clothesline. She'd walked the four blocks to the edge of town and followed the dirt path into Peterson's old pasture.

The empty pasture had been so quiet she could hear

her own heartbeat. She wasn't sure what she was there for, but no one would be needing her at the house for a little while. She had all the feelings of playing hooky. The small pleasure and slight guilt of absconding from a place where people would normally expect to find her; the puzzle of how she would explain herself if someone asked her what in the world she was doing wandering through the pasture. She wanted to stretch out on her back on the grass as if she were a girl and watch the clouds recede. But a grown woman didn't do such things – a mother, a mayor's wife.

She walked across the open grass toward the hollow that was prone to flooding in wet years; there, she felt sheltered by the bushes. She sat on the ground near a clump of wild roses. The grass around her was long, thin, sharply dry; she pulled out a handful and played with it, threw the feather-light blades in the air and watched them settle at her feet. A meadowlark's song rippled the stillness. Jean ran her right hand along the sloping ground beside her and stopped on a half-buried, rust-coloured stone. She tugged it free, brushed away the dirt, turned the stone over in her hands. It was long, one end rounded, the other end a dull point. She turned it this way and that until it settled into place, or rather her hand settled into place, cupped around the squarish end. Someone had long ago shaped this stone quite intentionally to fit a woman's hand. The fleshy part of her palm nestled into a depression on the underside; her fingers fit into the ridges scored across the square end; the pads of her fingers gripped a hollow on the top side and allowed her to control the pointed end. A scraper? Probably. Hard to say for certain. She experimented, scraped at the rough tufts of grass that burst through the sun-cured ground, pulled the skirt of her housedress taut across her knees and scraped at the fabric as if it were an animal hide. Her control of the tool was clumsy, but she could imagine that, with practice, a person would develop some skill in its use.

Jean had left the stone where she found it last summer, settled it back neatly into the dirt cradle from which she'd kidnapped it. She hadn't visited the stone again, but she knew it was there, nestled into the soil and the grass. She thought about it once in a while, the smell of the moist, uncovered earth where she'd lifted the stone out, the smooth, well-used feel of the tool, the mystery of who had used it and how. But of course she had no business going to the pasture just to play with a stone. How would a person explain spending time that way? She didn't tell anyone about her find. What was there to say? Didn't even tell her oldest, best friend, Lillian, who'd been her bridesmaid eleven years ago. Stood up for her, was how they referred to it. They didn't visit back and forth as much as they used to. Lillian and Howard's farm was four miles west of town. Might as well be forty.

NORMAN KNELT beside Susan in the yard one day after lunch.

"Digging to China?" he said.

Susan slid her arm down into her hole and scooped out a handful of dirt. "Not digging anywhere," she said. "We're burying things." But Norman was already back on his feet and on his way down the hill to the CPR station, without waiting around for his daughter's half of the conversation. Norman's life was like his railway, running straight like steel, clear into the distance. The children's enchanted summer lives were different, all bunched up against the present in piles of secrets and penny candy and castles underground. Jean's own life eddied around the others, taking its shape from whatever it whorled up against.

Norman Shepherd, community mainstay. Known to all as the most decent boss the CPR had ever hired, the most forward-thinking mayor the town could hope for, the fairest councillor. He was the strength behind the push for cement sidewalks and new street lights and running water. He was the one who made sure someone like Elsa Eriksen didn't have to worry about those back taxes, property taxes her husband hadn't paid in three years. (He liked to drink, Nels Eriksen did.) Norman held his own in arguments with councillors who were all for taking over the title to the house in a case like that.

Norman had tried to give up the mayor's job at the end of both his first and second terms. Let someone else take a turn, he'd said. Each time, two or three of the other councillors came by the house with a bottle of Silk Tassel. The first time it took only an hour to convince Norman that he should serve another term. The second time the convincing had kept him up past midnight, and Jean had put the children under orders to be quiet most of the next morning. When Jean poured him a cup of coffee just after eleven, he admitted to her that he was mayor once again. You had to think he liked it.

No one could complain about a husband like Norman. He might not weed the garden, but he dug it every May in plenty of time for Jean to do the planting. He wasn't one to scrub the pots when he did the dishes, but then how many husbands washed dishes at all? Norman even knew how to cook. A few things.

A man ought to help out in the kitchen once in a while, he'd been known to say to Howard and Lillian over a game of whist. A guy's got to give the wife a break. He had a repertoire of five or six dishes. He cooked once a month or so, on a Saturday or Sunday. Baked beans, soups, a stewy mixture he called slumgullion. His favourite creation, both to cook and to eat, was his own original version of hash. Its appearance on the menu depended on his being able to secure from Harvey, the butcher, a suitable combination of scraps and trimmings and offal.

Jean didn't mind most of what Norman cooked, but she could have done without the hash. To make it properly, you had to push all the odds and ends through a grinder, an implement that was, Norman often stressed, a must-have kitchen device. It ranked right up there with the cast iron frying pan and the pressure cooker. Proper use of a meat grinder demanded care, and scrupulous attention to cleanliness. All the implements down to the nut on the spindle of the mincer had to be soaped, then scalded, before and after every use. Norman took care of the before, but he wasn't keen on the after. Neither was Jean. "It's worth the bother though, isn't it?" Norman would say. Jean didn't agree, but she kept that thought to herself. Some things just irritate a person. The meat grinder was one of those things. There were others, if she let herself think about them: little bits of dark brown whisker in the basin after he shaved; the red handkerchiefs he wouldn't give up even though they had to be washed in their very own load; the way he cranked up the volume on the radio because, as he said, his eardrums were wearing out. Any number of things. Small things. Not worth mentioning.

THE CHILDREN were proud of the deep, narrow holes they dug in the yard. They competed for depth, and Jean found herself called in as judge, uncertain how to be fair, especially to Cindy, the youngest – her short, thin arms, her determined face, her limp, dark curls. The children coaxed, though, and Jean obliged. Knelt and slid her arm into the cool, brown tunnels one at a time. Gopher holes, rabbit holes, that's what they made her think of. Smooth sides that went down and down. She pictured Alice in the rabbit hole, wearing a white pinafore, like the one in the drawings in Susan's hardcover illustrated copy on the bedroom bookshelf; Alice reading signs that said EAT ME and DRINK ME, following instructions in the bewildering world of the rabbit hole, never knowing what would happen next; Alice reciting lessons that turned into nonsense on her lips; Alice explaining herself repeatedly to impossible creatures. Jean withdrew her hand from the last deep hole and told her children that they'd all won first prize, a judgment which satisfied neither the children nor herself.

In August, a new digger came along and put Jean's practiced young excavators to shame. A digger they couldn't compete with. It appeared first at the other end of the gravel street that parted the houses into facing rows. It munched out the hard clay core as it advanced down the middle of the road with indisputable efficiency. The trench the upstart digger gouged was three yards wide and almost as tall as Norman. A work crew came to lay a new core down its centre, the water and sewer lines for the town. "Human beings are traveling in space," Norman had said at the first council meeting of his second term, "and only four homes in Flat Hill have running water." They'd been working toward the water project ever since.

Jean pulled the living room curtains to one side as the machines growled awake one morning. "How long will it take, do you think?"

Norman didn't look up from last night's newspaper. "Oh, I dunno, a couple of weeks by the time they're all done. Not long."

The children called the trench in the street the Grand Canyon, and that's how it must have seemed to them. At first they went daily to the edge and peered over, while wonder and disappointment took turns on their faces. Jean spied on them from the petunia bed.

"Wow. Deep," Cindy said.

"Boring," Billy said. "You can see right to the bottom." Briefly, timidly, the children considered climbing down inside. They plotted strategies copied from TV westerns.

"We could tear up a sheet," Susan said. "You know, knot the lengths together and climb down. Like the Mavericks escaping from the top floor of a saloon when someone's after them. Or we could jump down and stand on each other's shoulders to climb out."

"But what about the last one?" Cindy said, worried

about being left behind. "How would the last one get out?"

"I don't wanna see you kids near that hole," Jean called through a blast of hot, late summer wind. "Just suppose you're down there when they come to fill it up…then what?"

"Then what?" She tacked that question on at the end of so many of her unfinished suppositions. Sometimes she took her own "Then what?" entirely too seriously, and frightened herself with some possibility that she conjured in response to it. The children *would* climb into the hole; one of them *would* break a leg, or hit his head, her head, on a pipe, end up with a concussion, who knows? So many things were outside a person's control. The best a person could do was supply whatever was required from day to day. Put a band-aid on a knee, kiss the world better, patch the pants when they wore through the knees. Keep the weeds down, do the canning when the vegetables came ready, clean the fish when Norm took it into his head to spend Saturday afternoon at Redwing Creek.

It wasn't a bad life. There were people all around with serious troubles to worry about. Elsa Eriksen down the street, coping with her husband's fondness for the bottle and looking almost unhinged herself by now. Anna Mueller, too young to be a widow, turning her living room into a seamstress's parlour. And there was Emerald Stevenson, curling further around herself from arthritis every year, a look of unescaped pain always on her face. Someone like Emerald couldn't play hooky even if she wanted to, couldn't sit in a still pasture with her legs tucked underneath her, couldn't pick up a stone and feel its weight and turn it over in her hands.

Jean knew very well how fortunate she was. *Mustn't complain. Mustn't mustn't mustn't grumble*. She'd inherited the standard set of maxims. *The devil finds work for idle hands. A fool loses her temper, a wise woman holds it back.* A checklist of proverbs, sound wisdom that stood the test of time. *A woman can throw out more with a teaspoon than a man can bring home in a wagonload.* That sentence skipped through Jean's mind each time she conscientiously swiped the rubber spatula through the bottom of a can or jar to force out the last smear of soup or tomato sauce. As a set of rules for living, her adopted grab bag of axioms tended to keep life humming smoothly along. *Always keep a black bobbin and a white bobbin ready at the sewing machine.* She wasn't one to complain when there was nothing to complain about, wasn't one to go against elementary wisdom, wasn't one to prove herself a fool by striking off in some untried direction.

SATURDAY AFTERNOON. Norman had been to the butcher shop. He'd boiled the kettle, scalded the various parts of the meat grinder in the dishpan, reassembled it, interrupted himself only to haul in some water from the backyard pump when Jean asked him to fill the washer. Jean stood in the kitchen doorway hugging her laundry basket and watching him. He steadied the grinder at the edge of table and tightened the clamp. He was on his way to making a mess. He bent one knee and rested it on the plastic seat of a kitchen chair, turned the handle to set the blades in motion. Into the bowl of the grinder sank offal and scraps and gristle and fat, and out of the side flowed smooth, mottled sameness.

Jean crossed the kitchen, swung the wringer arm out of the way and started loading children's clothes into the washer. She picked at a wrapperless candy stuck in a pair of overalls, shook the sand from a sock into the wastebasket, pulled a bent spoon out of a pants pocket. She looked over again at Norman; he was in full swing. She watched the extruder as thick ropes pushed their way out of the ring of holes. He swept his cutter up across the plate in a regular rhythm, chopping the greasy meat-ropes into bits that fell onto waxed butcher paper. The washing machine was only half-loaded, but Jean left it and retreated to the bedroom, lay down, pulled the pillow over her face and tried to smother the image of the meat slinking out of the business end of the grinder. Fat pink worms, slithery, twisty, like the earthworms on the front walk after a rain. Some things just irritated a person, some things you just wanted to pick up and throw across a room, break into bits.

Saturday night Jean scrubbed and scalded the meat grinder, packed it into its yellow box with the Good Housekeeping Seal of Approval, snapped a fat elastic band around the box to keep it all in place, and slid it onto the high shelf above the fridge. It stayed there until Monday morning, until Norman had left for the station and the children were out of her hair. Then she climbed the kitchen stepstool, retrieved the box, carried it out to the Grand Canyon, threw it in and covered it up. Left it there under the ground. Any excavator unearthing it in the distant future would see the meat grinder only as an object with a specific purpose, a tool used to make dinner. But to Jean it wasn't an object any more, it was an act – a clumsy act for sure, but she could imagine that with practice she might find more graceful ways to make her own mark.

She went back to the house and phoned Lillian. When Lillian answered, Jean jumped right in, told what she'd done, felt her face heat up, asked her friend, "Am I crazy?" But Lillian had to run; baby Joanie was squalling, there was a cow with udder trouble bellering down in the barn, Howard needed her help. "Probably as sane as the rest of us," Lillian said. Jean set the receiver back on the hook, then realized she'd just made a ridiculous admission over a party line. She went to the bedroom, fished through the tray on the dresser for bobby pins, twisted her hair into a bun and pinned it. Hair in place, lipstick on, she went to the kitchen and took down the big crockery bowl to make bread.

SUMMER BELONGED to the children, but Jean claimed the big white space of winter for herself. Winter was easier than summer, easier than fall. There was no digging in the dirt; clothes were cleaner; things ran according to schedules; the house was quiet during the week. She guarded a treasured space between nine and three-forty every weekday. Even this space – diminished as it was by the need to have lunch on the table for the children – shrank in at the edges, as if it needed to be stapled down.

On a Saturday afternoon a week after Christmas, Jean crowded pickle jars and plastic containers with snap-on lids from the refrigerator onto the countertop and the kitchen table, and turned the temperature dial to "defrost." She could only use one end of the table; the rest was polka-dotted with thimble-sized paint pots. Susan sat, her shoulders rounded over a cardboard panel, and brushed "# 3 flesh" oil paint onto the face of a girl who played with a cocker spaniel. "I hate this stuff," Susan said. "The hairs from the brush keep coming out and sticking on the picture." She let the brush roll across the table. "There's nothing to do."

"Go out and work on your snow fort, why not?" Jean's suggestion was designed to clear the kitchen for her own privacy.

"Can't. Sheila's gone to her grandma's in Zachary today. We have a pact that one of us can't work on the fort without the other."

"Well then, what about that puzzle Sheila gave you for Christmas?"

"Too hard. Can't tell the waterfall pieces from the cloud pieces." She was quiet for a few seconds; then: "I hate winter."

Jean sighed, gave it one more try. "What about your other presents, then?"

"They're all dumb. Sheila got a dartboard this year. Why didn't we get a dartboard?"

Jean turned back to her towers of plastic and Pyrex. You can't take boredom away from a ten-year-old with a tenacious hold. Through the window beside the fridge, she saw Norman coming up the lane from downtown, his figure framed by the plastic lace of the curtain. His arms swung loosely from his shoulders. In his right hand, he held a pinkish-brown paper bag that flicked up and down in the afterthought that followed each swing of his arm. It was a fine, sunny day, almost a January thaw, and Norman's heavy coat was open and flapping. He was grinning the way Billy did after a good hockey game. Jean braced, just slightly, for the invasion.

In a moment she heard the slosh and stomp as Norman shook the wet snow from his boots out on the verandah. He came in whistling, hung his coat on the hook behind the door, and stepped out of his dripping black boots. He slapped his paper bag on the table next to a green bowl of something forgotten that had recently occupied a far reach of the fridge. "Jean, can you get out the meat grinder? I've got some odds and ends from Harvey at the locker plant. I'll do up some hash for supper."

Jean looked over at the table where Susan was cleaning her brush to switch from "flesh" to "forest green." Norman usually mounted the meat grinder at just about the spot where the bottle of paint thinner now stood in its own sharp-smelling puddle. Jean felt her face go warm and heard the buzz of a fly fooled out of a winter crack by the extra measure of sun.

Norman waved his hand in front of her still eyes and made his request again. Jean turned, sat down in a chrome and red kitchen chair, and faced her husband. Time to confess. She pumped her mouth to draw enough saliva to swallow. She stifled the rising giggle that belied the seriousness of her situation.

It was a comic picture, she thought, herself in her summer housedress with the rose-red stripes, standing at the edge of the Grand Canyon holding the meat grinder in its cardboard box, the whole thing so heavy that once she let go it had fallen faster than you can see motion. The heel of her brown everyday shoe working into a crack near the edge of the trench wall, loosening a clod

of dirt. The clod breaking up as it hit the yellow cardboard.

She'd have to tell Norman now.

"I can't get you the meat grinder." The giggle she'd
stifled was still close to the surface.

"Tell me where it is and I'll get it myself."

She didn't answer. Norman tilted his head at her,
bent down a little to look into her face. A line formed
between his eyebrows. "What's up?"

"I buried it." Jean let out a nervous laugh.

"What do you mean?" He straightened up.

"Just what I said. I buried it."

"What d'you mean?"

Across the table, Susan had set her paintbrush down
quietly. I need to put together a simple, clear statement,
Jean thought. So she told Norman what she'd done, that
she'd thrown the meat grinder into the hole in the street
last August and covered it up so she wouldn't have to
look at it anymore. A confused smile crossed Norman's
mouth and quickly left. He stared into her face for a
long moment. She could think of nothing more to say,
and she looked away from him, looked out the window
to where the snow was melting in the lane.

"Why would you go and…?" Norman gave a huge
shrug, slapped the table, said, "Honestly, I don't know
what…!"

He found the cutting board, got out the butcher
knife he'd bought on a previous trip to the meat locker
plant, ripped open the bag he'd brought home, and set
to work chopping. He worked around Jean, who sat and
said nothing, and around Susan, who said nothing and
started to paint again. Once in a while Norman crossed

the kitchen to fetch an onion or find a cooking utensil, each time leaving an exaggerated berth between himself and the table where they sat. He whistled a breathy little whistle.

Presently Jean got up, found a cloth and went back to defrosting the fridge. She didn't want to think too hard about why she'd thrown the meat grinder down the hole, or the reasons would slip away on her. Jean wiped at the melting frost on the grey metal of the freezer compartment. Her breath made transient clouds when it met the bits of ice that still clung to the walls. She watched water trickle down metal, and as she watched she chased thoughts and attempts at logic out of her head. She didn't want to try explaining the unexplainable to Norman. She hummed a little, no particular tune and not so loud that anyone would hear. Just enough of a sound to fill up the space in her head where thinking usually happens.

MARKING TIME

January: winter slouching along at the pace of a tortoise. High on the wall of the grade eight classroom hung a round black-and-white clock. Above it, someone had taped up solid black construction paper circles to look like Mickey Mouse ears. Time might be nothing but a joke.

At the front of the classroom, Ox Kovach faced nineteen other grade eight students and wore a crooked grin as he brought *Webster's New Collegiate Dictionary* repeatedly down on top of his own head…six…seven…eight. Off to the side stood Mr. Constable, a smirk on his face – the teacher who'd walked into the room on the first day of school in September and said, as he said every year to every class, "This here is Russia. And me, I'm Khrushchev." Took off a shoe and slammed it on the desk to make sure the message got through.

Never mind that Khrushchev had had to make way for someone else a few years ago. Irrelevant. No one was about to mention it.

Nine…ten. Muffled thumps. Ox lowered the dictionary, looked over his shoulder for a nod from Constable, received it, and returned to his desk at the back of the room. Combed his fingers through his flattened hair.

A solid book, the dictionary, at least two inches thick. Constable made you hit yourself over the head with it if you didn't finish your homework or if he caught you eating a chocolate bar in school hours or scratching your initials onto your desk with the tip of a compass. You weren't expected to hit *hard*; it was discipline by embarrassment as much as anything. Some, like Ox, even knew how to capitalize on it, use the opportunity to be the centre of attention.

Stephen Parker, who sat two rows over from Ox at the back of the room, had never been ordered to stand at the front and pound himself with *Webster's New Collegiate*; hoped he never would. He wasn't smiling now, the way the others were, as Ox plopped back into his seat. Instead, Stephen sat at his desk with his legs crossed – no, not crossed, twisted around, his right ankle locked behind his left, like a little boy who has to pee.

Except he wasn't a little boy. He wasn't big for his age, wasn't small. Had the kind of looks that blend in. Brown hair with a slight wave, blond streaks in the summer, uniform brown now midway through winter. Eyes an inconsistent blue. Not much for muscles; those were still to come, he supposed; not fleshy either, ribs he could bump his fingers over in time to the music when he lay on his bed listening to *Sgt. Pepper*.

UP ON THE WALL, the mouse clock stared. The second hand measured its way around from one stop to the next, but hardly fast enough for Stephen. Keep moving, clock. Get me out of here.

A few feet away from the clock, above the tall wain-scoting that ran along the west wall of the classroom, was a reproduction of a painting, a dull-looking picture with a brass plate on the frame that said *The Gleaners*. Stephen looked at the picture now, the way he did once in a while when he wanted to be somewhere else. Not that staring at the painting did the trick, not nearly. He wouldn't have wanted to be one of those people anyway. Bent figures, each holding a few straggly stalks of grain, their backs to the soft, full haystacks way off in the distance.

SOCCER AT RECESS TIME on the frozen schoolyard. Stephen feeling invisible, as he often did. There he'd be, right in front of the goal, wide open, not another player near him. All he needed was the damn ball. *Here*, he'd yell. *Over here!* But nobody would see him, not unless the ball bounced off him by accident. Once in a while, a pass down the sidelines from Dutch, the classmate most in the habit of acknowledging his existence.

They played hard to keep warm, gasped for breath, munched handfuls of snow to wet their dry throats. "Hey Ox," Shiner yelled between plays. "How come you had such a grin on, hitting yourself over the head with that big sucker of a book? You musta' been thinking about page 295."

Laughter from the others. Ox had shown page 295 to the rest of them one morning before Constable came in.

The word that had caught his interest was "décolletage." None of them knew how to say it, but that didn't matter. What did matter was the picture beside the definition. A very small line drawing, but one that nicely illustrated the meaning.

Though in the end, even a picture like that didn't show Stephen anything he really wanted to see. It left the crucial parts hidden, which was no surprise. So often, just when he felt he was about to sneak up on some impressive discovery, the main idea would wink out of sight, vanish around a corner.

HOCKEY THAT NIGHT, the men's league at the Flat Hill community rink. This season Stephen had fallen into the good graces of Paul Tredwell, who ran the record booth upstairs. Stephen had gotten to know the routine by hanging around outside the booth, watching Tredwell through the glass pane in the door. Tredwell played "Oh Canada" before the puck dropped at the start of the game, used an album of organ music to liven up line changes, played selections from the hit parade between periods while other boys Stephen's age pushed wide tin scrapers around and up and down to clean the ice surface.

Tredwell let Stephen run the turntable once in a while. Handed it over to him and stood outside the booth with his coffee cup in his hand, dipping his head to look in every once in a while, nodding with a serious expression on his face to show his agreement that things were going fine.

Tonight Tredwell turned things over to Stephen right

at the start. The instant the last word of the first verse of "Oh Canada" slid out of the singer's throat, Stephen lifted the needle off the spinning record, cut it short the way old Tredwell said to do it. Even so, one or two players had already done a cross-cut or two backwards and glided back to the blue line. Couldn't stand still. Sticks slapped the ice, players tossed their heads. *Hey hey, let's go. Get this show on the road. Show these turkeys what it's all about. Get rolling.*

Stephen's body wouldn't stay still either. His knee bounced up and down underneath the table, his heel softly slapping the floorboards, pum-pum-pum-pum. He gave the booth back to old Tredwell, walked over to the counter where Katie Mueller was helping her mother manage the concession, and bought a coconut bar from her. It occurred to him that since a coconut bar came already divided into two pieces, he could offer one piece to Katie. He didn't, though, just stood a few feet from the counter and ate both halves himself, shifting his weight from one leg to the other, sliding the zipper of his olive-green canvas parka up and down, watching the game through the long upstairs window that looked down onto the ice. Watching Katie once in a while too, out of the corner of his eye. Her back to him, moving onions around on the grill with a spatula. Wearing some kind of orange dress; always wore those clothes her mother made – different from everyone else's, but she wore them as if they were normal.

FEBRUARY: a trough of cold stretched from Saskatoon to Winnipeg, settled in, refused to move. Stephen's mother not walking, this latest spell with her hip well into its third week. She spent hours propped in the armchair, a Perry Mason novel in her lap, the TV set playing whatever happened to be on. She was a moving statue, adjusting her bifocals, readjusting and resettling them as she moved her attention between her book and the TV.

Noon on a Saturday and Stephen made bacon and eggs, got Francie to watch the toast, butter it, stack it.

"Francie, go tell Mom the food's ready."

But there was Mom on her way in already, navy bathrobe still on, tasseled belt hanging undone from the side loops, pink flannel nightgown on display. Stephen had thought of going in to help raise her out of the armchair; didn't. She'd had Stephen's dad take apart a broom so she could use the sawed-off handle as a walking stick, which she leaned on now as she made her way to a kitchen chair. Thud shuffle, thud shuffle, thud sit. Hair in curlers, as if she had plans to do herself up and venture out this afternoon with her sugar-pink cosmetics suitcase and make a few sales calls. The curlers had been in for two days now. Scatter of pink and white plastic picks sticking out of the brush-and-wire rollers.

"Go uptown after lunch and get some potatoes and bread, can you Stephen? And some kind of meat for supper. Take Francie with you."

Stephen nodded at his mother, scowled at Francie. Francie looked past him and out the window. "Dad's coming," she said.

"My scarf, Francie," their mother said, and Francie hopped up and ran to the bathroom, came back with a gauzy blue square which she folded into a triangle and knotted over her mother's curlers. Their mother straightened in her chair and closed her robe around her waist. Stephen's father came in with a smile that looked as if he'd just tried out the muscles for it as he opened the door. He put a pot of coffee on before he sat down, left for work again before half an hour was up.

SCHOOL THE FOLLOWING MONDAY. Mickey not moving the clock along in any kind of a hurry. Finally three-thirty. Bright and cold outside, cold enough to make Stephen hesitate before walking home. His parka still undone, he ran up the half-flight of stairs to the library, a small room off the landing between the two floors. Light knifed in through the window and made everything else in the room too dark for a moment. Four short walls. Against one, the desk and the two sets of encyclopedias ranged on the shelves above it. On the desk, a wobbly globe with a screw that always needed to be tightened. Someone had taken the sphere off its stand and replaced it upside down so that Antarctica was at the top. Greenland and Russia and the deep pink that was Canada all crawled up into view from underneath. Stephen liked that. Who decided the North Pole was at the top and the South Pole at the bottom anyway? You could think of it as just the opposite, couldn't you? Then we'd be the upside-down ones, not those people in Australia.

Three more walls, mostly filled with slump-spined books that were rarely disturbed. A four-paned window; a locked cupboard where paper and glue and models of the planets sat in the dark for months on end. The interesting books were on the two shelves on the right as you came in the door, the space reserved for the block of books from the unit office. They changed every month. These were the only two shelves where it was worth looking for something interesting to read. Sci Fi, Hardy Boys, anything *new*. The unit office books lay across each other at angles, some with their backs to the wall, some open, spines straining under the weight of the volumes piled on top of them. Stephen searched through this landslide for science fiction. The future, that's what science fiction was about. The future, which was a lot more interesting than the present. Had to be.

He found a book by Ray Bradbury. Might be worth a look. He'd read *Fahrenheit 451* before Christmas. It wasn't too bad, "outstanding" in fact, just as the cover promised. The part near the end where the fireman put on someone else's dirty clothes, doused himself with whiskey to throw the hound off his scent, and floated down the river and out of town – that was the scariest part. The man floating down the river. Frightening to a guy who'd never learned to swim and who did his best to hide that fact any time he ended up at a place where swimming was the main activity. Last summer at the school picnic at Horseshoe Lake, Stephen had slipped off the raft and been trapped underneath. Whirled and swirled, hung on with his fingernails to a two-by-four on the underside, worked his way along it to the edge, hauled himself back up, his arms feeling like stretched elastic bands, his leg muscles quivering. He'd tried to act as if it was no big deal, but had to sit curled over with his forehead pressed into his knees to stop all the shaking.

After Horseshoe Lake, he'd concluded that muscle development was what he needed. He'd resolved to strengthen his arms. The Parker house had one bedroom without a door, and that room was Stephen's. There was a door on his parents' bedroom and one on Francie's – privacy is supposed to be more important to a girl – but none on his own and no one could say why the house had been built that way. In his open bedroom doorway he installed a chin-up bar. Bought it on a trip to Regina when he took the bus in with his mother for one of her doctor's appointments. "Home Gymnasium Muscle Bar," the box said. The metal surface of the rod was scarified to make it easier to clasp. Rubber grips on each end held it in place inside the door frame.

THE BRADBURY book Stephen picked up was a collection of stories. He flipped to the beginning of one, read the first page, stopped at a reference to "women's hidden wonders." He read the sentence over twice, knew from the tone that whoever put this book in with the lot that went from school to school for junior high students hadn't looked too closely between the covers. Stephen scooped the book into his stack of homework and took it home without filling out the card.

In his room that night, lying on his bed, he picked up the book again. Despite the lack of privacy, Stephen's room was a refuge of sorts, a place where he played his records, worked away at his current model (67 Shelby GT-350, bright blue), read his books, stared at the ceiling, watched the cobwebs take shape in the corners. Right now, if he had a door on his room, he'd close it. He turned to the story he'd been looking at that afternoon. A couple in a hotel room in Mexico, the woman naked, fresh from her bath. By the second page, though, that part seemed less important. This story was not at all about a woman with no clothes on; it was about other things. Something frightening and unexplainable was about to happen, Stephen just knew it. There were descriptions of coffins, graveyards, mummies. Threats bulged underneath the sentences like muscles stirring under skin. He stopped reading, slid the book underneath his bed.

MARCH: the first beat of spring, but only if you could sense it way inside the trunks of the trees where the sap was getting ready to soften.

Another hockey game against Blake. Stephen went upstairs at the rink to have a look around. Katie Mueller wasn't at the coffee counter. He should go back downstairs, shouldn't be hiding up here anyway. Up here where the little kids and the old people sat in a single row in front of the glass, where other people's mothers fried burgers and onions and dished out pie and coffee. He should be down below, standing out there somewhere along the boards, close to the ice, stamping his feet to get the circulation going, sneaking a smoke, shouting easy insults at the ref or the fans from Blake. *There* was the group he should be standing with, out past the penalty box, leaning against the boards where they'd rolled back the chicken wire that was supposed to protect them from flying pucks. Hiding their cigarettes inside curled hands, waiting with their skates laced up, ready to hop the boards and clean the ice at the end of the period.

Tredwell was inside the record booth. When he saw

Stephen, he reached for his thick green coffee mug and started to push himself out of his chair, but Stephen lifted his hand in half a wave, shook his head, pointed down to the ice, turned and descended the stairs. He swung open the door that separated the lobby from the arena; the heavy spring above him squawked and slapped the door shut after he passed through. Stale, cold air touched his cheeks; Stephen took a breath and puffed out a wisp of white. He stood near the door for a few minutes, then walked the plank, made his way down the rink behind the straggle of fans lined up along the boards. Squeezed himself behind the players' box, past the empty penalty bench. Wondered as he approached the others whether he was supposed to have some kind of invitation, or could he just go stand there at the edge of the group and pretend he belonged? No one paid much attention when he walked up. Ox looked over at him, said hi. Stephen stood beside Dutch, who nodded at him and asked him if his cousin Vic would be on the ice for the game.

"Yeah," Stephen said. "It was just a one-game suspension." There, he thought; he could do this. No invitation necessary after all. He took a drag from the smoke Dutch offered, inhaled, let it out past the slight burn in his throat and handed it back without coughing.

APRIL: the rhythm of tires on pavement. Around, around, around, with a shake in the chassis every time the tires passed over a pothole. Under the authority of Shiner and Ox, Hallowe'en-style pranks with raw eggs were the chosen after-hours amusement for Easter weekend.

"Got 'em," Shiner yelled. "You see that? Smack in the middle of the windshield!" He'd been half-standing, leaning out the front passenger window. Now he pulled his head and shoulders back inside the car and flashed a grin at Donnie, sitting between him and Ox in the front seat. He turned then, and looked back to be sure Stephen and Dutch had taken note of his accomplishment.

Ox, who was two years older than the others and had passed his driver's test in March on his second try, was driving. (He was doing his second year in grade eight. He liked to refer to this as his "advance" year; a few years earlier he'd completed his "advanced" grade six.) He'd got hold of his dad's car for the evening.

Shiner supplied the eggs. His mother had bought two dozen for his little sister to colour for Easter, but Shiner thought of a better use, carried them out to the car in paper bags. Left the cartons empty in the refrigerator, his idea of a joke.

The lights of the car Shiner had bombed with a raw egg flashed past, stopped for a second, then carried on as if the driver had made a sudden decision.

Ox in the driver's seat and Shiner at the front passenger window were the two doing the actual egg-throwing, targeting buildings, signs, other cars. They'd gone through almost a dozen and there was another dozen hidden under the blanket on the back seat between Stephen and Dutch, whose job it was to keep them from rolling into each other, and to pass the ammo up to Donnie whenever he asked for it. Donnie passed it along to the two at the windows. Stephen had shifted from thinking a few weeks ago that these guys didn't want him around to realizing they didn't care one way or another about him so long as he wasn't in the way. A good audience is hard to find.

Ox pulled into an approach and turned to head back to town. Shiner took a few more shots at road signs on the way in; Ox heaved an egg at a truck on the way by, but missed; Shiner dropped another by accident - shit! Back in town, with half a dozen eggs still nestled under the blanket, they were pulled over by the Mounties. Ox rolled down his window and cool spring air spilled into the car, followed by the flashlight beam that cop number one bounced from face to face.

"You boys aren't up to any mischief tonight?"

"No officer," Shiner said. Sudden humility.

"No drinking going on here?"

"No drinking," said Ox, sliding a shaky finger into his wallet to find his licence. Donnie unsuccessfully stifled a laugh, converting it into a series of painful-sounding nasal snorts.

Cop number two opened the rear door without warning and shone his flashlight in. Stephen blinked. "Had a complaint," the cop said. "A complaint about someone throwing eggs. That wouldn't be you, would it?"

"Not us," said Ox, taking back his licence from number one, lifting his chunky hips to stash his wallet in his back pocket again.

"You boys won't mind getting out while we have a look."

The five of them got out and watched as number two leaned first into the front seat with his flashlight, then into the back, where he moved the beam of light over the floor and the blanket on the seat. He patted the blanket lightly, then whacked it repeatedly with the flat of his hand until there could be no doubt that anything underneath would be sliding and spreading and soaking through the upholstery.

Once he'd done a thorough job, he withdrew and said to his partner, "Nothing in there. These boys have nothing at all back there. Can you believe it?"

"I'll just make sure of that," number one said. He leaned in and patted the blanket lightly, then slapped it hard. "You're right," he said to his partner.

"Have a nice evening, Mr. Kovach," he said to Ox. "Don't rack up any points against that new licence of yours. You'll want to keep it clean. Just the way you keep your dad's car."

Stephen would be in shit six ways from Sunday when he got home, but it didn't seem to matter right now. For now, nothing was more important than to sit here at the edge of the empty grain field and listen to the frogs chirp, listen to Shiner perform fragments of Rolling Stones songs, as much as he could remember, humming to fill in when he ran out of words, beer bottle as a microphone, blonde hair swinging a split second after the beat. "Jumpin' Jack Flash." The air was frosty, but Stephen had his winter jacket on, which was long enough he could pull it down between his butt and the cold ground. Stars by the millions out here away from the street lights, a few raggedy clouds up there too; the tangled branches of half a dozen dead trees near where the old house was falling into the basement; a stack of bales off in the field, gone silver after a winter of sun and snow and wind.

They'd been to the water pump near the town office,

soaked the blanket and used it as a clumsy rag to scrub the back seat of the car as well as they could. The more you work at egg whites, they'd discovered, the more they turn to foam. Finally Ox had said it was good enough. They'd washed the blanket under the pump and wrung it out, two boys twisting at one end, three at the other. Rubbed their hands together afterwards to warm them, crossed their arms and tucked their fingers into their armpits. They hadn't *really* done a good job on the back seat at all, it would dry all crusty, but that was between Ox and his dad. They'd pulled off a country road into an old yard at the edge of a field and made themselves a party out of a few bags of chips, half a pack of cigarettes, a couple of Cokes; also three beer Donnie had scoffed from his parents' fridge on the way out of town.

The soggy blanket hung from a tree, barely moving in the breeze, its fringes letting go of a drop or two of water every once in a while. They'd opened all the doors of the blue Pontiac that belonged to Ox's dad, the better to chase out both the damp and the smell of raw egg. Not a hope in hell. Stephen looked across the field at the stack of bales. He shivered against the cold wicking up through his jacket. He thought of standing up and walking across the field, not stopping until he came to…where? To someplace else. Maybe the hotel room in that Bradbury story. The book was still at home under his bed where he'd left it. Once in a while the beginning of the story would flash through his mind, but by now he'd forgotten how it had frightened him. What he did remember was that it was about a man and a woman together in a room. How did a person get from here to a hotel room in Mexico?

Across the yard, Dutch and Donnie sat in the shadow of a maple tree, leaning against the trunk. They might even be asleep, it was too dark to tell. Shiner, whose Mick Jagger performance had wound down, stood looking across the field in the same direction Stephen had been looking. Maybe, Stephen thought, Shiner was thinking too about where he'd end up if he headed out over the stubble and kept on going.

Shiner turned and caught Stephen's look, flipped his bottle upside down as if to say, "Sorry, none left or I'd give you a sip," and walked back to where Ox sat with his back against the car.

"Ox," he said, "you're up shit creek with your old man. Up shit creek and down piss river. Let's go."

MAY: a pulse pounding in Stephen's temples when he woke up. How's a guy supposed to sleep on a Saturday morning? TV going full volume in the living room. Francie across the hall with her squeaky friends and their Barbies. Stephen kicked away the covers, got out of bed and stomped across the hall in his undershorts. Three girls, their high small voices singing "Lemon Tree"; three hands holding Barbie dolls on a shoe-box stage, stiff, synthetic doll-hair moving with the music. He shouted at Francie, "You've got a door, use it for Christ's sake," and pulled it shut with a slam. An instant of silence before giggles exploded inside her room. He wanted to hit his sister, his mother; he'd hit his father, really hit him, if his father wasn't at work. Shut them up, get some privacy. How could they all stand each other, the people in this house? His mother with her hip out again. His father coming and going with that smile he picked up off the doorstep before he walked into the house. Coming home from the elevator and making supper, proudly cutting little nicks in the edges of the baloney slices or the pork chops so they wouldn't warp in the frying pan. Raising his eyebrows as he set things on the table. Doing *such* a fine job of adapting.

Stephen went down the hall to the living room, still wearing nothing but his shorts. He ignored his mother sitting in her chair with her detective book (she ignored him back), searched through the drawers of the sewing machine cabinet and took out four old diaper pins. In his room he took the ribbed green spread off his bed, fought with its slipperiness, its shifting weight as he held it around the chin-up bar, and made himself a hanging door. He worked to push the spread properly over the rubber grips at either end of the bar so that the strips of light at the sides of the door frame disappeared. A solid, dark curtain. Stephen looked around. The colour of the light in the room had changed for the better. He could simulate twilight if he closed the navy curtains at the window. Sleep longer. Sleep until he got old enough to leave.

SOUND PASSED THROUGH the makeshift door as if there were no barrier, but Stephen was soon good at pretending it didn't. He acted as if the suspended bedspread caught household noises and his parents' questions, commands, and demands the way a spider web arrested flies, held them there outside the room.

He played his music louder than he had before he'd hung the curtain. *Sgt. Pepper*. Stephen liked to trace his finger over the small faces on the front of the album, turn it over and read along with the lyrics on the back, open the gatefold sleeve and look back into the four pairs of eyes that stared out at him. He listened to this one more than he listened to his other albums, never failed to hear the beginning of the next song in the ending of the last one.

Dutch came over to listen and said his favourite song on the record was "With a Little Help From My Friends." Stephen said it was his too, but that was a lie. His favourite was "Lucy in the Sky With Diamonds." He'd memorized all the words, had no idea what they meant. Waltzing horses, marshmallow pies, the sound of a circus. Maybe you weren't supposed to understand it, maybe you were just supposed to let it slide past your ears. Take a breath, let it out slowly. Wait.

JULY: fireworks for Dominion Day. Explosions like rifle shots, one after another in the hot summer night, setting off a ringing in Stephen's ears. Now, the excitement is over and the sky is strewn with stars that look as if they're remnants of the light show. Most of the town has gone to sleep. Stephen leans against one of the massive wooden beams that shoulder the water tower near the railway station. Old wood, exposed to decades of winter snow and summer heat. He tilts his head back almost to the point where his neck hurts, looks up at the dark underside of the tank above him. Catches his hair on a splinter; frees himself, then uses the inside of his wrist to wipe sweat from his forehead, his upper lip. He and the others are waiting for Dutch, who should've shown up by now if he's coming. Dutch told them his dad wanted him to stay and help clean up after the fireworks, but no problem, he'd get away no matter what, wasn't going to miss this.

The swim in the water tower was Ox's idea. His older brother did the same thing last summer. A cool place on a hot night. Celebrate Canada's hundred-and-first birthday. The tower is in its last days. Built first to supply the steam locomotives, it long ago outlived its original use; now it supplies the station and the twelve-man bunkhouse with running water, after a fashion. But they're about to run the town water pipes out to those two buildings and the tank will soon be out of service for good.

Ox, leaning against another wooden beam, drops a couple of Aspirins into his Coke, takes a swig, makes a face. "Nothin'," he says. "Doesn't do anything. Supposed to be such a big deal."

"Well, you gotta wait," Shiner says. "Drink the whole thing."

"Looks like Dutch isn't going to show up," Donnie says. "Come on, you guys." With a quick motion he pulls off his T-shirt. Shiner kicks off his shoes, pulls at his socks, unzips his fly.

Stephen kneels – in no hurry – to untie his runners. He peers down the road looking for Dutch. What the hell is he doing here without Dutch? Should've stayed with him after the fireworks instead of expecting to meet him here. He's sure he could figure his way out of this, if only Dutch would show.

Ox puts his pop bottle down and the glass clinks against gravel. He grabs Donnie's and Shiner's shorts as soon as they take them off, stands in the middle of the tracks with a pair in each hand. "How do you do that semaphore thing?" he says. "Like the boy scouts." He stiffens his arms and moves them about in jerky motions; the shorts flap stupidly in his hands. He speaks out a message, one arm movement for each syllable. "Time-for-a-swim. Where-are-you-Dutch?"

Donnie and Shiner scramble around him wearing only their sweat, both of them half a foot shorter than Ox, pulling at his arms, jumping to grab at their underwear, yelping as their bare feet land on gravel. This would be the time for Stephen to leave, walk away down the road with his untied shoelaces flicking against the gravel. They might not even notice.

Finished with his joke, Ox stops the game suddenly, throws the shorts down and strips. Stephen slips out of his shoes...socks...shirt. Pants. Shorts. By the time he finishes the others are on their way up the ladder.

"You coming or what, Stevie?" Shiner says from halfway up. "Grab the rope there."

Stephen slings the coil of rope over his shoulder and starts to climb. Can he take the rope up to the others and then just say he'll wait at the trap door for them? Offer to be the lookout? Watch for old man Shepherd, the station boss? Never mind, he'll figure it out once he's up there. He doesn't *have* to go down into the tank.

His memory latches on to the incident at Horseshoe Lake. That time, he'd resurfaced once or twice before he'd sunk down again and found himself turning around and around underneath the raft. Maybe a person just floats of his own accord, as long as he doesn't panic.

Two dozen smooth wooden steps up the ladder, then

a long stretch of the torso to work his way over the eave. Wood scraping against his belly. Reach out and grab the first two-by-four bolted to the roof. The others are waiting, crouching on the tapered roof panels. Shiner takes the rope from Stephen and fixes it to the last two-by-four, drops the free end through the open trap door. They hear the rope hit the water down below.

"Me first," Ox says. He crouches near the trap, grabs the line in both hands, lowers himself awkwardly to loop his legs around the rope lower down, and disappears. The others hear him shout when he reaches the water.

"Hell with the rope," Shiner says. "Look out below!" he yells into the echoing tank and drops feet-first through the opening without benefit of rope. His splash sets the tank vibrating.

"After you, Stevie," Donnie says. "Let's go."

"Go ahead," Stephen says, crouching beside the opening, wiping his damp forehead. He's aware of sweat prickling in his groin, his underarms. What to say? Get in or get away.

"Go on, chicken-shit." A good-natured insult.

Dark beyond the trap door and hard to see. Smell of wet wood. Echoing laughs from down below. Donnie behind him. What now? Make some excuse, some explanation. But he doesn't. Instead he thinks of what his dad said once, how *his* father taught him to swim by throwing him off the dock into the river. Said he'd resurfaced of his own accord and that's all there was to swimming. Stephen pictures a chunky toddler with his father's rough face and dark green work overalls thrashing for a moment, then calmly floating with the current. His father knows how to keep from drowning all right.

Look at him now, bobbing and breathing, bobbing and breathing, moving where the water takes him.

The thought gives a perverse lift to Stephen's spirits. He lets his arm take hold of the rope, tells himself he'll climb down carefully, stay close to the rope, not let go if he doesn't feel safe. Out over the water now, leg half hooked around the line. The rope burns his hands as he slides along it for nearly a foot, drives wiry slivers of hemp into his fingers, provokes an uncontrollable reflex that loosens his grip. He tries to clench his hand again just as Donnie, above him, yanks the rope and says, "My turn."

Quick now, deep deep breath. Into the water. Under. Down, thinking of nothing, an impression of dark, double-dark green inside his head – no feelings, neither fear nor panic, just the colour. And then he's back up to the surface without having done any work to get there. He kicks, dips under again, comes up, gets a breath, and now he's moving arms as well as legs. He's doing it – staying up, almost – as long as he moves his legs and arms about. He *does* know how to do this. He's under again now, for a second, but now he's up again. Takes a breath. This is working. He's stayed up so far, must be at least a minute.

He's off to the side, he realizes, away from the others with their shouts and sputters. He can stay up long enough to make out their shapes in the dark tank. Kicking up waves, skimming their arms across the surface to throw water in each other's faces. He's bringing his initial frenzy of paddling under control. No need for help, he has it now. He's up, staying up. Man! his arms are tired, moving, moving, can't slow them down or....

Under he goes, feels a swirling and up again, his arms turning him half around in a corkscrew. Looking for air to call for help. Under again, then up. Chest muscles screaming. Time to get a breath but no time to shout. His bladder swelling, releasing itself. Something on the side of the tank to hold onto? Opens his mouth to cough and in comes water. A burn in his nose. Straining to shout but he's under again. Splashing for attention but his arms are underwater where they can't make a noise.

His heartbeat a frantic wet percussion in his ears. His gut tearing at itself. Get to the top get to the top. Burning in his throat, his chest. A losing battle. Get to the, get to, get to the.... Which way up? Dark. The square of night sky long gone. The pile of folded clothing, still, abandoned at the foot of the tank.

BUT BEFORE THAT, JUNE. Days counting themselves off to the end of the school year. Two more weeks starting Monday, but this day had been a Saturday and there was no use rushing through the weekend. In his shirt pocket Stephen had carried two Export A butts he'd scavenged from his mother's ashtray. At the schoolyard, leaning in the shade against the cool brick of the building, he'd fished out one of the butts and lit a wooden match with his thumbnail the way he'd been practising. He took a drag, inhaled, tried a smoke ring. Not bad. Tried again. Perfect. Once more. Hopeless. A few more puffs, and then his stomach told him it would rather be anywhere else but in his body. He crushed the butt in the dust and stood up thinking he'd head uptown to find something to do. He left the shadow of the building, squinted in the bright sun, automatically raised his hand to shield his eyes.

There was Katie Mueller over at the swings, all by herself. Once before, he'd seen her alone in the school-yard, drawing little pictures in an exercise book, con-centrating, ignoring the blue ruled lines as if they weren't there. When she'd seen him, though, she'd put the book down and started pumping on the swing, maybe to relieve them both of the need to say anything to each other. Pumped sitting down with her yellow skirt tucked under her thighs. He'd watched the fabric rise a little with each forward motion, but her legs held the skirt down so well there was nothing to see, not even a wink of underpants as she swung forward and back.

Today she was sitting on the swing. Just sitting, not drawing, not swinging. She looked at him as he crossed the yard. He thought if he had a real cigarette, a fresh one, not just the leftover butt in his pocket, he'd ask her if she wanted a smoke. He didn't have one though. He walked on past her but he said hi on the way by just to prove he wasn't totally invisible. Told himself that next time he'd think of something more to say, something that would make her get off the swing, walk over to him and...what?

Katie said hi back and for all Stephen knew she said it because she was another one who had to prove she wasn't invisible. Like she might be. Not a chance. He kept on walking and the possibility of a conversation between them rolled away like a drop of mercury.

Stephen changed his mind about going uptown,

walked aimlessly for a block or two, then turned and wandered home. The book of stories he'd neglected to take back to the school library lay under his bed, covered in dust. He wiped the cover on his jeans, opened it and started over with the story he'd given up on months ago: the hotel room again, the naked woman, the expectations he'd had the first time he picked up the book. But once more the story wasn't what he'd hoped for. Instead, there was that same desperation spiraling off the page like smoke; a graveyard, skulls, corpses. Stephen kept reading, holding his breath for half a page at a time. The woman had fear sewn up inside her, knew she wouldn't get out of that creepy, isolated town alive – was so certain of her future she was making it happen. Rushing at it full-speed ahead, and all she could do was be sorry about all the things she'd always wanted to do and would never do now. Just stupid, Stephen thought when he came to the end. She was just plain stupid. He shut the book and threw it out of sight, mad at her, even madder at himself for getting so scared for the sake of someone like that.

He thumbed through his records but couldn't find a single one that might help him unscramble his feelings. He wanted to hear nothing but quiet. He took his new model kit down off the shelf (a T-bird this time, colour still to be decided). He opened the box, spilled out its contents, and caught the smell of plastic fresh from the factory, a smell he had always found satisfying. He snapped the pieces off their rigid trees and arranged them on his desk. All the little components laid out in front of him on the brown painted plywood surface, waiting to be attached to each other. This would be, as usual, an exercise in patience. He'd tried not to be in too much of a hurry; he'd held in check the appetite that made him want to see the finished T-Bird now, without delay, without all the monotonous movements it would take to glue the bits together.

EDGES

On more than one occasion, Frances had tried to repeat slivers of Abigail Larch's wisdom to Bill, but the fragments became nonsensical in translation. Then she'd asked Abigail around to the house so Bill could hear for himself. The older woman had leaned forward on the wooden rocking chair in their living room and talked for almost half an hour, working her wrinkled fingers through her sparrow-coloured hair the whole time. She told them there are trees that produce seed pods that will only break open in the intense heat of a forest fire. She told them a panda had died in a city zoo somewhere in the United States and the bear's keepers were at a loss to explain it, but Abigail knew it was lack of stimulation, pure and simple. She told them how every once in a while a person needs to be presented with some awful possibility to brace herself against.

"What do you mean, dear Abby?" asked Bill, who at that point seemed at least willing to play along. "What do you mean by 'awful possibility'?"

"All I mean is that without some small calamity from time to time, some real or imagined fear, you can run out of reasons for just getting through one day after another. Frances understands, don't you Frances?" Abigail looked at Frances, then at Bill, then back at Frances, who had no answer, but who remembered to herself how she'd felt when the biopsy last November had shown that the mass in her ovary was a mere cyst. Benign. For weeks afterward, every detail of existence had been more vivid.

"I have *no* idea what you're talking about," Bill said to Abigail.

"Sometimes it takes something frightening," Abigail said. "Say you pull a lamp plug out of the wall and for some reason it's live and it knocks you out cold for a second or two. Once you come to again, you think you know what it must be like for those people up at the Arctic Circle when they see the sun break the horizon after all those months of winter."

"I haven't had the pleasure," said Bill, looking at Abigail with an expression that Frances had to admit hadn't crossed the line to mockery just yet, a look that might at any second either cloud over with impatience or ripple into a grin.

"Or even just thinking about the cold," said Abigail. "In the winter just the frost in the air can be enough some days to remind me that without a good overcoat a person would die here.

"Summer is harder, because of the heat. Sometimes in the summer I have to go out on the bridge. I go in the evening. If the air is too dull even at the bridge, I have to climb right up on the edge and look over.

"Don't look so alarmed," Abigail said to Bill. "It isn't as if I'd jump. It's just a way to put myself back in balance."

"NOW WHAT was I supposed to get out of that?" Bill had said after he closed the door behind Abigail. "Is that the kind of gibberish you've been listening to during your afternoon teas in her living room? You meet a stray lady on the bridge and it isn't enough you spend every third Friday afternoon listening to her, you have to bring her home too?"

"She doesn't make any sense at all to you, does she?" Frances said.

"None at all. And if she makes sense to you, I hope you stop short of standing on the balustrade of University Bridge."

"You don't need to worry about that."

"But I do. I do worry. Are you coming upstairs?"

"Soon."

She should have kept Abigail to herself, should have kept her a secret, but she'd told. Challenged herself to make Bill understand Abigail's take on life. Challenged herself to put into words what drew her to this woman and her compulsion to make herself feel more of what there was to feel, to test the edges of things the way a chef will check a blade for sharpness by drawing it across the back of a fingernail.

NOW BILL AND FRANCES have come to a northern lake for a few days away from the city, as they do almost every year at this time. Frances floats on her back not far from shore and thinks of Abigail. She holds her breath and feels the stillness of the lake around her. This is pungent northern air, water cold enough to bite flesh. She should be able to open her lungs and pull life inside along with the sharp smell of pine, should be able to rinse away the mildew of the day-to-day with an icy swim. She thinks of Abigail standing on the bridge in the city, of Abigail's soft hair curling around the updraft, of Abigail looking for some sharp sensation to brace herself against.

From time to time Frances kicks her legs to keep herself afloat. Oh, she's a good swimmer; her lessons started when she was nine and continued every summer for five years, daily drives to Horseshoe Lake, trips for which her father used his entire two weeks vacation every year. The first day of lessons, she balked, afraid to sit on the dock with the others as they kicked their legs to splash water over themselves. The second day of lessons she refused even to get in the car. "In," her father said. "Now." Short, no-nonsense commands. His surviving child would learn to swim.

When Frances waded into the lake today, the shock of cold had quickened her muscles for a moment, but she acclimatized in no time. Now, feeling more comfortable than she'd like to feel, she arches her neck back – way back – so the water washes her eyebrows and she glimpses the shoreline, the pine trees, the green canvas tent, the picnic table, the whole scene upside down. She backstrokes until her hands catch in the sand.

On the beach she stands in her wet bathing suit and allows a prolonged, cold shudder to move through her body. She wants to let the air at her skin until she can feel the cold inside like needles. Bill wraps her in a towel, too soon. He leads her to the fire, pours her a cup of coffee from the tin pot they've used over campfires for nine years now.

He stirs the fire and talks the way he always does on the first morning of a camping trip, about how satisfying it is to get back in touch with nature, about how right it is to have a proper view of the sky without buildings in the way, and a proper view of the ground without lawns and sidewalks and pavement covering it up. Out here a person can really get in touch with himself, says Bill.

Frances says nothing. She turns to the nearest pine and presses a cluster of needles into the soft pad of a numb middle finger. When she stops, small red polka dots fill the indentations. Abigail says the only way to get in touch with yourself is to jolt your whole system awake, to brush up against some extreme discomfort or even an outright threat. Last night Bill had moved his log stool upwind of the campfire as soon as the breeze changed; Frances had waited five minutes with smoke in her eyes, welcoming the sting and the spontaneous wash of tears it called up.

ONCE UPON A TIME, forever ago, there had been a brother, Stephen. When he died, Frances, bewildered rather than grief-stricken, had been unable to conjure a tear. She'd waited for the mystery of grief to engulf her. She would know it when it hit, she was sure. During the funeral she stared at the coffin, spoke to herself inside her head. *Now I'll cry. Any minute. It's just I'm waiting for it to hit home.* They followed the coffin out the front door of the small white church with the black painted trim and the black iron handrails. *Now, maybe.* And then at the cemetery when the minister rested his warm hand for a moment on her shoulder. *For sure now.* She went home feeling cheated that grief had let her down. Didn't it owe her some kind of feeling? Maybe if she'd known him better. A fourteen-year-old boy is such a long way away from a nine-year-old girl.

"Poor girl," Aunt Lydia had said to her when they were all back at the house and Frances had watched a tear brim out of her aunt's eye, hesitate on her round cheek as it looked for the path of least resistance down her face, then slide quickly to the corner of her mouth. *Poor me,* Frances thought in an attempt to convince herself. *Poor me, poor Stephen.* She thought she might like to see him for a minute, find out how pissed off he was over the whole thing. He'd be mad all right.

ABIGAIL LARCH had come into Frances's life four months ago. Frances had been walking downtown on her Friday off, trying to think what to do with herself, going on faith that merely by walking across the bridge she could force the day to present her with some purpose.

She'd seen a woman – sixtyish she guessed – standing still, facing full into the wind off the river and staring downstream. She was layered against the March weather in only a short denim jacket, unbuttoned, and a long purple cardigan over her dress. As Frances approached, the wind whipped a gauze scarf out of the woman's hair and blew it against the first obstacle in its path, which happened to be Frances's arm. Frances had allowed the act of returning the scarf to lead to conversation.

"Your scarf likes me," she said, watching how the fabric wanted to stay curled around her arm as she lifted it away.

The woman turned and thanked Frances, and her shoulder-length hair blew thinly across her features. Without further preliminaries she said, "I come here to feel the wind." With an ungloved hand she cleared the hair from her face. "Now it wants to steal my scarf."

Frances turned toward the river, face into the wind, as the woman had been standing before she approached. The early spring current was shaving snow and ice away from the east bank. The relative warmth of recent days had lifted with the clouds this morning and cold had rushed in to fill the space. "Chilly," Frances said.

"I know. I love it."

They'd had a strange, brief conversation, agreeing that cold had its attractions and that yes, the wind could steal your breath, but if you faced into it long enough and purposefully enough you could steal it back so that you felt a breeze running inside along your veins. Frances was aware she was talking with this woman in a way that would embarrass her with anyone else she could think of – the others in Payroll, the women from her stitch and bitch group, the people she met for drinks on Friday afternoons. She decided not to think about this. She didn't want to break the spell.

The woman made another observation: she told Frances that tea takes on the power of a tonic after a person has had a long meditation in a cold wind. So Frances had surrendered to the momentum of this unforeseen meeting and accepted the woman's invitation to share a cup at her house downtown, the little yellow house on the big lot in among the high-rises not far from the foot of the bridge, the house that resisted real estate agents year after year. The house that was to become familiar to Frances over the next few months.

During the visits that followed, Abigail served tea and muffins and taught Frances arcane embroidery stitches: bargello, trapunto, cut-work lace. Abigail told Frances she'd learned them all as a girl, her mother's belief being that the art of needlework made a woman more desirable on the marriage market. "I showed her," Abigail said. Meaning, Frances supposed – though she didn't ask directly – that Abigail had never explored that particular market, or hadn't explored it successfully.

The walls of Abigail's rooms were festooned with giant fabric hangings, embroidery samplers of the most contrary sort. Stitches ran off at absurd angles, cut-work interrupted daisy-stitch, loose flaps of material in unlikely colours obscured whole areas of meticulously knotted patterns. Frances could hardly stop looking at these adornments. "You should do something with these," she said finally one day.

"What do you mean?"

"I don't know what I mean. Put them in an art gallery somewhere. Take pictures of them and make a book. People should see them. They're worth looking at."

"Oh, I know. I look at them all the time," Abigail said. "And now you can look at them too. There's no need to show them anywhere else; I've made them and I've put them where they are so I can see them every day.

"You know what I like most about them? On days when I don't feel good they help me remember that there are endless possibilities out there. And that's just with needles and fabric. Endless possibilities." She rose from the armchair she'd been sitting in and leaned across it to inspect the hanging beside her. "Some days I need a reminder."

Frances looked at Abigail and nodded.

WHEN HE DIED, Stephen left a roomful of things, hardly disturbed for at least a year after he drowned, everything there to remind her who he'd been: his records, his model cars, the poster with the cartoon figure wearing beads and yellow bug-eyed glasses, captioned *How has the guru affected you?* The jar with the four-inch nail he'd been trying to dissolve in Coca-cola – the soft drink evaporated, the spike still intact. Press on the tip of it, convince yourself the impossible has happened.

She was nine when Stephen died, fifteen when she walked the half-mile out to the cemetery with a group of friends. The sound of shoes on the gravel road in the dark; the smell of chilly evening damp wafting out of the ditches; the chirp of frogs somewhere unseen and surprisingly close. They were on an expedition to watch for the rumoured ghosts that people said hovered above the graves. At the cemetery, Frances and her friends sat in a row on the stone fence, lined up boy-girl-boy-girl so that nature could take its course if anyone needed to give or take reassurance, or if they pretended to need to. All this to the musical accompaniment of "Band on the Run" and "Hooked on a Feeling" and "Bennie and the Jets" threading out of a transistor speaker the size of a quarter.

She was self-conscious, a little, about the fact that she had a brother there. The others must have been self-conscious as well; at any rate no one mentioned it. He wasn't buried in the original walled area where they sat and kept watch. That part of the cemetery had reached capacity years ago. Stephen and all those others who'd died since the mid-sixties were outside the stone wall in an area surrounded by immature spruce trees. Frances didn't look in that direction, didn't catch anyone else doing so either.

AT THE CAMPGROUND, standing barefoot in the sand, still wrapped loosely in her towel, Frances pushes another clutch of pine needles into the pad of her finger. Wanting to feel her muscles work, she sets her melmac coffee cup on the picnic table, slips her feet into rubber-soled thongs and walks across a patch of gravel to the bin of firewood supplied by the park administration. The hatchet feels too light in her hands. It should be bigger, more powerful, should require more strength to lift, but it will do. Without speaking, she steadies a log on the stump that serves as chopping block, braces her left foot on the stump, and begins to split off kindling. She concentrates on the power of the first blow each time, satisfied when she buries the head, pleased with the hollow crack every time the wood separates. Then a slim twig of slippery birch underneath her right foot rolls sideways and pulls her off balance. The hatchet glances off a knot and catches her left foot. The pain is immediate, searing.

This wasn't supposed to happen. She was only wanting a little bit of exertion. Frances is calm though, as she sets the hatchet on the ground and watches a thin red line fill the fresh cut on her toe. She feels the blood pool in the depression the ball of her foot has worn in her thong. Bill is there to help, wrapping a shirt, then an arm around her shoulders. He scolds her just a little for chopping wood without proper shoes on. As she walks to the car, Frances' foot slips back and forth on the slickness; blood, rubber and skin slide against each other. She props her foot on the dash and twists a kleenex tightly around the bleeding toe.

Bill drives to the doctor in La Ronge. It's a small cut, worth two stitches only, hardly any blood after the first puddle. The hatchet left a clean track the way a properly keen blade will. Look away while the needle goes in. Stare at the ceiling tiles as the doctor takes the needle and thread in his antiseptic hands. Steal a glance or two before it's over. The edges seal up nicely.

On the main street they find a place that supplies them with take-out burgers and fries, which they wash down with root beer as they drive back along the treed road. Bill and Frances are back at the park in no time. The campsite looks as comforting as home. A breeze coaxes this morning's fire-logs to turn red again on the undersides. Frances walks down to the edge of the lake, lurching awkwardly, holding her newly-mended toe clear of the sand. She looks at the water, thinks of Abigail on the bridge, climbing to stand on the balustrade, hopes she won't lose her balance reaching for something.

For some people, Frances thinks, things never seem to get all that complicated. There's Bill, rummaging in the tent, shoes sticking out the door so as not to leave dirt and pine needles on the canvas floor. But maybe she's not being fair. No doubt he carries his own set of complications inside himself, layered out of sight the way an oyster covers a piece of grit.

Bill brings Frances her running shoes and a pair of socks. She tells him thank you and wishes she could tell him more. That she didn't intend to hurt herself, though he must wonder. Dipping her sutured foot in the lake, she feels the cold rush up her leg. Feeling an energy she hasn't felt for months, she towels off and slips on her socks and shoes. There is so much to be done – clean the scattered breakfast dishes, brew a new pot of coffee, rinse out yesterday's T-shirt and hang it to dry, carry the canoe down to the water for an afternoon paddle. Maybe they'll go all the way to the bay at the north end of the lake and hunt for wild strawberries hidden under round, delicate leaves.

"Let's get going," she says, reaching for her cold coffee cup and pouring its contents onto the dirt with a no-nonsense flick of her wrist.

HARD FROST

The crawl space underneath the house wasn't big enough even for a child to move around in. A twenty-one-year-old woman with expanding hips didn't have a hope. Getting the cat out wouldn't be easy. Evelyn couldn't think how the stray found its way down there in the first place. Her father didn't care, he said, as long as she got it out before it died and rotted there. He didn't want no damn bloody stink in the house, he said. *Old King Cole was a crabby old soul.*

There was only one way for the cat to get out, as far as Evelyn could see. He'd have to come up into the kitchen through the cellar door. She left the trap door in the floor open these days, hoping to tempt the cat out with warmth or company or food. The opening made a square black hole that gave off a chilly smell of old dirt and burlap sacks. Fusty hints of potato sprouts working out through the weave.

Maybe a little bait would work. Evelyn knelt and

held a squat salmon tin with the juice still in it down into the cellar hole. A wasted meow came from underneath the floor about where the stove was, or maybe further down, underneath the wringer washer in the corner.

"Come on, kitty, hasn't anyone ever told you you're a cat? – supposed to be able to find your way out of anyplace." The muscles in Evelyn's arm strained in their contrived position. She gave up. Maybe the cat would get too hungry to stay down in the cellar. Maybe a late spring frost would drive the damn thing out.

"Where's lunch already, Ev?" The question came around the corner from the living room. Evelyn looked at the kitchen wall, pictured her father on the other side of it, close to the radio, slung into the stretch of green vinyl between the wheels of his chair. Moving nothing but his lips. *He called for his pipe and he called for his bowl.*

"Almost ready," Evelyn said. "I have to run out back for some lettuce."

"Lettuce won't be up."

"It's up," she said. "Little teeny leaves. I planted it in the fall the way you said."

At the edge of the garden, Evelyn stooped and leaned across the mud to pluck a curly handful. The early lettuce and onions were in a small patch in the front corner. Weeds already twisted across the soil behind them. The garden was a leftover from the days before her father lost his feet. It was Evelyn's responsibility now, weeds and all. Through spring, summer, and fall, Evelyn's father instructed her week by week on what the garden needed. He had opinions about the results of her efforts. Last fall he'd said the carrots were too long, the corn was a poor variety, wasn't it, and if she'd watered the tomatoes when she should have, she wouldn't have lost so many to blossom-end rot. He ate them, though – the corn, carrots, onions, and beets, the tomatoes that hadn't succumbed – with nearly the same appetite he used to have for vegetables he'd grown himself.

On her way back up the path, Evelyn stopped to brush away the dry leaves she'd used to blanket the columbine after the first hard frost in the fall. Her father had warned her a columbine was every bit as delicate as it looked. Right now it didn't look too good. It would be a week or two before she knew if it had winter-killed.

Evelyn finished putting lunch together and wheeled her father to the kitchen table. He took the top slice off his sandwich, lifted the lettuce out of the way, scraped half the salmon out with his fork to make a small heap on his plate. It took him a long time.

"Well, I heard a good one this morning," he said eventually. "The Swap Shop on the radio says some nut over in Ripley's looking for old whiskey bottle caps. Says he's collecting them. Says he's going to build a statue out of them." He looked up. "What's the sense in that?"

"What's he swapping for them?"

"Didn't say. You see any sense in making a statue out of whiskey bottle caps, Evelyn?"

"Something to do, I guess."

They were quiet for a long minute. Then her father said, "So…Saturday."

"Uh-huh."

"S'pose you and Louie'll be going out. Going over to Ripley to the movies?" He turned his head far enough to see the movie calendar taped to the fridge. No further.

"*The Longest Yard*, they got. Football and Burt Reynolds. Something for each of you."

"It's old, second time around. We saw it last fall."

"Down to the café then." He pronounced it "cuffay," and the last syllable lay heavy and flat.

"Nobody goes to the café on Saturday night."

"Beer parlour then."

"I hate the beer parlour."

Her father chewed for a minute, moved his crusts around on the plate with his fork. "What d'you plan to do?"

"I don't know." Her voice was at the near edge of impatience.

He broke a rag of bread with a tiny smear of salmon on it away from the crust and set it on his tongue. He swallowed. "Parking, that's where you're going," he said, sounding matter-of-fact. "I know what goes on behind the grain bins at Hunters' old place. I grew up in this town too." He looked up. "Next thing you know, you'll get yourself in trouble."

Evelyn's father took a cigarette from the stack she'd made for him that morning with his little one-at-a-time stuff-it machine. (Load, slide, release. Load, slide, release.) He tapped his cigarette twice on the table and lit a match. "Stray cat's making a racket down there in the cellar again."

"They moved the grain bins off Hunters' old place years ago," Evelyn said. Her father had a lot of opinions about her behaviour for a man who'd put himself in a wheelchair through his own drunken carrying on. He was close to the mark, though. Already she was trying to think how she would handle Louie's back seat press and fumble tonight.

It was a tricky balance Evelyn maintained, hanging onto the same date for this long and not "giving him what he really needed," as the Flat Hill boys described it. Three years out of high school, she was, and running out of excuses. It wasn't the idea of the sex itself that was the problem; she just couldn't see herself in the part that comes after the bit where you sweat in the back seat. The part where you set up housekeeping.

Louie would cajole. She would say no, not yet, maybe when they got engaged for sure. He would say, okay, let's get engaged for sure. Evelyn would say, no, she wasn't quite ready. So it went. *Polly put the kettle on. Sukey take it off again.* Would it be so awful? he wanted to know.

Would it? Most of the girls from the class of '72 hadn't wasted any time. Her best friend Myrna had her own family by now. And so did Lynn and Gail and Julie. A few nights in the back seat and they all ended up buying clothes from the maternity rack at Woolworth's in Ripley. Cooking Easter eggs, Myrna called it. Enormous round ovals under brightly coloured blouses.

EVELYN DUMPED the crusts from her father's sandwich into the garbage, left the dishes soaking in the sink, and headed downtown. Tredwell's Hardware had merchandise on the shelves that had been there since the day Evelyn was born. Dusty belts for old model sewing machines, cracking where they curved out of their cardboard sleeves, cast aluminum vegetable juicers that came with hand cranks and promises of overnight vitality, fuses you couldn't trust the age of. Evelyn fished in the fuse bin, found a ten amp for the stove and took it up to the counter.

Old Paul rang up the sale. Young Paul was setting out packets of seeds on a wire rack. Old Paul touched her elbow the way an uncle might, wanted to know if her father ever used those plant pots and garden tools they fixed him up with last spring.

"No," she said. On her way through the porch that morning, she'd stepped around the pots, still nested in the stale-dated Greyhound schedules Old Paul had wrapped them in to keep them from breaking. The little tin shovel still had a price tag stuck on the blade.

Evelyn reached over to Young Paul's rack and picked out seeds for corn, carrots, peas. She'd have to plant more than that to keep her father happy. She took down radishes, reached for beets from the top of the rack. The stretch made her arm tired.

Old Paul was still looking at her. Now he wanted to know if she'd heard about that fellow in Zachary who lost his feet in a railway accident a couple of years back. "Doctor in Regina fixed him up with peg-legs and canes," he told her. "Gets around pretty good. Maybe your dad could get something like that."

"You could come by the house and talk to him," Evelyn said. It was no use bringing it up herself – her father didn't hear advice when it came from her. He wanted his own legs, not sticks. He wanted a real garden, not plant pots. He wanted his job at the mine, not a welfare check and a seat at the seniors' card game down at the Legion Hall.

"I'll get over for a coffee," Old Paul said. It wasn't the first time he'd said that. There were lots of promises, but only the people from the roster the United Church

Women had set up followed through. *Please to put a penny in an old man's hat.*

NURSERY RHYMES ran through Evelyn's head on circuits she'd never seen any point in shutting down. After all, most such rhymes were made up for adults in the first place, not for children. Remnants of off-colour drinking songs, Mr. Murphy had told them once in lit class – drinking songs and street cries and conundrums from the days when people still found word puzzles a suitable pastime for grown-ups. *All the kings horses and all the king's men couldn't put Humpty Dumpty together again.* Just a riddle about an egg. Of course, some of the rhymes really were meant to be lullabies from the very beginning. *Rock-a-bye Evelyn.*

When Evelyn's mother died, Evelyn had stayed home from school for three days. The funeral was the third day. For the first two days she sat in a kitchen chair and stared out the window into the back yard, trying to guess what was expected of her and wondering why none of the ladies who came and went with foil-covered casseroles and date loaves and turkey sandwiches could tell her what she was supposed to do. She held on to her mother's embroidery hoops, still clamped to the half-finished piece of work that had knocked around the house for years. (They used to sit together with their needles and embroidery cotton. Used to move their hoops into a column of sunlight to inspect rows of stitches that looked like fine ropes. *Sit on a cushion and sew a fine seam and feed upon strawberries, sugar and cream.* Until her mother's hands had curled so far out of shape the needle was impossible.)

Just before noon the day before the funeral, Mrs. Elliot from next door came in with lunch and told Evelyn she looked like she hadn't stirred since yesterday. Of course, she *had* moved, been to bed and got up again, even had different clothes on. But since breakfast she'd only moved once and that was to go to the bathroom.

By late afternoon of the same day, Evelyn still didn't know what to do with herself. Eventually she left her chair, but only because her bottom had gone numb from so much sitting. She tucked the bit of embroidery away in her room, did so because at twelve she was old enough, just, to be embarrassed by the melodrama of the picture she must make holding it. She told her father through his bedroom door that she was going for a walk. Once outside, she had trouble finding a destination. In less than half an hour, she was back at her kitchen chair, watching Mrs. Elliot and Mrs. Moore, the minister's wife, spread buns for the people who stopped by to offer sympathy. Evelyn listened, still as a doll in her chair.

"Peter doesn't know the first thing about raising a girl," Mrs. Elliot said. "There's no reason to such a death."

"There's a reason, always is," Mrs. Moore said, as if she could see an invisible plan she wasn't telling about. She swished the empty egg salad bowl through the dishpan.

Evelyn had her own opinions about reasons. She'd heard her mother's ideas about why people do things. About why, for instance, Tillie Wilson stayed with her husband against all common sense. "She stays with that old lout because it's easier than leaving," Evelyn's mother had said to Mrs. Elliot. "One day the balance will tip over. One day Tillie will get so tired of doing for Charlie that she'll decide it's easier to leave him than it is to stay."

Evelyn figured her mother had died according to the same rule. One day she saw it would be easier to be dead than to live with all that arthritis pain inside her, so she found a way out. Not to say that was how she got sick in the first place, but it just might be the reason things sped up so quickly at the end. The fall that broke her hip had come in August, the cold that came with lying in bed took hold in early September, and pneumonia took over before the month was up. If you can't stand it, get out.

LOUIE HONKED from the alley Saturday night just after nine-thirty. The passenger door on the Dodge wouldn't budge when Evelyn pulled at it and Louie kicked it open from the inside with his cowboy boot.

"God, it's good to get out of there," she said. She slid across the vinyl seat and set the quickest kiss she could manage just beside his furry sideburn.

They drove the regular circuit: a couple of tours up and down Main Street, a short weave back and forth on the four streets either side. The Dodge was the only car on the streets. The CPR station dead-ended Main Street, solid and important. Louie made a last pass down Main and pulled into the lot in front of the building.

He parked with the car facing the street, motor idling. Johnny Cash slid through the eight-track. They weren't waiting for anything in particular, just Saturday night to start. Around ten o'clock, Louie squinted down the street and said, "Two-headed driver."

A new girl was squeezed up against Donnie Gunther in the front seat of his old Studebaker. Donnie pulled in facing the station so the two drivers' doors were even. Louie revved his motor and the Dodge blew a cloud of exhaust from its rear end. Donnie spewed an answer from the Studebaker's tailpipe.

"What you got under there?" Louie shouted. It was a joke by now. There wasn't a guy in town who didn't know the details of everyone else's motor. They spent Saturdays with their heads stuck under each other's hoods, taking turns in the service bay at Donnie's father's garage, trading wrenches, advice, insults. Louie was the only one in the unmarried crowd who had a real job and Evelyn wondered how much of his salary from the mine went into chrome polish and spark plugs for other people's cars.

"Meet Allison, you guys," Donnie said. "Allison's from Ripley."

Allison's hair, parted perfectly down the middle, hung smoothly to her shoulders. There was, Evelyn knew, some simple secret about hair that people like Allison knew and people like Evelyn didn't. She wondered how Donnie had got to meet Allison. A date from Ripley was one of the most exotic things that could happen to a Flat Hill boy.

"You guys want to get in the back over here?" Donnie asked.

Louie grabbed the plaid car blanket and they moved across. Who wouldn't jump at a chance for the back seat, no steering wheel in the way?

It made Evelyn nervous.

Donnie twisted around to talk, but he managed to

keep his right arm around Allison.

"You guys been sitting here long?" he asked.

"A while. Evelyn couldn't stand being in the house with her old man."

"Yeah? Old Stumpy's not up to much these days, is he?" Donnie grinned.

Evelyn shrugged.

Donnie spun out and drove down the block to the hotel. Louie went in to pull a dozen Pilsner. He got back in the car, matched the caps of two bottles, and used one to open the other. Foam hissed around the caps and ran down a fold in his jeans. All the cars Evelyn knew smelled of beer.

"Any bush parties tonight?" Evelyn asked as they crossed the tracks and headed north. Safety in numbers.

"Doubt it. People are still hungover from the burnout last night," Donnie said. "Big party out behind the old bins at Paveliks'."

"We never knew about no party,." Louie said. "We got stuck playing rummy with Old Stumpy." He tucked the blanket up around his and Evelyn's shoulders and pulled her against him. Evelyn couldn't see the wheel or the gearshift any more. She felt the car pull into third.

Things were quiet for a while, except for the clink of stray gravel against the undercarriage. Evelyn liked the rough silence. Donnie slowed down to turn in at Paveliks' road. He'd mastered an awkward, left-handed technique for shifting gears and steering on gravel at the same time, without taking his right arm off Allison's shoulder. Louie knew the same trick. Evelyn had asked him once if the guys had to practise this or did the third generation of driving men in Flat Hill inherit the ability? "Little of both," he'd said.

Once they were on Paveliks' road Allison turned around, disturbing the quiet and dislodging Donnie's arm. Her hair was backlit by the dash lights, and it glowed an unreal green around the edges. Her face was all in shadow. As if there'd been no break in the conversation, she asked, "Who's Old Stumpy? And how-come you call him that?"

Evelyn felt caught in the light, as if the dash-glow that ghosted around Allison's head must converge on her own face. Caught in the light like Louie the time the two of them drove over to see *Gone With the Wind* in Ripley and the Roxy was so crowded he had to sit behind her. When she turned around to talk to him, she could see his open stare and his shaggy mustache silvery clear in the light reflected from the screen. Her face must be as naked to Allison as Louie's had been at the Roxy. Her blouse was unbuttoned by now, and she dipped her chin a little to make sure she could feel the blanket right up tight at her neck. She didn't answer Allison's question.

"Stumpy's Evelyn's old man," Louie said, and left it at that.

"Know how he got his name?" Donnie asked Allison.

"No. Are you going to tell me?" Allison looked at Donnie.

"He's got no feet." Donnie's voice sped up. "Cut off below the knees on both legs."

"That's awful! How did it happen? Was he in the war? Or was it a railway accident or something? There was a guy over in Zachary that worked on the trains and he lost both feet when he jumped out of a moving freight."

Donnie laughed. "Nothing like that. And the only thing it had to do with the war was the fact he passed out in front of the cenotaph."

Evelyn sat up straight, adjusted the blanket, matched the hems of her blouse so she would get the buttons in the proper holes. She didn't speak.

Louie waded in. "Come on, Donnie," he said. "Leave it alone, eh? He got caught in a storm, Allison. Froze his feet, that's all."

Donnie wasn't to be stopped, not by Louie nor by grace. "Caught in a storm all right – in the middle of town. My older brother found him. There was Freddie on his way home from taking Mom to Zachary to catch the passenger train to Edmonton. The train was late in from Winnipeg, so he wasn't on his way home 'til about three in the morning. Don't know what would've happened to Old Stumpy if that train hadn't been a few hours late.

"Anyway, Freddie's driving back into town and he turns the corner in front of the cenotaph there." Donnie parked and pointed ahead as if you could see the ornamental iron gates and the snow-capped hedge right there where his headlights shone on Paveliks' grain bins.

"So he's turning the corner and his headlights pick up this big rock. Only thing is, there never was a rock there before. Well, Freddie gets out and tramps through the drift, figuring a guy's gotta investigate. When he sees it's a person, he brushes the snow out of his face and starts shaking him."

Evelyn walked her fingers up the front of her blouse underneath the blanket. Two more buttons, if she'd counted right.

"Well, when Freddie sees that it's old Pete – that's

Stumpy's name from before we started calling him Stumpy – when he sees it's old Pete, he figures what happened was he got tight and set out to walk home from the beer parlour. Figures he sat down for a rest and fell asleep."

Allison giggled, then stopped abruptly. Evelyn looked at Louie. He shrugged and Donnie ran on.

"So pretty soon old Pete's awake and whining and trying to stand up. Well, of course he can't do it, 'cause his feet are frozen solid by now. But what happens when he tries to get up is that a six-pack of Pil falls out from under his overcoat. He was all curled up around it to keep it from freezing, see?" Donnie leaned back against his door and grinned at a tear in the vinyl ceiling. His teeth shone, yellow and slightly wet, in the dark. *The little dog laughed to see such sport.*

"Anyways," Donnie said, pushing away from the door with his elbows and leaning toward Allison, "the beer ends up okay, but his feet hadda be chopped off so he wouldn't catch whatchacallit. Gang-a-rene."

"That's awful," was all Allison said.

"Let's go for a walk," Evelyn whispered to Louie.

"Want to take a beer?" Louie asked. Evelyn nodded.

A path ran between the bins and down to the edge of the old dugout. There were no other cars, and Evelyn and Louie picked their way through a scatter of empty bottles knowing they'd be alone. They checked for broken glass beside the dugout and Louie spread the blanket. The two of them lay down and pulled Louie's siwash over top to make a scratchy wool sandwich. The nighttime voices of frogs came up through the ground into Evelyn's bones and sang inside her head. She hadn't said a word since Donnie started his humiliating account. Now she took her note from the frogs' watery whine.

"Did Donnie make up that part about the six-pack?"

"Forget about that, Evvie." Louie rolled to face her, nuzzled in, kissed her neck.

"Not right now, Louie." Evelyn used her shoulder bones to rock herself a few inches away from him. "Did Donnie make that up about Dad being curled up around the six-pack? I never heard that before."

Louie turned onto his back again. "It's no big deal," he said quietly.

Evelyn traced the Big Dipper with her eyes, then the Little Dipper, star by star, deliberately focusing to make each point hard and bright. "Old bastard," she said, "always looking after the wrong thing. His beer instead of his feet. His garden instead of his wife. All that time Mom was sick and he was out there digging in peat moss, seeding lettuce and onions in the fall. Old bastard."

THE DAY AFTER Donnie's performance, Evelyn sat in Chan's and stared across the table into Myrna's Coke. Myrna took a drag from her cigarette and blew the smoke down through her straw so it came up through the Coke and sat in the top of the bottle, trapped by the narrow neck. It was a trick the two of them had been doing for years.

"I got a letter from Kate," Evelyn said. "She got a scholarship to go to Halifax. A master's degree in art."

"I saw that in the *Ripley Advance*," Myrna said. The baby fussed and she gave him a french fry. "Imagine a girl from Flat Hill getting a master's degree. I've never even *met* anyone with a master's degree. And us, we're just the old married ladies of Flat Hill. Me anyway and you soon enough." The baby spit out the french fry and Myrna jingled her keys in front of his face to distract him. "Pretty soon you'll be married to Louie and looking for a house to fix up."

Evelyn dipped a fry through the skin on the gravy at the side of her plate. "I won't marry Louie," she told Myrna. She waited to be surprised at herself for how final it sounded. She failed to be. All that happened was she wished she hadn't said it out loud in front of anyone. She tried to take it back in a roundabout way. "I can't leave Dad alone in that house. He can't look after himself." For one thing, she thought, he'd never get the cat out of the crawl space.

"More like *won't* look after himself, isn't it? Seems to me – and I know I'm *completely* outside the situation – but it seems to me from certain things you've said that he hardly lifts a finger anymore. You can't help a guy who's up and quit, Ev." The baby let out an energetic wail and waved his pudgy arms until he knocked Myrna's glasses askew. She surrendered her keys entirely into his greasy fingers. "If all he wants is someone to wait on him," she said, "he can get that in the nursing home at Ripley. Or work something out with the church ladies. Or go it alone, why not? Use your imagination. He's got a phone, he's got neighbours, he has ramps to get in and out of that place."

Evelyn was overwhelmed by the number of options someone *completely* outside the situation could name. She looked for a way out of the conversation. She doubled back on herself. "Well, Dad aside, I can't marry Louie."

"I'm surprised you haven't *had* to yet." Myrna looked straight at Evelyn until she looked back. "I mean, look what happened to the rest of us." She put the baby on her shoulder, said, "little Easter egg," into his fat cheek, patted his bum as if to make her point. "You can't keep Louie flopping on the line forever, Evelyn. He's an okay guy. I bet Christine would be glad to take him. She must be tired of working over at the drugstore and chasing after every new credit union trainee that comes to town."

Myrna was right about Louie. Not a thing wrong with him, was there? He had a job; he had a car; he looked okay. He would never lift a hand against Evelyn.

"Christine can have him, then," Evelyn said and immediately saw the pair of them together. She saw herself too, how it would be for her in two or three years – even one year – if she were still in Flat Hill. She was used to picturing herself in between Louie and her father, no room to move on either side. When she took Louie away and put him in the back seat of the Dodge with Christine, she started to slip out of her form a little on that side. She saw herself walking into the café all lopsided like that. People would stir their coffee in the thick white crockery mugs and say to each other, "There's that poor Stevenson girl who never got married." They'd speculate on matches between Evelyn and the small set of bachelors who showed up at wedding dances, shy and hopeful, in their twice-a-year suits. *Evelyn Stevenson, whom shall you marry?*

EVELYN HELD HER COLLAR tight around her neck when she left the café. She stopped a little way down the street in front of Tredwell's. The store was closed for Sunday, but the Greyhound schedule taped inside the window above the painted ashtrays and ornaments showed a morning bus to Regina every weekday at eight-thirty. *Where are you going my pretty maid, pretty maid?* She wondered how long before it would seem easier to leave than to stay in Flat Hill. She didn't know where people lived when they showed up in the city, what they did for money until they found jobs. She tucked her face out of the wind.

At home her father had the *Leader-Post* from the day before spread on the table. "You're home," he said when she walked in. He moved his magnifying glass over the newspaper columns, stopped at a story in a bottom corner.

"Listen to this," he said. "There's a man who's been standing outside the government building in Regina every day for a week, wearing nothing but a barrel. Says it's all he's got left, now he's paid his taxes. Says he had to give the government the shirt off his back." Evelyn's father shook his head. "The things some people do."

"I heard about that," Evelyn said. She hung her coat on its hook. She opened the cellar trap for the cat, reminded her father to watch out for the hole in the floor, and sat down across the table from him. She could hardly picture the legislative building. She'd been there on a class tour when she was in grade eleven. A big black dome, she remembered, a foyer that might have been marble, tall columns on either side of the main doorway.

"You see any sense in standing in front of the government building wearing a barrel, Evelyn?"

"Not really."

"Louie called," her father said. "He said it was noth-ing important."

Nothing important. In her imagination, Evelyn went looking for Louie, found him on Main Street, walked up to him and told him she was moving to the city. He laughed out loud. It made sense to Evelyn that he would laugh. It was, after all, a far-fetched idea. She tried to think where she'd stored her mother's old hard-sided suitcase with the open-weave finish and the leather bumpers. She couldn't imagine putting anything into it. Jeans, sweaters, skirts, books, underwear? She couldn't imagine.

She told Louie something else in her mind. She told him maybe it was time he gave up on her. Louie didn't laugh this time; instead he said, "I expect that's true," and, "see you around then, Evelyn." A smile broke underneath his mustache and he turned and walked off. See you around.

"No sign of that damn cat yet," her father said.

"No," Evelyn said. "I don't expect so." She got up from her chair and went to the fridge, took out the roast she'd bought the day before, fished out the roasting pan from the corner cupboard, and turned on the oven.

People did leave Flat Hill; it wasn't so unusual. Mellie Sonter left, found a job in Saskatoon right away. Judith Eriksen even went to university and now she's a teacher in Saskatoon. And there was cousin Kate away at art school – though people did seem bewildered by her – by her very odd paintings and her new haircut and her city boyfriend.

Evelyn made herself busy while she waited for the oven to heat – refolded the yellow tea cloth embroidered with the word "Thursday" and hung it back on the towel rack, wiped and arranged the canisters with the red lids and the flower decals on the sides, still with the oatmeal in the sugar tin, the sugar in the tin that said coffee, and the coffee in the one that said tea, just the way her mother had set them up years ago according to some logic of necessity. Evelyn thought about how leaving was an idea a person had to get used to gradually. A person could only expect herself to take one step at a time. One more summer tending the garden here in the back yard couldn't hurt.

Her father shook his head again about the story in the newspaper. "Must be bloody breezy wearing nothing but a barrel."

The oven made its familiar small expansion noises as it heated. Evelyn took the seed packets out of the drawer she'd put them in yesterday, found a pencil and paper, and laid them on the table in front of her father.

"You draw out where you want things in the garden," she said. "I'll plant next week."

WHEELS

I t's Tuesday, so there's a letter for Pete from his daughter Evelyn. A page and a half in her unlovely, squarish handwriting. Evelyn's letter makes the usual demands of Pete: promise to get out of the house at least once a day; wheel yourself out for a trip down the sidewalk and back again; sit on the front step for half an hour and get some air; go to the card game at the Legion Hall on Wednesday. It will do you good, she writes. Other people do tend to think they know what's good for him. *A lot they know*, Pete thinks. *Here's what Evelyn's letters are good for: irritation.*

He folds the letter in on itself and holds it that way. In fact, he *will* get out of the house, but he'll wait until later in the day. He goes out every day in the summer, weather permitting, though Evelyn doesn't necessarily know it. For now, Pete's parked his chair in his favourite spot between the radio and the end table where he keeps his cigarette rolling machine, his lighter, and the big brown glass ashtray. This is where he likes to spend his mornings when there's nothing else to occupy him. Some days Phil Gunther brings Pete small repairs from the garage – sit-down jobs he can do at his low work table in the kitchen – but there's been nothing for a week or so. Today is a day for sitting still, for listening to Swap Shop on the radio. A day for looking out the window.

In the ten years since he's been in the wheelchair, Pete's spent a lot of time staring out the window, looking past the green-black shingles on Shepherds' roof across the street, watching the sky. He knows the sky, the clouds, as thoroughly as he knew them when he was a boy. Clouds and sky make more pleasant company than people do, he sometimes thinks. They have fewer expectations of him. He doesn't look for pictures in the clouds the way he did when he was young; no bug-eyed frogs or tractor shapes or rifles or maps of Newfoundland. Instead he receives them now simply as clouds – one day thin films with edges frayed against the hard blue sky, another day cotton softness stacked layer on layer, holding sun and shadows. Yellows, whites, greys and silvers, shades of deep blue underneath where the rain builds up. He should have a hundred words for clouds, like the Eskimos with their words for snow. Evelyn, he supposes, would be able to tell him the precise name for each type of cloud, just like that, she has that sort of a mind.

Today the clouds are few and scattered, so thin they're about to disappear. Pete sets Evelyn's letter on the end table, sets it between the ashtray and the chunk of potash ore, about the size of a fist, that also sits on the end table. The ore is a piece Pete brought home from a town hall meeting years and years ago when potash was still a new word in town.

There'd been a big turnout for that meeting way back, people dressed up as if it were some kind of occasion, kids running up and down the aisles in clothes that would normally be saved for Sunday school, grown-ups holding chunks of ore, turning them over, holding them up to the light, putting them to their noses to sniff. The company men from Carlsbad stood up on the stage beneath the portraits of Queen Elizabeth and Prince Philip and made promises about the future, based on the past. Hundreds of millions of years ago, they said, a massive sea had evaporated and left behind a layer of milky crystals. The men ran a film that showed a map of the world with a letter "K" superimposed over New Mexico, another one superimposed over Russia, and a third, giant "K" right there on Saskatchewan. By the time the film was over, everyone in the hall knew that the "K" stood for potassium and that soon there'd be a potash mine a few miles down the road. It would put them to work, those who wanted work. There was more: the company told the people they were part of a grand project, making fertilizer to feed the world.

When the men from the company had finished saying what they had to say, there was coffee in the big urn and talk and smoke at the back of the hall. Not many of the people who gathered around the urn talked about their mission to feed hungry people, but a lot of them talked about the jobs and about the new construction that would come to town. Houses, maybe even apartment buildings. New families, new businesses, new money. Cement sidewalks. Asphalt on Main Street.

As for Pete, he'd been willing to close up his own shop and put his mechanical skills to work on that massive equipment he'd seen in the film.

The promises made in the name of potash had come true, after a fashion; in the years since that meeting there'd been steady work for some. There'd been new construction too, four houses right away in '62. No apartment blocks, though; those were built in the towns closer to the mine if they were built at all. People say Flat Hill might see its apartments yet, though, if the company sinks the shaft they talk about sinking south of town, the shaft they've talked about sinking for years now. These days about ten people from town work full time at the mine. Secretaries, miners, janitors. Pete worked there for five years too when he was still able-bodied, up until the night he'd lain down for a rest in a snowdrift on the way home from the beer parlour and woke up the next morning in the hospital down the road in Ripley. Found out they were sending him to Regina where the doctors were going to take his feet off, he'd frozen them that bad.

THERE ARE FIST-SIZED CHUNKS of potash ore sitting in living rooms all through Flat Hill. Some of them are glued to plaques beside stalks of wheat; some are sawed off smooth with a clock face on the front and the works embedded in the back; most are just ragged pieces of raw ore sitting on windowsills gathering light and dust. Children in the houses pick them up once in a while and lick them, for the salt. Pete picks his up too once in a while and does the same.

There's little else for ornament in Pete's living room. Em used to have figurines – china birds, porcelain dancers in long, solid skirts. He's managed to break most of these items; he's in control of his chair now, but he'd bumped around a lot when he first came home, even with Evelyn still around to help.

A photograph of Pete sits on top of the big console television, a colour photograph, and in it Pete is slim and sound and smiling. He leans against a verandah rail; his red hair lifts in the wind; he wears a golf shirt with blue-and-white stripes and two buttons undone at the neck. In those days he walked about with a self-possessed gait, walked about the town, the golf course, the countryside during hunting season. Walked about inside his own house, tended properly to his garden, did a good day's work for a good day's pay.

For the five years that he was on the company payroll, his good day's work took place three thousand feet underground in the heat of the maintenance shop – a cave like a cathedral, five hundred feet long with a ceiling as high as a two-storey house. Nothing was small down there in the big room where he did repairs on the personnel carriers and continuous mining machines. The men who operated the machines, chewing out double circles of ore, creating caves barely taller than their own heads, reminded him repeatedly how much tougher their own job was. In a friendly way, of course, because in fact they envied him. Mechanics worked straight day shifts for the most part and the maintenance room, warm though it was, registered a few degrees cooler than the tunnels.

EMERALD'S PHOTOGRAPH sits where she placed it years ago, looking out from inside the low walnut china cabinet at the end of the living room. Her sister took the photo a year or two before Em got really sick. It looked to have been taken on a fine day, a happy day – the type of picture a person keeps for display precisely because it has a fine and happy quality to it. The photo doesn't look much like Em the way Pete remembers her. But then she'd hardly recognize him either if she were to resurrect herself and walk in through the front door.

A snapshot of Evelyn leans against Em's picture. Evelyn in the red-and-white prom dress she made for herself. Beside her in the photo is Louie, the fellow she went around with for three years before she moved to Regina. Evelyn's life is in the city now. She broke up with Louie in the spring a couple of years ago, left Flat Hill in the fall. As she packed, she'd explained her reasons for going. She'd mentioned the lack of job prospects in a small town. Mentioned the tech in Regina, though she'd never enrolled. She'd even said, who knows, maybe it's warmer in the city. He'd asked her what the hell would make her think that, and she'd said maybe the buildings block some of the wind. Prairie is prairie, he'd told her. The buildings just make the wind all the more fierce trying to find its way through.

Off she'd gone. There's a letter a week, sometimes a phone call. She found a job right away, in a store where people come to buy the wherewithal for handicrafts – drawing pencils and paintbrushes and embroidery threads and such. A place where she can put to use all those fine points about needlework she learned before Em died.

Evelyn works most Saturdays, has a floating day off. She says again in today's letter how it's too bad she can't get home for the weekend more often. She took Pete to the doctor in Ripley last time she was home. She didn't like the way he listed to one side in his chair. "I think I know how to sit," he'd said. "I'm a damn bloody expert at sitting." But she'd insisted, borrowed a car.

"Windswept deformity," Doctor Gopul had announced. "Windswept deformity, from the hammock effect of the soft chair seat. It makes the pelvis tilt to one side, like a tree in a prevailing wind. Do you have trouble with a sore back?"

Yes, he had a sore back. Of course he had a sore back. Doctor Gopul had sent him to rehab where they'd fitted him out with plywood and a cushion. He couldn't say he always used it. He suspected it just moved the pressure sores to a different place. He'd left it leaning at the foot of the bed this morning.

Swap Shop doesn't let Pete down today. It's an hour-long friendly radio chat, where everything happens on a familiar, first-name basis, and Pete gets to listen without taking part. The host is nothing but respectful of the people who call in with their assortment of idiosyncratic needs. Pete wonders, though, if the man doesn't chuckle behind his hand when Carol from Ripley calls for the third time this month looking for an old cream separator she can shine up and make into a planter for her front yard. Or the flat-voiced woman named Valerie who's always looking for plastic vinegar bottles. She cuts the sides into triangles, she says, punches holes in them and crochets them together to make tote bags. You have to laugh at the things people do to kill time.

As Swap Shop wraps up, Pete switches off the radio. He looks at the pictures of his wife and daughter in the china cabinet, says to them, "Time for my trip up the sidewalk and back again." He thinks ahead, imagines himself rolling back up the ramp after completing his short tour of Main Street. Imagines wheeling back in the door, back to his spot by the radio, then saying to Evelyn's picture, "See, I went out and came back and I'm still in the same place I've been for years. Didn't get me anywhere." The imaginary conversation satisfies him somewhat and he rolls himself out the door.

A few summers ago, six new lengths of sidewalk had appeared in Flat Hill, a product of the mining money spreading through the town. One sidewalk passes Pete's house, connects with his ramp, and carries on up to Main Street. It used to be that Pete could only go out when someone was around to help, but the sidewalk has changed his life, at least during the summer months when he can count on it being clear. He considers the sidewalk to be his leftover share of what the potash brought.

Pete turns right at the end of his ramp and wheels uptown, pushing slowly, taking it easy. Ginger Mack passes him in his Chev, honks and waves. In this town there are people who'll get in their cars just to drive two or three blocks. People regularly joke with Pete that it must be handy to have his own wheels with him all the time. Built-ins. It's hard to see that as an advantage.

Uptown, Isabelle Turner waves from inside the post office, then opens the window and asks, just to be sure, whether Paul Tredwell dropped Evelyn's letter off to him. Yes, thanks, he says and keeps going, since he doesn't normally enjoy a conversation with Isabelle Turner. He passes the Texaco and Phil Gunther comes out to say hello, tells him he'll bring over some electric motors in a day or two for Pete to do the copper winding, maybe some other bits of sit-down work.

There isn't much to see or do after that, is there? It's a hot day and Pete sweats against the vinyl seat of his chair. His wet shirt hugs his back; his legs itch. He turns around and wheels himself in the direction of home. On the way he hears rude shouts and laughter from three kids who spot him from down the block. He knows that the names they have for him alternate between "Stumpy" and "Grumpy," and those are just the ones he knows about. He knows it isn't the fact of the wheelchair they're making fun of. It's how he ended up in the chair that makes him worth laughing at. He stops his chair, swings sideways to take a look at them. There's a heat in his neck and in his ears that wasn't brought on by the July sun. He wants to shout, wants to throw stones and make the damn bloody kids run away in three directions. Here's what an excursion like this is good for: reminding a man he's got years and years to get through. He pushes hard at his wheels – around, around, around – builds up some speed to make it easier to climb the slight rise at the end of his block and the ramp up to his doorstep.

JUST AFTER TWO in the afternoon, Paul Tredwell comes to Pete's back door carrying a toolbox. He knocks and lets himself in. "Be right back," he says. He leans out the door for a second and comes back in with a couple of pieces of conduit pipe and a hacksaw. Paul's been leaving bits of pipe outside the door for a few days, telling Pete only that he intends to make an improvement to the wheelchair.

"My chair doesn't need improving," Pete says now, seeing that Paul is serious about his project.

Paul moved into the vacuum when Evelyn left home; he sees to some of Pete's needs. Not that Pete can't do most things for himself. He stuck with rehab long enough that he doesn't need help to get himself in and out of the bathtub and the bed or to move between his chair and the toilet. They even taught him to locomote on his knees and he can climb up and reach things in the high cupboards.

Paul's in the habit of dropping off Pete's mail – when there is any – on his way home from the post office. Pete had been abrupt with Paul at first, then grudgingly more tolerant as Paul found out where things were, made the coffee, showed up with store-bought cookies once in a while. Pete was genuinely surprised the first time Paul stayed at the door instead of giving his usual wave and moving on. He didn't get many visitors, especially unannounced. He and Paul had known each other well enough, though, years ago when they were both setting up their own shops. So he'd tolerated a short conversation – about Paul's newest grandchild, about the new bridge over the creek, about the car accident the week before out at the highway turnoff.

Pete was even more surprised at Paul's second visit. He didn't think he'd shown much welcome the first time. On the third visit, he watched Paul mix up instant coffee for the two of them and said outright, "You're just looking for something useful to do, now Young Paul's taken over the hardware." Paul had given over not only the store but also his big house to Young Paul and his family, and moved in next door to Pete, into Mrs. Elliot's little house after she died.

"You may be right," Paul had said.

Now Paul comes in for a visit twice a week or so, and here's what he's good for: passing time with. Other than that, Paul knows a lot about what other people ought to do. A real silver-lining man, a count-your-blessings man who thinks everyone else should do the same and it's a sin not to. He even tried once to give Pete a silver-lining nickname. "We should call you Wheels," he'd said one day as they sat, cups in hand, looking out the kitchen window. Their view took in the overgrown back yard and the empty garden where Pete's wheels wouldn't take him.

"Well. Haven't you got a rosy view of life," Pete told him. It wasn't a question, wasn't an exclamation, just a statement. "You know what my name is around here. Stumpy's what they call me."

Paul looked at him for a moment, then looked down at his own coffee mug and wiped at the wet spot his mouth had left on the lip.

"That or Grumpy," Pete said. "Or worse."

"That's the kids. They don't know any better," Paul said.

"I s'pose you think I earned it. Look at *you*, though. You've got your name spelled out right there on your shirt, just so there's no mistake." Paul still wears the dark blue work shirts he used to wear in the hardware store. Each one has an oval crest with his name on it stitched to the pocket.

SIGHTLINES

"I'll get some crests made up for you that say 'Wheels,'" Paul had said.

"You're joking."

"Yeah."

PAUL PUTS HIS TOOLBOX and his pieces of conduit down on the mat inside the door and starts in making coffee. "What's this in the sink?" he says.

"Bea Millar brought beef stew yesterday for my supper. I didn't finish it. She'll be back for the dish."

They sit, the two of them, looking out the kitchen window, Pete with his stumps resting in front of him on their boards and cushions, Paul with his long legs crossed and tucked under his chair. Paul shifts around in his chair, looks over at Pete, then away.

"You never have much to say, do you, Pete?" he says finally. "It's like trying to get these coffee cups to talk."

"Wheelchair makes me grouchy," Pete says. It's his usual reply, but today Paul calls him on it. "You were a grouch before you ever had to sit in a chair all day."

"You know a lot about me, you think, don't you?" Pete half-smiles, only half though, because he half means it. "Okay, so I was a grouch before the wheelchair. Must have been the war that turned me into a grouch." They lapse back into silence, watching the hot wind pull at the branches of the Russian olive tree in the back yard.

"Whose turn to bring dinner today?" Paul asks.

"Don't remember. I'll find out when they show up."

"You're lucky," Paul says. "Lucky to have so many people looking after you."

156

Pete doesn't respond right away. Finally he says, "It helps, I suppose." After a pause he says, "They wouldn't do it if they didn't want to. Besides, I give them a break, I get my own dinner on Wednesdays."

BEA MILLAR, yesterday's dinner-lady, is just as polite on the surface as any of the others who take their turns coming by with a meal for him, but she gives off a chill; anyone would notice it. She has a habit of staring into the corners, of looking past Pete into the living room, of straightening things on the table, and not out of help-fulness. She knows the same set of things about him that everyone in town thinks they know. She knows he wouldn't have lost his feet if he hadn't turned into such a drunk after Em died – that's what it came down to after all. She probably knows he wasn't good at seeing to all of his daughter's needs when she was a girl, and that Mrs. Elliot had to tell her about things like underarm deodorant and see to it she had the women's things she needed at the appropriate time. Bea knows, as everyone knows, that Pete didn't make a very good job of looking after Em at the end. But Pete himself knows all that as well as anyone. It's old news now, isn't it?

That's not the whole of his history, though. He ran a good, honest business when he had his own shop. He did the best work and didn't charge too much. Agreed to take venison in trade two winters in a row when Nels Eriksen couldn't afford the parts for his truck otherwise. He never took a sick day from the mine until the morn-ing he wound up in the hospital.

And there are things people don't know about him

now. For instance, the fact that he says a little something to Em's photograph just about every day. He's adopted Em's old Gruen wristwatch, expanded the band so it'll reach around his wrist. He takes it apart every six months or so and, just for the satisfaction of the work, cleans with toothpicks and fine wires all the wheeled gears that keep it ticking. The watch isn't the only accessory of Em's that he uses. He wears her reading glasses to look at the paper, her last pair with the black frames that are almost like men's glasses anyway. Evelyn, who's impatient with him more and more, makes some remark about the watch and the glasses every time she comes home. He tells her they're good company. He doesn't say out loud that they're better company than actual people.

PAUL'S LEFT HIS COFFEE to go cold and he's laying things out on Pete's work table, sorting through the dies that go with his pipe bender, walking around to look at the back of the wheelchair. He's fiddling with different sizes of conduit, marking lengths of pipe with his hacksaw, making drawings of angles and fasteners at the kitchen table. Presently he gets up, brings a drawing over to Pete where he sits looking out the window. "Here's the problem," he says. "The way they make these chairs, they're just about impossible to push. A tall person like me, I've got to lean way over. Gives me a sore back." He hands Pete the drawing, pulls out the chair, with Pete in it, and pushes it a foot or two across the linoleum to demonstrate. "And the handles are too close to the back of the chair. I end up knocking my shinbones."

"But *you* don't push me, Paul. I push myself."

"You never know when you might want company," Paul says. "You might want to go for a walk with someone else sometimes." He goes on without leaving room for Pete to comment. "Here's how she'll work. I run these two lengths of conduit up the back of your chair on either side. Then I telescope a smaller piece inside each one, bring them up past the existing handles, bend them back and extend them." He's smiling at Pete. Beaming. "The new handles will be further out and higher up, easier for the person pushing you."

"Evelyn's not that tall."

"Ah, but here's the beauty of it," Paul says. He takes the drawing from Pete and picks up a bolt from the table to use as a pointer. "I'll make holes, say, two inches apart. You can use the bolts to set the handles at whatever height you want. It's adjustable."

"No handle grips," says Pete.

"Garden hose," says Paul. "I'll make the handle grips out of garden hose. You'll see. We'll be going to the races with this gizmo."

"I'm not so sure about that," Pete says. It looks like a lot of bother. He doesn't recall saying he's looking for someone to go walking with.

"Trust me," Paul says. "When I make a thing, it works. You never saw the carpet sweeper I made for Doreen, did you?"

"No. I never saw that. But I saw the pea sheller you rigged with the wringer washer and the bed sheet."

"There's another one," Paul says. "That was a dandy."

"Whole lotta mess, I thought. Doreen thought so too, didn't she?"

"I won't argue the point. I just want you to give this a try, that's all."

"Here's what you want," Pete says. "You want to show off a new apparatus you've figured out."

"Could be."

PETE CHECKS HIS WATCH, Em's watch. Three-fifteen. He moves the bracelet around on his wrist, looks at the dial again. *Love and Enemies* comes on at three-thirty. Paul's measuring a piece of conduit, looking like he's deciding where to cut it. If Pete wants to get Paul out of his way in the next fifteen minutes he'll have to start now.

"That's enough work for today, don't you think?" Pete says. "You've got other things you should be doing. You don't have to spend all your time putting that rig together."

"Don't worry, I'll get out of your way in a minute here. The next part's maybe better done at the shop any-way." He puts his pencil and his tape measure into the tray in his tool box and closes the lid. "I usually watch the TV at three-thirty anyway, the same story Doreen used to watch. I never realized 'til after she died that I like it just as much as she did."

"Stay if you want. I sometimes watch it too."

On *Love and Enemies,* a man has been murdered and three detectives are assigned to the case to work around the clock. A woman who was paralyzed in a car accident has learned to walk again. The driver of the other car, a woman presumed dead, has shown up in town very much alive six months later.

"She doesn't even look a bit like she did before she got killed," Pete says.

"Not a bit," says Paul.

"I guess they couldn't get the same girl back to play the part," Pete says. "Makes you laugh, doesn't it?"

"Yeah. It does."

BEA MILLAR knocks on the door about five as expected, says hello to Pete – who nodded off in his chair sometime after Paul left – retrieves her stew bowl, shakes her head over the leftovers and goes on her way with little conversation. Anna Mack comes by a little after six and leaves a plate with two slices of meatloaf, carrots, and boiled potatoes. He salts it and peppers it, eats every bite and sets the plate on the counter by the sink. He doesn't go back to the living room. Tuesday nights aren't so good for TV this time of year, so he wheels out the front door, stops on the platform at the top of the ramp, and sets his brake. When Pete first had the ramp put in, it struck him how much it was like the flat hill over across the tracks and down the road, the hill the town was named after. As hills go, it's insignificant, doesn't even have a real crest to it. You finish the climb before you should – find yourself on a level plateau, flat as a sheet of curling ice and no bigger than the average living room. Still, it's a place with not so bad a view – the golf course, the houses, the station, the railroad tracks running off into the distance. People like it for that reason.

From his vantage point beside the front door, Pete looks up and down the still street. There's hardly a sound, hardly a movement, and the breeze he watched in the branches earlier in the day has dropped away.

Paul Tredwell might not know it, but Pete does think about his blessings now and then at quiet times like this, on a full stomach: there's the sidewalk; there's Phil, who brings him the odd bit of work – from what used to be Pete's own garage years ago; there are the people who do for him what he needs to have done; there's a good chuckle once in a while from the radio or the TV.

But those are just the blessings, and once you've given them the nod, you have to turn around and count the aggravations. A person has to give some proper respect to all the aggravations. The damn bloody sores on his backside from sitting and sitting. The kids and their name calling. This isn't the life he'd planned on, and he's yet to find a consolation prize as big as the one those prospectors stumbled on when they went looking for oil and found potash instead. He can't let it matter too much, though, can he? – the things Bea Millar sees in corners, or the fact that "Stumpy" might not be the worst nickname some people have for him. If he's got years to go yet, he damn well better not let it matter too much. Nothing he can fix. Nothing he can take a wrench to, tighten the gears on, grind a new bit for.

ANOTHER OUTING is in order tonight, Pete thinks, though not the sort Evelyn would have in mind. He has-n't been to the beer parlour in two years, not since Ginger Mack agreed to take him one night and Pete got so tight Ginger swore he'd never do that for him again. He'll go by Paul's place on the way uptown, ask him to come along, get him to back the chair up over the steps into the hotel. The man's moved into Pete's life just the way the clouds have and Pete's gotten used to him without even knowing it. Paul's so worked up about this wheelchair improvement idea that Pete will have to let him give it a try just so he won't be disappointed. Maybe Paul's right, maybe a little company's good for a person once in a while. Once in a while. It's one way to keep time pushing along in such a way that the aggravations aren't so noticeable. Pete takes off his brake and rolls down the ramp.

At the end of his ramp, though, he turns left instead of going right toward Paul's place. He'll take a little fresh air roll first, something he can report to Evelyn if she calls later in the week. Give Paul a minute to digest his supper. He wheels all the way to where the sidewalk stops, down where the schoolyard ends and the town proper ceases to be. Empty pasture stretches in front of him. The ground – except for a footpath dwindling off the end of the sidewalk – is dotted with tufts of coarse grass that crack the soil where they push out. Beyond the pasture, ripening barley marks the horizon. Above the fields, clouds darken from silver to purple. He feels the heat building itself into rain. A group of kids plays and shouts over in the schoolyard not far from where Pete sits in his chair. Maybe they're shouting things about him, or at him.

Underneath the pasture, a long way down, lies a conglomerate of milky white crystal and glassy bits of halite, all held together with prehistoric red clay. It took ten million bucks to get the first shaft down to the ore, through everything from boulders to quicksand. Two and a half years to get through the quicksand alone, and then ten more underground rivers to plug.

Somewhere down there and a few miles to the south, in a different kind of heat, miners are shearing potash off the walls with massive, side-by-side digging wheels and sending it up in skips to the mill. Crush; sieve; float out the sylvite with the potassium in it. In a huge room near the shaft, the maintenance crew is cleaning and retool-ing a parade of equipment and rolling it back out into the mine. Pete can feel the grease on his fingers, can hear metal ring against metal, can smell the salt.

He shifts his gaze from ground to sky. The clouds are moving closer and a breeze has started up. It chases in across the pasture, carrying the smell of the storm. Lightning plants a fork way off on the horizon. When the first big raindrops fall, Pete turns and heads up the sidewalk for home. He'll take Paul down and buy him a drink another night, maybe once the new rig for the wheelchair is finished. For tonight he wants nothing more than to wheel himself close to the living room window and see what kind of show the thunderclouds put on this time.

PASSING ON

"Auntie, the others won't come to play anymore because of the bees' nest by the fence."

"Then we will remove the bees' nest."

Elsa was eight years old when Aunt Eleanor showed her what faith was about.

She had watched as her aunt lifted the skirt of her long housedress clear of her sturdy, honest knees, knelt on the painted verandah boards, and petitioned God to keep her safe. Then Aunt Eleanor rose, walked directly down the back path, detached the remarkably quiet hive, and carried it calmly into the woods beyond.

That was more than sixty years ago.

ELSA CAN HARDLY hold herself back now that her daughter Judith has finally come. They need to talk things over, talk many things over. "Sit down, sit down, dear," Elsa says and points an unsteady finger toward the yellow vinyl chair by the window that looks out onto the back lawn of the hospital. Judith sits.

"Is your teachers' convention done with, then?" Elsa asks, or thinks she asks. No response. Maybe Elsa is forgetting to say things out loud again. The nurses say she does that. ("You didn't *tell* me you needed the bathroom." "You didn't *say* to pull the curtains." *Yes I did. Three times I did.*)

She tries again, tries with something else. "There's so much I want to talk to you about. From the beginning on down. I want you to tell me everything you wish had been different."

This time Judith responds. "Just like that?" she says. "As if we're talking about something we can change, like the colour of the curtains?" Judith's tone is not particularly sarcastic; but she doesn't smile to take the edge off what she says either.

Elsa changes direction. "Did I ever tell you about your Great Aunt Eleanor?" she asks.

"Many times. You talked about her yesterday."

Yesterday. Judith was here yesterday and Elsa has forgotten. Must keep better track. Pay attention.

"Aunt Eleanor was a woman, Judith, who believed in possibilities. And in herself," Elsa says. "She was a woman who didn't give up easily. Aunt Eleanor told me I had persistence built into my nature because my last name was Will. Used to be Will. Before it was Eriksen." Elsa closes her eyes. She can see so much more when she closes her eyes, can call up the deep green of her aunt's dress, call up the sincerity in her face, call up whatever she wishes, without the pastel details of the hospital room obscuring the picture.

"You look tired, Mom," Judith says. "Just rest."

"But you're here now. We should talk."

"I'll be here later too."

ELSA ERIKSEN, née Will, was twenty-eight and preg-
nant for the first time when Nels came home and told
her he was out of a job. It was 1949. She heard him –
earlier than he should be home – come up the outside
stairs to their apartment. Heard him pause at the landing. He came in and hung his hat behind the door. Said
he wouldn't be going to the railway yards any more.
They'd let him go because the foreman caught him
drinking in a boxcar, and not even on a break. Rye
whiskey from a mickey Young Carl carried around in the
big front pocket of his overalls. So Young Carl was out
of a job too, but he hadn't started a family yet, lived with
his parents still. Carl was not in dire straits.

Nels sat down in his regular chair, the one they had
to shift out of the way whenever Elsa needed to get at the
pots in the bottom cupboard. "It's a real piece of bad
luck," he said. But he'd always had good luck until this,
he reminded her, and he'd be lucky again. Elsa felt com-
pelled to go outside, where there would be more room for
the huge piece of news Nels had brought home. She
picked up the slop pail and edged around Nels.
Pregnancy hadn't made her cut back on the amount of
lifting she did. The water slapped back and forth inside
the pail's thin lips, but didn't spill. Elsa went out the
door, down the stairs, across the dirt and dandelions. She
tipped the slops into the trough at the back of the yard
and watched as what didn't sink in right away ran into

the back alley, leaving a bubble scum on the gravel.

She rubbed the soft little rise in her abdomen and said out loud, "We will all be fine." Fine because, in spite of this latest, Nels was a good worker. More honest than some. Hadn't tried to hide what happened, had he? Other men did things like this all the time. Nels had the bad luck to be caught, that was all.

The job wasn't the only thing, Elsa had to admit. Marriage hadn't changed Nels the way she'd hoped it would. He refused to see a dentist about his loosening teeth; he had a habit of wearing long-sleeved underwear with short-sleeved shirts and seemed not to realize how unkempt this made him look; he smoked so many cigarettes the lock of hair that hung over his forehead had a streak of yellow. The two of them couldn't get through a week without shouting at each other. But that wouldn't go on.

Elsa wrote to her sister, "He's always kept a roof over our heads, Pauline. He's looking into new business opportunities."

Her letter showed the same stubborn faith, fastened way back to Aunt Eleanor's simple demonstration, that had seen Elsa through so far. Through the endless stretch of high school, as it became clear she couldn't blame her lack of friends on a bees' nest in the back yard – people just did not gravitate toward her. Girls didn't ask her along when they went to the drugstore hoping to see the pharmacist's son James at the counter. James with his orderly teeth and his shiny black hair with the wave that stood up so dramatically above his forehead. Nor did her classmates invite her to sit with them in upstairs bedrooms and shape each other's hair into finger rolls before a big night out. Young men were polite but paid little attention to her. A fellow would dance with Elsa only if the partner he'd crossed the floor to ask was scooped away in front of him and Elsa stood so close it would be just too rude to walk past her.

Elsa knew how things stood. Nevertheless, she wrote down the details of every dance she did have and some that she didn't. The entries in her diary blended fact and fiction in a way that Elsa herself sometimes couldn't sort out. After her father left the household, she wrote about him as though his absence was only temporary: "Dad will be so pleased to see how well the garden is doing." And, "I've organized the tool shed so Dad will have everything within easy reach. It's never been so orderly."

During the times when she had no address for her father, Elsa composed letters to him directly in her notebook. Hopeful letters. News of her mother, her sister Pauline, her younger brother Frederick. News of the library job she had convinced the town council to create for her. She listed for her father the speedy engagements and weddings among her contemporaries as local boys signed up for the air force and the army and prepared to leave. She wrote that she was looking forward to seeing him back home as soon as his finances improved – which surely they would any day. This last sentiment she expressed to Pauline.

You have quite an imagination, her sister said.

David Will had closed his insurance office in Bridgewater in 1937. His desk had collected more dust than business for three years before that. He worked his way through the rest of the Depression with longer and longer stretches of odd jobs away from home. He picked up intermittent work at insurance offices in the cities and larger towns, answering letters, clerking. Talked his way in the door on the basis of what he knew about the business. It wasn't reliable work, it didn't pay well, and the checks he sent home were sporadic.

ELSA THOUGHT of her father as her real friend in the family. Her sister Pauline and her brother Frederick both seemed so young, and her mother didn't invite confidences. Elsa kept company with her journal and her embroidery, her novels and poetry anthologies. She quietly saved her money and ordered Silver Birch china by mail from Eaton's, one or two pieces at a time, for her hope chest. She spent two years optimistically waiting for attention from an Englishman who walked her home one evening after she paid a visit to his mother.

She wrote: "I had a sudden wish to walk the hills and footpaths of England with just such an amusing, reliable companion." Her fanciful nature compressed half a courtship into that single evening. Before she put her notebook away she wrote, "He told me I had a good gait."

John Jacobs had lived all his life on the Canadian prairies, but both his parents had grown up in England. To Elsa, this heritage implied a certain set of traits that had to do with education, afternoon tea, manners, and something less tangible that Elsa thought of as decency. In the local militia regiment, John Jacobs was an important man. He was also a teacher, as his father had been, and one of her most regular patrons at the library. She watched to see which books he borrowed – Rudyard Kipling, John Buchan's many novels, new British

Penguin editions by almost anyone. Elsa added the titles to her own reading list.

On Sunday mornings when the rest of her family went to the unadorned, white Presbyterian church, Elsa walked across town to the unfamiliar Anglican church with the brown brick steeple. She went partly because she wanted to know that aspect of her Englishman's life, and partly for the opportunity simply to be in the same room as him. She sat in the last pew and watched so she would know when to kneel. John was tall, his shoulder so high it was level with the deep green netting that stood away from his mother's felt hat. The two of them sat near the front in the same pew every Sunday, a small, proper family. On the rare occasions when John Jacobs' head turned and his eyes ran past Elsa sitting at the back of his church, she read a greeting in his expression.

Even after he stopped turning his head, she kept on attending for a month. Finally Elsa had to admit that what she had insisted to herself was special attention was really only courtesy, and even the courtesy was growing more dilute with each visit John Jacobs made to the library. She wrote him out of her diary and moved her optimism to someone new. Nels Eriksen was a solid-looking Norwegian with early wrinkles in his leathery face, a back that was broader than the Englishman's, and a set of seasoned work boots. He had built the fires for her in the library through two winters. At the end of the second spring, he asked her if just anyone could borrow things to read. He took home back copies of *Popular Mechanics* two at a time.

Nels was a reserve man too, the same regiment as John. He had a slight limp and a chronically ill father.

Elsa guessed that it was one or the other of these that kept him on this side of the Atlantic. The relationship developed slowly, sometimes seeming as if it was not a relationship so much as an assumption between them. Nels still lived with his mother and father on a farm at the edge of town. The running of the farm was up to him, and he would not shut it down, would not entertain notions of change while his father was still alive. Old Olaf died in 1945. Nels and his mother ran the place for another year before they rented the land out and bought a house in town.

The war had been over for almost three years when Elsa and Nels married. They moved to Flat Hill for the CPR job and took the apartment over the post office. Elsa had her very own home to keep. She left most of her books stored in her mother's attic in Bridgewater. The few she took with her stayed packed in their moving-day box, along with her own journals, underneath the bed in the apartment.

Elsa knew how to be frugal. When the pair of old sheets her mother gave her "for starting out" wore in the centre, she split them and turned them to, so that she and Nels slept with a seam down the middle of the double bed. She grew fewer irises than her mother had, used most of her patch in the landlord's yard for carrots and potatoes, for peas and beans and beets that she canned in the fall. Elsa regularly carted Nels's overalls down the street to mend the knees on Isabelle Hepburn's Singer; the crochet hooks Aunt Eleanor gave her stayed folded away in paper. She read less than she liked, but Elsa was fond of the poetry of her new name, the way its syllables rolled up and down. Elsa Eriksen.

Nels's mother came to visit, clattered up the outside stairs and into Elsa's kitchen carrying enameled tubs and heavy cast-iron pans. Cooking lessons. Elsa was introduced to foods her own mother had never even been in the same room with. She learned to soak the *lutefisk* overnight before she baked it at Christmas time, to take out the strong lye taste. She learned to bring it to the table with butter so hot it ran like whiskey. She learned to stop imagining a sharp pain in her front teeth every time she saw Nels sip his tea through a spoonful of sugar.

"We need to find someone who will carve you a rolling pin," Nels's mother said. "You can't make proper *lefse* without a fluted rolling pin. See, thin and strong like a linen napkin is how the dough should be when you're through with it."

LOSING THE RAILWAY JOB had been a setback, no question, but Nels had been on steady as a welder at Brackman's three months to the day when Judith was born. It was long enough to recover, almost, from the stretch when they'd been on relief, although they still owed two months back rent.

Elsa's water broke just as she brought Nels's spare overalls in from the clothesline. She stood a moment in the kitchen, feeling the stream turn from warm to cold on her legs, checking the stitching on the long patches she'd sewn inside the thighs of Nels's pants to line the scattered burn holes the welding sparks left. He'd grunted and thrown them on the table without a word the last time a patch had come away. Elsa left a note on the kitchen table to tell Nels where she was, put on a coat to hide where the wet made her dress turn dark, and walked two blocks to the cottage hospital. By the time she arrived, she was bent low with back labour.

It was small and homey, the cottage hospital – well-named – the smell of medical clean buffered by the gentle scent of baby powder.

UNIVERSITY HOSPITAL, where Elsa is now, bears little resemblance to the old cottage hospital back home. It helps Elsa sort out the two, the fact that they're so different. She knows just where she is, most of the time. She opens her eyes and sees white gloss paint on the ceiling. Her gut hurts, as if tiny creatures inside scrape at the walls. She raises herself on one elbow and tries to guess the time of day from the light and shadow in the room. Afternoon?

There's Judith, asleep in the chair beside the window. It's good she has finally come. There's so much to talk about when she wakes up.

Elsa knows enough about Judith's current troubles to guess at how things are in the schools these days. Students out of control, parents on your back about every little thing. Judith says all her energy goes to what she calls classroom management, nothing left for teaching. Elsa wants Judith to know there will come a day when everything that makes her anxious now will seem far, far away. But there's no use saying that to someone who's right in the thick of things.

Suddenly Judith is there beside the bed. "What is it,

Mom? I didn't hear what you said. Can I get you something?"

"Just thinking out loud," Elsa says. She must have been doing just that. Judith's voice brings her back in touch with the real and the physical, including the real, physical pain she's been trying to ignore. There is no question she's dying. The cancer must be everywhere inside. Perhaps a doctor has even told her so, she can't remember. It hardly matters what doctors say at this point, because Elsa herself is certain. Her imminent death is one reason Judith is here with her. They don't normally see much of each other. All the more reason to talk now. Concentrate. Get to the point.

"How was your teachers' convention?" Elsa says.

"Not so great. People listening to themselves talk."

Elsa closes her eyes but stays in the conversation. "Do you still want to quit teaching?"

"I don't think that's a choice I have. No fall-back position. No partner either."

"Sometimes a husband is no help anyway – certainly your father wasn't much help."

"So you've told me. More than once." Judith says. "We don't need to go into all that again."

"Would you rather talk about this?" Elsa lifts her arms a few inches off the bed and gestures feebly at the air, as if by doing so she can describe the room, the bed, her body on the bed, the reason they are in this particular place together. "Because *I* would rather not," Elsa says. "Feels like an excavation going on inside me."

"I'm sorry," Judith says. "But I already know how things were. I don't need to go mucking through history all over again, and I can't understand why *you* want to talk about it. You were always so…mad all the time."

Elsa opens her eyes and looks at Judith. Looks and listens. She doubts her daughter would believe her if she tried to tell her how all that anger has thinned out. Evaporated into little patches. It's evaporating still.

Her daughter shrugs. "It's what I remember," Judith says. "You mad at Dad. You mad at the town. You mad at anyone who had better luck than we had."

This is true. Elsa must have been about the same age Judith is now when she stood on the church steps after the service and told Reverend Moore that faith is only good so far as it goes – there are some things it just isn't equal to. And maybe even younger when Elsa called her sister Pauline just to say that even a strong last name like Will couldn't keep a person going forever. Judith probably heard both those conversations. Likely remembers them.

"I can't use up our little bit of time making sense out of all that for you," Elsa says. Her whole set of old grudges has shrunk. Anger seems less important all the time. Some memories are still sharp when they surface, but they grow dull with exposure.

The dozen small pointed blades that have been stabbing Elsa from the inside merge into a single keen sword. She draws a sudden breath, squeezes Judith's hand. Judith pushes the button for the nurse.

THE WHISTLE of the one o'clock train vibrated through the dark house like a blue note. Elsa sat at the kitchen table, the baby sweat-warm against the front of her nightie. The train sounds sent a shiver across her back. She nursed Judith in the kitchen at night, so as not to disturb Nels's sleep. She wondered who would be down at the rail yards with the train. Not Young Carl, she'd seen him go by on his way to the station just after lunch. He'd be home by now. Carl had talked his way back on with the boss within a month of being let go for drinking. They'd checked his pockets for the clink of glass every day for the first two weeks, he'd told Nels and Elsa, then left him alone. Why don't you come back too? he'd said. The pay's better than you'll ever get from Brackman. But when Nels went by, hearing they needed help coopering grain cars, the station agent told him he had a full crew. Lucky bugger, Nels said about Carl, crediting the difference between their two situations to nothing more predictable than a throw of the dice.

Judith fell asleep at the breast. Elsa ran her finger around the ring Nels's whiskey glass had left on the table. She licked her finger to wet it, traced the ring again, and licked a second time. Her tongue puckered.

The next morning Elsa told Nels she didn't want him to drink in the house anymore. The whiskey bottle, still with two inches of amber in the bottom, went into the fridge and stayed there. Nels followed to the letter her request not to drink at home. The hotel was a ten-minute walk from the house. By law, the beer parlour closed between six and seven. Weeknights, Nels arrived home at ten past six for supper and left again at ten minutes to seven. Elsa poured her family into this small reservoir of time. She recounted Judith's latest accomplishments to Nels, talked about her daily round of errands, coaxed him for conversation about work. When Judith was two, Elsa painted the little wooden corner cupboard yellow for her to use when she played house.

"See," she showed Nels when he came in. "I even did the shelf inside."

She wrote to Pauline: "He wants to make Judith a set of play dishes to put in her cupboard. He has me saving the lids of tobacco tins and peanut butter cans so he can paint them green."

Elsa waited three weeks before she painted the makeshift dishes herself. She was outside stirring turpentine into the paint with a scrap of wood that had split off the back fence, when she saw Young Carl go by across the street. He was on his way to work, stride long, shoulders loose. The word was he'd made an offer on the empty McCallum house and everyone knew that charming Anna Spencer would say yes to him any day. Elsa stirred and stirred until the sharp-smelling turpentine blended with the paint in a thin, even mixture.

WHEN HER SECOND PREGNANCY miscarried on the same day Aunt Eleanor died, Elsa felt everything behind and in front of her buckle and shake. There was a fight the night before the funeral, as there had been the Sunday before and the Sunday before that. The rolling pin that Nels's Uncle Herman had carved – the one with the hard ridges for making *lefse* – made a dent in the plaster in the kitchen wall. Elsa was never clear afterward if the dent happened when Nels threw the rolling pin at her or when she threw it at him. Nor could she say who threw first. What stayed with her afterward was the picture of little Judith scrambling in and out amongst their feet. Screaming. Crawling under the kitchen table to hide. Elsa wanted to quiet her somehow

– wrap her small shoulders in a blanket, brush the hair back gently from her forehead – but the greedy roar inside her own head swiped away her best intentions.

It was a question of pacing, Elsa concluded. She could give Judith a decent start as long as she could stretch her own energy across a known time frame. An article in *McCall's* said that if you can get a child safely through to age three or four, then the pattern will be set. Your child will always know who she is and who loves her, and that will carry her through anything. Elsa resolved to hold herself together until Judith's fourth birthday.

The shouting and shoving between Elsa and Nels continued and Judith still screamed in the centre of it, but Elsa made it her job to manufacture security through little acts of will. She stuck to firm routines, listened when she hardly cared to, pretended delight at Judith's drawings, gave her elementary cooking lessons – breaking eggs, stirring pancakes. She ordered herself to make sure there was a story, a kiss, and a bedtime prayer every night. As soon as Judith learned to count well enough, they played games together from the cardboard chest, *Ten Games for Children*, that Judith's Grandma Will sent one year for Christmas. Steeplechase and Parcheesi. Snakes and Ladders, which made Judith impatient and which Elsa told her was about persistence, about keeping on.

The house Nels had put the down payment on before she lost the second baby was bigger by half than the apartment, and Elsa moved her things into the tiny third bedroom. She did better than her promise to herself about Judith's fourth birthday. In fact, her daughter was almost nine by the time Elsa retreated to a state where she spent most of her time in her room. After that, though, she rarely came out when Nels was in the house, spoke to him only when necessary. She did what she had to do to keep things running: made sure Judith was fed; washed her clothes but didn't mend them; helped with homework when she could muster her resolve; tried to manufacture conversations with her daughter, but failed more often than not. Occasionally, Elsa even made it to Sunday service or to a meeting of the United Church Women, avoiding certain people and keeping up a thin connection with those who were kind enough to make small talk, tactful enough not to mention her irregular appearances.

The year Judith was eleven, Elsa's sister Pauline, whose husband had a good desk job with the post office in Bridgewater, supplied two yards of mint green velvet and a packet of rick-rack to outfit her for the Explorer Girls' fashion show. Elsa made a rare excursion down the street with Judith in tow to put the dress together at Isabelle Hepburn's house. When she was finished, she folded the leftover pieces and stored them in a corner of her own room, where they were soon covered with piles of attendant mending and scraps intended for quilts.

THERE WAS A FIGHT about the house. Elsa said the neighbours would complain soon about the peeling paint and the cardboard taped in the hall window if they didn't do something. And the mayor living just down the block. Nels said there was no money for paint and who had time to do it anyway? Elsa sat in her room with Judith's old box of wax crayons and drew pictures of houses. None of them looked at all like her own. She drew irises in front of the houses, tiger lilies, tulips. Then she left the houses out of the pictures completely and drew only flowers, big ones that filled the whole page. Some she drew by making patterns of little x-marks, so they looked crudely like the cross-stitch pictures she used to make before she married Nels. When Judith stopped in the doorway of Elsa's room and asked what she was doing, Elsa gave her a verbal lambasting and sent her away.

Elsa unpacked her old books and kept them close around herself in her room. Kipling, Housman, Buchan, *The Oxford Book of English Verse*. She liked the calm, matte feel of the Housman pages, was drawn to the tissue-thin leaves of the *Oxford*. Her mother supplied her each year at Christmas with subscriptions to the *Saturday Evening Post* and *McCall's*. Elsa tore the short stories from every issue and kept them laid flat in apple boxes. She packed a suitcase one Thursday and wrote to Pauline that she'd be on the bus on Monday. Get away, maybe for good. When Monday came, she didn't make the bus, but she did make it out of the house.

She borrowed a doddering Smith-Corona from Reverend Moore, who had acquired a new typewriter and assured her there was no inconvenience. Three weeks of drill brought her typing speed back up to what it had been when she made book lists at the library. For practice she reproduced, word by word, entire chapters from Judith's copy of *Emily of New Moon*. She wrote imaginary letters to Aunt Eleanor. *Judith continues to do well in school. She is a favourite with the teachers. It is some trouble keeping her in clothes, but Mom has knit her a new*

sweater, which helps. The house is very cold in this weather.
Nels's work is steady still, but his eyesight is deteriorating.

Elsa searched out work in bits and pieces. She set up shop on the kitchen table during the day and made out invoices for Morgan's Farm Equipment, shifting the carbon periodically to keep it fresh, darting a hand up to flick the metal arm back into place every time the "t" stuck. She typed and retyped a thesis for a local farmer who grew special plots of seed during the summer and spent his winters off at the university. She paid off three months of past due grocery bills; bought a piece of glass that she puttied into the hall window where the cardboard had been; learned to pass Nels in the kitchen without speaking at all. And she began to accept that Judith almost never spoke to her.

Elsa and Nels carried on their co-existence, sometimes flaring at each other, sometimes just stirring the coals. Elsa kept Reverend Moore's typewriter clattering in the background with one small job after another. Judith didn't scream any more when her parents started up; she just left the house – late at night, early in the morning, Sunday afternoon. She must have had places to go.

"Where have you been?"

"Out. Around."

"Where did you sleep last night?"

"Donna's."

"You weren't with that Sonter boy were you?"

"No, I wasn't with that Sonter boy."

It might be true. It might not. "Next time tell me where you're going. You have to tell me where you're going."

"Right."

LIGHT SEARS Elsa's eyes when she opens them. She closes her lids quickly, then opens them again just enough that she has a slit to see through. Something in the slant of the rays looks like late afternoon, early evening. This can't be right – she has always arranged things so that her bedroom window faces east. She squints across the room. Her window is the wrong shape. The curtains are no colour at all. The hospital. University Hospital. Judith is here. Has been here long enough to fall asleep in that awful moulded plastic chair. She looks so uncomfortable. If Elsa could move more easily, she would find Judith a pillow, tuck a blanket around her shoulders. Rock her.

Elsa pulls herself out of bed and, leaning on the wheeled bedside table, attempts to use it as a walker to get herself over to the window. The IV line in her arm stops her after two steps. The noise wakes Judith. "Mom, you're up," she says, pushing her legs straight out in a stretch.

"Judith…."

"Yes Mom?"

"Thank you for coming, Judith."

"Of course, Mom."

Elsa focuses on a scratch in the table's surface. She concentrates on speaking out loud so Judith will hear her.

"Judith?"

"Yes." Judith comes to stand beside her, puts a hand lightly on her arm.

Elsa doesn't go on. Leaning on the unstable table makes breathing difficult. It rolls ahead a touch and Elsa's legs begin to shake.

"Let me get you back into bed," Judith says.

"Judith…?" There is something else. She wants to talk to Judith about Aunt Eleanor, about faith, even, but she can't. Religion embarrasses her. She suspects any discussion of faith would embarrass Judith as well.

"Yes, Mom?"

Elsa doesn't answer. Judith helps her back to the bed and settles her in.

"Do you want a drink? I'll get you some fresh water."

"This is good just like this," Elsa says. She closes her eyes. "This is good…. Good to lie here quietly now." Maybe she'll try again to talk to Judith. A little later. It occurs to her that what she practises might have nothing to do with religion, with faith, the way other people think of it. Just some stubborn idea that she must keep at it. Whatever *it* might be. But maybe Judith doesn't need to talk about this. Maybe determination is built right into Judith's nature. At any rate, something has brought her this far.

"You're all right, aren't you, Judith?" Elsa says.

There is a short silence.

"I'm fine," Judith says. She pauses, then says, "Most of the time I'm fine. You sleep, Mom."

Unsteady hands adjust Elsa's blanket; she senses the fatigue in the hands. Judith will need a good rest after this many hours waiting in a hospital room. Is it hours? Must be days. A good rest after this many days at the bedside.

Elsa's heard her daughter, she's almost certain, singing old lullabies beside her bed sometime in the last few hours. And she's heard her reciting a children's prayer. Where she learned the lullabies heaven only knows; Elsa was never one to sing them. But didn't she hear a line or two from "All Through the Night" in Judith's unstable alto a minute ago? And the spoken words, "Now I lay me down to sleep," a phrase that can comfort even an atheist if she's repeated it often enough as a child. Can comfort against all odds, built as it is on the possibility of death each time you put your cheek on the pillow.

Judith must be as tired as tired. The girl needs rest. She doesn't need talk about aunts who died long ago, or how to find your way out of a low spot or about what you can learn from a game of Snakes and Ladders. She'll dredge up the details of the past and make her own sense of them in her own good time. The best thing Elsa can do for Judith now is to depart.

Her stomach feels a little better for the moment. They must have given her something easier to manage for lunch today. She sleeps. She wakes. The sheet feels heavier than cotton ought to feel. There's movement beside the bed. Someone settles her hair away from her forehead, wets her dry mouth with a swab. Elsa focuses what attention she still has on the soothing cool line of water on her lips.

THE UNRULIES

Just how, Judith wondered, was she supposed to feel about all this? How, especially, was she to feel about the diaries with which she'd been presented? It took her by surprise, didn't match up with memory, the way her mother's old notebooks tempered war and domestic tribulation by recording their events alongside girlishness and gossip and romantic delusion. She came across her mother's notebooks, or rather, her cousin Maggie came across them, a few weeks after the funeral, buried several layers deep in the older house, the one in Flat Hill. Judith and Maggie had sorted through at least three feet of stacked papers, the sediment of decades, when Maggie said, "What about these?" and handed Judith two dark red exercise books.

They were smaller than the notebooks Judith's students used, finer somehow. Judith brushed her hand over the cover of the first one with the same motion she'd used all morning to dust needlework patterns and crayon drawings and bundles of old telephone bills. The surface was embossed with thin, horizontal lines. The name "Elsa Will" appeared in blue ink in the upper right-hand corner.

Maggie had called a week earlier. "You shouldn't do this alone," she'd said. "I'll drive down with you and help with the house in Flat Hill." Judith had hardly protested. She'd already dealt with the Saskatoon house on her own, an undertaking that had taken several days. Elsa had kept nearly everything that came into her hands over her seventy years, and none of it was organized; it took its only order from the chronological layers in which it was laid down.

Judith had gone to the Saskatoon house with an economy box of green garbage bags and a borrowed half-ton truck. There wasn't much worth keeping after the auction house carted off the furniture – dishes for the Salvation Army, tax files and pay stubs for the lawyer to look through, drawers full of yarn that Judith sent to Evergreen Lodge. Most of her mother's books had been in the basement through a spring flood three years ago and the pages were fused together. They smelled of mildew. After trying to force two or three of them open, Judith had given up and thrown them all out: *Captains Courageous*, *Rilla of Ingleside*, *The Golden Treasury*, *Memory Hold-the-Door*, *The Book of Myths*. On and on. There must have been a hundred. *Death of an Expert Witness*, *Treasures of Britain*, *Gaudy Night*, *Puck of Pook's Hill*. She stacked them into boxes and more boxes, shuffled them out the back door into the warm afternoon, and made trip after trip across the overgrown lawn, past the spent tulips, and out the back gate to heave the cartons up and over the high green wall of the rented dumpster.

Emotion had hardly come into it. Judith herself had never lived in the Saskatoon house, hadn't even spent that much time there. She and her mother had acted out their rare visits at Judith's apartment during these last years.

The house she and Maggie were cleaning today, the older one in Flat Hill, the house Judith had grown up in, was the tougher one. Her mother had never quite managed to clean out the last of her belongings and get the property ready for sale. It wasn't worth much anyway. She must have convinced herself she'd be ready one day to come back and deal with it. Judith had seen Maggie's wonder at the disorder as they slid the plastic folding door aside and looked into what had been Elsa's room. "Wow. I knew Aunt Elsa had her own way of doing things, but what's all this?" Maggie's head turned a little as if she was trying to look at Judith, but her eyes stayed fixed on the clutter.

"Her room. Where she slept. I don't remember them ever sharing a room. She holed up in here, piled her life around her."

It was a tiny, chaotic space. A series of wall shelves, poorly anchored, had torn loose from the plaster and spilled onto the single bed. Judith's first step into the narrow path between the bed and the stacks of paper on the floor knocked a slippery tower of old *Life* magazines sideways, releasing a damp odour that had been trapped in the papers underneath.

"Let's get started," she said. She flipped a garbage bag so it snapped open; she had this down to one motion by now. "Most of it's junk. Anything you're not sure about, ask me."

Throughout the morning, Maggie did ask. She found an old edition of Housman's *A Shropshire Lad* under the collapsed shelves on the bed and asked what to do with it. Judith looked at the woodcut illustration on the book jacket, an idealistic youth gazing toward some symbolic place beyond the edge of the picture. Her mother's favourite poet. The missing copy. The volume had gone astray the summer Judith's father died and her mother moved to Saskatoon, and Elsa had brooded over the loss until Judith searched out a replacement. Judith had no taste for Housman's old laments over lost youth and fallen comrades, but there was no sense throwing away a perfectly good book. She slid it into her carry-all.

Moments later, Maggie showed Judith a Christmas mug, the red paint flaking away from Santa's hat like week-old nail polish. "I'd forgotten all about that," said Judith. Maggie held it out, but Judith didn't take it. "I don't know what use it is, but I won't rule on it just yet. Put it on the floor here."

Maggie asked next about a tintype of an unknown relative, a woman with shadowed eyes and a mountain of light hair.

"I don't know," Judith said. "What do you think – someone we have in common?"

"Don't know," Maggie said. The tintype went on the floor beside Santa. Judith came across a handful of tatting shuttles and set them on the floor as well. Her mother hadn't made lace for years.

Maggie asked next about a painted porcelain rabbit.

"Can't decide," Judith said, and Maggie set the rabbit down with the other things.

Maggie held out a Westclox windup alarm clock. "Vintage?" she asked.

"Whatever," Judith said. "I'll make a ruling on it later." From then on, Maggie referred to the assortment on the floor as the unrulies.

If she hadn't brought someone along for company, Judith thought, she would have risked growing physically smaller as she ploughed through the residue of her family's past. As it was, when she found her grade six report card, her fingers started to itch in between, the way they had with that rash she'd had such trouble with the winter she was twelve. And when she dropped a box of crochet hooks so they clattered across the floor, she pulled her shoulders up and waited for a scolding. She stuffed the fear reflex back down inside, made her muscles relax, composed herself. She arranged the hooks back in their places in order of size, snapped the cover shut, and set the box on the floor with the other unrulies.

They'd been working for hours when Maggie passed her the notebooks. Judith, daunted by the idea of another decision about what to put in a box and what to send to the garbage bin, sat down cross-legged on a clear spot of floor. She could feel when she folded her legs that her jeans had more give around the thighs than they'd had a month ago. She opened the first notebook on her lap and recognized a younger version of her mother's hand; the curves were rounder, the loops on the tall letters less angular than those on the grocery list she'd found on her mother's fridge in Saskatoon.

March 9, 1940
Dad took me to see the railway hotel in Saskatoon,
the one they named after the Earl of Bessborough.
The ceiling in the rotunda is over a storey high,
maybe two, and the carpet is more than an inch
thick. The 64th Regiment could cross it and you
wouldn't hear a sound unless they were talking.
There's even a room where anyone who wishes can
go and have tea. We watched for a minute from the
doorway, saw the people sipping tea from china cups
painted with little pictures of the hotel. I hear there
is a ballroom with mirrors on all the walls, so people
can see the dancing dresses reflected over and over.

JUDITH IS DRESSING for Sunday school. The blue dress
that came in the mail on Friday from her cousin in
Bridgewater is almost new and it has puffed sleeves that
you can see right through and it makes her feel fine and
frilly and very clean, as if she were one of those girls who
come into the back room of the church on Sunday
mornings wearing shiny black pumps on white-
stockinged feet. Her mother kneels in front of Judith,
takes her by the shoulders. The stiff fabric of the puffed
sleeves scrunches into Judith's skin.

"Judith, suppose someone came to you one day,
someone like Mrs. Waigle, and asked if you would rather
live with your mom or your dad." Her mother pauses,
lets go of her shoulders, but her face is still there, close
to Judith's. "What would you say to her?"

Judith doesn't want Mrs. Waigle to ask her anything.
Mrs. Waigle who stands over her and the other kids in

beginners' class at Sunday school, thick and tall like Jack's beanstalk, and silences them with a rough "sh-sh" and a shake of her finger.

She looks away from her mother's face, fluffs her sleeves, waits for the question to go away. It does.

"WHAT'S IN THE NOTEBOOKS?" Maggie asked. She tied off a garbage bag and came around to look over Judith's shoulder.

"Diaries, it looks like." Judith could feel Maggie close enough to see the writing. She started to flip the pages. In the back, Elsa had ruled out a ledger that ran back to front. Letting the book rest open, Judith ran her finger down one of the columns. Her mother had kept a meticulous account of how she spent her part-time salaries from the coal office and the library. Life Savers (wintergreen) .05; stockings .60; Aspirin .24; church .10 – all penciled in with proper zeros and decimal points. There were necessities: shoes half-soled, .76; and indulgences: six small red star buttons, .16. Judith saw that her mother, a woman she never knew to go to the movies and rarely saw laugh, paid thirty cents to see *The Great Dictator* one day, and, a few days later, put fourteen cents toward something she recorded only as "foolishness."

JUDITH'S DAD is watching Ed Sullivan, laughing at a comedian with a Spanish name. Her mother comes in from the kitchen, storms across the living room, pulls the plug on the set.

"Sit there and laugh," she says. Says it to the room,

not directly to her husband. "Taxes aren't paid and we'll all be out in the snow by the end of the month."

The television picture collapses into a sharp white dot in the middle of the dark screen and when Judith stares into it she sees her father sitting outside in his armchair. Little mounds of snow rest on his thighs and on the toes of his work boots. Snow drifts off his forearm when he lifts his hand to call Jack Tompkins over for a game of cards.

THE FIRST ENTRY in Elsa's second notebook was a list of books that ran to two full pages. Some were checked off with red pencil. "I think the ones she ticked off are the ones she'd finished," Judith said to Maggie. "See – Kipling, Buchan, DuMaurier, Stevenson. She set herself an ambitious exercise and got about half through by the looks of it."

"I'll tell you what's ambitious," Maggie said. "Ambitious is you and I doing anything more before lunch. Does your old home town have a good café?" She wiped her hands on her jeans, took a comb out of her purse.

Judith looked at her, raised an eyebrow.

"Okay, does it have any kind of café at all?"

Judith shrank at the thought of running into people she used to know, people who had known her mother, people who had known the girl who grew up in this house. Wiping her hands and combing her hair wouldn't be enough to make her feel presentable. "Couldn't you just get me takeout? A hamburger and some fries?"

"Sure. Tell me where."

"Try Chan's. Main Street, across from the grocery

store. Take the thermos and get a refill."

Maggie left the inside door open when she went out and the light June wind threaded in through the screen door. The quiet swish of the air as it crossed the wire mesh was the sound of childhood summer days, made more emphatic by the backyard smells of gravel and grass that the breeze carried in. Judith put the notebooks aside and walked through the small rooms, hoping some clear task would present itself. In the living room: a folded ironing board, a collapsing couch, a desk covered with crazy piles of papers. She'd need to arrange for someone to haul the old furniture to the nuisance grounds. In the kitchen: odd pots and mismatched dishes Elsa hadn't seen fit to take along when she moved. In her dad's bedroom: fishing tackle and a bent rod, clothing that had never been dealt with, a dust-covered curling trophy, engraved with his name, *Nels Eriksen*. In her own old room: a painted blue dresser – beautiful glass drawer pulls, but the drawers themselves jammed unless they were opened with great care. Judith wanted everything to vanish without having to pass through her hands. There was too much for one day, but Maggie had to go back to the city first thing tomorrow. Judith would have to make a second run at it some other day.

She returned to her spot on the floor in her mother's old room and picked up a notebook.

May 10, 1940
No word from Dad for months, no cheques. Looking for work in Winnipeg, last we heard. We'll hear from him soon.
    I sat down on the front porch to knit on

Frederick's sweater. He's such a good help to Mother now that he's the man of the house. I'm glad he's too young for the service. I hadn't been sitting more than five minutes when the water man came by. He said, "Looks like it's busted wide open, Elsa," and handed me the paper. "NAZI FLAMES HIT LOWLANDS." Belgium and Holland invaded. Wide open war for Europe." I kept on knitting and all I could think was how relieved I am that the sweater, with my brother in it, will not be crossing the Atlantic. More noble feelings, I'm sure, are expected of me, of us all, under the circumstances. One day, perhaps.

May 28, 1940
Frederick says John Jacobs has gone to another artillery course. Suppose they take him. Frederick will mope for days if JJ goes overseas.

Tuesday was hectic at the library. JJ came in and parked his books. He was in uniform, with a raincoat and debonair wedge cap. I was busy and when I turned around he was gone. N.B.: Next time ask him about books by Buchan; show him the new British Penguin editions.

JUDITH STANDS outside her mother's bedroom door. Her mother is inside, reading – she can tell by the occasional sound of a turning page. It's the only sound she's heard from her mother in days. She must come out sometimes, must come out during the day, at least, when Judith's at school. Judith shifts her weight and a floorboard creaks.

"Judith?"

"Yes."

"What are you doing out there?"

"Just standing here."

"Why?"

"Are you coming out, Mom?"

"Why? What do you need?"

"Nothing."

"Then go away."

"Aren't you coming out?"

"No. Go away now, will you?"

WHEN SHE HEARD Maggie pull up in the truck, Judith jumped like a snooper caught at the teacher's desk. She slid both the notebooks spine-first into her carryall behind the Housman, careful not to strain the staples.

In the kitchen, Maggie spread a fresh garbage bag on the floor and unpacked their lunch onto it.

"Chan's?" Judith asked.

"There is no more Chan's. Place called Murphy's by the gas station. I bought the Saskatoon paper too. Want a section?"

"No thanks."

Maggie opened to the op-ed page and settled in. Her sweatshirt hardly showed the dust from the morning's work; her jeans were new and still looked fresh; her short hair sat neatly in place. Judith lifted her own hair out of her eyes and redid her pony tail. Maggie managed to look solid and sane after trowelling through chaos for three hours. Her easy acceptance, after initial surprise, of the state of Elsa's house invited Judith's confidence.

"I read the obits yesterday," she confessed to Maggie. "Every word of every one. People I didn't know, hadn't ever heard of. I've never done that before. They're funny things."

Maggie set the newspaper aside. "Grandma Will told me once that she read the obituaries because they make death seem normal. Everybody ends up dead sooner or later. Everybody's last act."

"Maybe. I don't think that's what I was looking for."

"What then?"

Judith shrugged. "How the people who are left over afterward write a person's life into three or four column inches, how they make it manageable with strings of words like 'educated at' and 'lifetime interest in.' As if you can parse someone into credentials and descendants and club memberships." She paused. "Although... there's something attractive about the neatness of it all. I felt completely inadequate when I wrote Mom's. Even though it was printed weeks ago, I still keep going back to rewrite parts of it. I even thought half-seriously of asking my grade tens to write obituaries as a composition exercise. To see if they could give me any ideas."

"Tell you a secret – " Maggie said.

Judith nodded, smiled slightly, looked at her cousin across the space where secrets had passed before, but so long ago she could remember nothing about the confidences except how important they were. Important to girls of a certain age, an age where at family reunions they had hidden together under the stairs, run through hollows in hedges to shake unwelcome younger cousins, pooled their dimes to buy their first pack of cigarettes.

Maggie smiled back. "Mom's written her own obituary," she said. "Dad's too."

"Seriously?"

"Seriously," Maggie said. "Cross my heart. Checks every year to see if she needs to update them, same time as she writes the Christmas letter."

"Mom always said Pauline was the practical one," Judith said. "Are you going to use them when the time comes?"

"Don't know. Maybe. I'm practical too."

THAT NIGHT in the motel room down the road in Ripley, Judith eased the notebooks out of her bag and crawled into bed. Maggie was already settled in the other bed. Judith's eyes stung from sifting all day through dust and mildew and her mother's life, but she blinked twice and focused on the page. Her mother had written in blue fountain pen; the pattern on the page reminded Judith of the lace she could just remember her mother making when Judith was tiny. An ink blotter was caught in the spine a few pages in. "Nagle's 5¢ to $1.00 Store," the card said. "Reliance, the ink you can rely on."

The entries were separated by spaces of time, some-times months; the matters with which they dealt came together in unexpected combinations. One entry that began with casualty counts, lists of bombings, and spec-ulation that the Italians were low on supplies, gave way two thirds down the page to an extended consideration of which dresses Elsa could make over so they'd last another season. Another page was half-filled with dark, wartime jokes: "Old Mother Hubbard went to the cup-board, to get her poor dog." Full stop. Followed by,

"Democracy sausages: They're going to skin the dictators and stuff them with their own baloney."

John Jacobs appeared in entry after entry.

July 22, 1941
Heard a program tonight about the Home Guard in Britain – about a pacifist vicar who dies defending his ancient Norman church from Nazi parachutists. The hero's name was John, of course. It makes things all just a little too real.

Soldiers passing by remind me of JJ, last February, when he was recruiting for the 64th. He wandered into the library, in khaki, with a disgruntled expression. Someone said, "Rope in many?" "No. Sat there all day – two recruits. We're not those Air Force blokes, y'know."

August 3, 1941
Pauline and I were having a cup of tea with Margaret Duncan at the hotel, when I saw a tall man in khaki go by the window. I could only see his back, but I rushed out and, as I'd thought, it was JJ. I was wearing the dress I'd restyled from Mother's old yellow print. He had to rush away, busy with reserve duties, but he said he'd be in soon for another stack of reading, and could I think of something nice for his mother to read, something to remind her of England, before the war?

August 12, 1941
Ross Murphy has been killed in a crash. Sylvia seems to be taking it very well, but I expect it hasn't

become real for her yet. I remember her saying once that she never let herself worry about him, because such a life wouldn't be worth living. Two months ago she came over to give Pauline and I pieces of her wedding cake to put under our pillows. Pauline said that sort of thing is for dreamers; she slept like a rock. Now Sylvia is closing up the apartment in Saskatoon. The plane was struck by lightning and just went to pieces, 10 miles NW of Prince Albert. He was instructing at the time.

There was a service here, the casket covered with a Union Jack. And his cap on top, the same cap he flipped onto our kitchen table when he came over to look at Frederick's model planes.

This makes the first of my schoolmates "killed in active service," though two others have been reported missing. The Air Force people are all over town.

JUDITH IS EIGHT. Her mother has found a job, but it's thirty miles away, and it's only six months' work. She grumbles about the long drive, with the sunrise in her eyes on the way to work, the sunset in her eyes on the way home. "But it pays the taxes on the house," she tells her daughter.

"It puts the groceries on the table," she tells her sister on the phone. "Heaven knows, Nels doesn't." Judith waits for what her mother will say next to Aunt Pauline, the thing she always says. "All the good men died in the war."

JUDITH CLOSED the first notebook and, hearing a rustle as Maggie rolled over in the other bed, she tipped the lampshade to keep the light on her own side of the room. Close to the bed sat the box of unrulies she'd brought, finally, from the house. She'd looked hopelessly at the accumulated collection at the end of the day. The mug, the clock, the hooks and shuttles, the rabbit, the tintype. And more: an array of antique buttons mounted on cardboard; a copy of *Life* from the year of her own birth; a wine-coloured glove with a ruffle at the wrist; a blue tin wind-up cat; envelopes full of old postcards and photos.

She'd sat on the floor and resorted and rearranged, thumbed the dust off each of them, done everything but really look hard at any one piece. Finally she had released the breath she'd been holding, muttered, "What the hell," and said she'd throw them out after all. Maggie had left the room and reappeared a moment later with a cardboard box that decades earlier had brought an electric frying pan home from Tredwell's Hardware. Gingerly, she'd packed the collection of odds and ends inside, using pages from the newspaper where the job called for cushioning. Judith had watched with relief as Maggie closed the box and she could no longer see the contents.

Now, finished with the first notebook, Judith leaned over and set it on top of the box of unrulies. Where would a young Elsa have gone to write in her book? Would she sit at the kitchen table? Lie on the bed as young women do, chin on her hand, notebook in front? Would she take herself away from her mother and brother and sister for privacy's sake and perch on the stool in the rickety shed that used to crouch in the back corner of Grandma Will's garden in Bridgewater? Judith kicked the blanket off her legs, rearranged the sheet, and took the second book from the bedside table.

November 28, 1941

I have a new man to build fires at the library this winter, a Scandinavian fellow who's in the reserves, Eriksen. JJ recommended him, after leafing through the troop roll with his finger hooked over his pipe all the while.

I have an odd idea that JJ brings me luck, but whether it's good luck or bad I can't decide. I had an argument with him – nothing really, just a few words about the new mayor and council, but a disagreement nevertheless – the night before I broke the brush from Mother's dresser set. On the other hand, he walked me home last night after I visited his mother, and this morning the library board voted me a pay raise.

I was so surprised by John's unexpected gallantry that I'm afraid I forgot to wish his mother goodnight. It was a chummy, companionable walk. When we came to my favourite spot on the hill, where you round the corner and get the breeze from the west, I had a sudden wish to walk the footpaths of England with just such an amusing, reliable companion. He told me I had a good gait.

But whenever I throw an apple peeling over my shoulder to find the first letter of my future husband's name, it comes out C or L.

December 15, 1941
It seems the 64th has really been mobilized. I don't
believe JJ went, or I'd have heard of it, or seen his
mother go down to the train. Frederick will know
something, the way he idolizes him. If he has gone,
I must be sure to visit his mother regularly. She will
be so lonely. He is so very good to her.

JUDITH'S MOTHER is raging.

"Your father gave the house away Saturday night in a card game in the back room at Chan's. Can't depend on him. Can't depend on him at all. Now I have to go begging to Dick Pavelik to get it back. Down there every Saturday night with all his buddies, drinking next week's groceries. His greatest friends, as long as he's got money to lose."

IN THE OTHER BED, Maggie stirred again. "Aren't you going to sleep?" she asked.

"In a minute."

The girl in the notebooks was as close as the pillow, closer, right inside Judith's head. Judith was almost asleep. Her eyes and the journal fell shut at the same moment. Her hand twitched; she jumped awake, squinted to wet her eyes, focussed, and continued to read.

When finally she finished, switched off the lamp and closed her eyes, she saw a young girl with dark, careful curls. The girl sat on the front porch of Grandma Will's house, knitting a sweater, talking to the water man. The scene changed. The same girl walked along a winter street with another girl, threw an apple peel over her shoulder, followed a man along a sidewalk. She dusted a shelf of books in an oak-lined library, smiled and looked over toward the doorway, watching for someone special to enter.

IN THE MORNING, Judith splashed her eyes repeatedly with cold water and came out of the bathroom with a washcloth pressed against the puffiness above her cheekbones. Maggie said she would do the driving on the way back.

They filled the thermos at the service station on the highway and left without breakfast. Judith poured coffee into the plastic cup once they were on the road. She offered it to Maggie, but not before she had held her face over the warm steam for a second.

"No thanks," Maggie told her. "Have some yourself. Did you finish your mom's notebooks last night?"

"I finished them as far as she did. There's a lot in there about a man I've never heard of. This guy named John keeps popping up."

"Talk to Mom," Maggie said. "She'll know who the guy was. Or Uncle Fred."

"It isn't that important, I guess. So long ago it hardly matters. Let me know if you want me to drive."

"I'm fine. You close your eyes, have a nap."

JUDITH'S MOTHER picks her up outside the high school, drives through town, turns onto the highway.

"Mom! You're scaring me!" The old Meteor has a squared-off dash with a squared-off speedometer. The needle looks like it has to stretch itself longer to get out to the corner where the higher numbers are. Judith watches the needle reach over to seventy miles an hour. Seventy-five. Eighty. Even at her best, her mother is not a steady driver. Judith is afraid that to say anything more now would be like throwing a lighted match into a wastepaper basket. Maybe just say something careful, quiet. She measures out four words, gives them an even tone. "What are you doing?"

"I'm going to kill us both!" It comes out in a shout, but her mother's hands are still clenched at two and ten on the wheel. "We can't show our faces in this town after today. Your father had another set-to with Tank Morrison over the taxes. Right out in public, in Chan's, at 10:30 in the morning when the whole of CP Rail was sitting down to coffee." Her mother punches the pedal ahead at the word "coffee," then lets the car settle back to seventy. Judith knows if she just stays quiet they will ride this out.

BACK IN HER APARTMENT, Judith slid the box of unrulies into the hall closet and closed the door. She told herself there was no edict that said she had to open it. It was late June and she held her students sternly in line until almost the end of term, then let them explode into their summer holidays two hours early on the last Friday afternoon. At home that evening she walked past the closet six different times in the course of cleaning up, changing clothes, retrieving a magazine from the bedroom. She was practised at ignoring troublesome things until they went away on their own. She poured herself a glass of wine, opened her magazine, pointed the remote at the TV. Nothing presented a diversion strong enough to crowd out the presence of the cardboard box in the closet. Finally, she went to the hallway and pulled it out.

A brand-name her students were fond of came to mind: NO FEAR. The NO FEAR logo had begun to appear that spring in the usual places where brand names are found: on students' backpacks and baseball caps, on bumper stickers, on the T-shirt the muscle-bound, dark-eyed girl in grade ten composition sometimes wore to class. NO FEAR. Emotion sent packing by a bare, two-word command. Forbidden. No smoking/no minors/no pets. No fear. Judith touched the cardboard box with one hand, then with both hands, and braced herself. Braced herself against her mother's untidy legacy and against her own disorderly scatter of recollections. Braced herself against the possibility that the unrulies were really the Furies, come to set her spinning for not honouring her mother the way a daughter ought to.

She opened the box and stared. Nothing sprang at her. There they lay, these few things from her mother's house, seated in their newspaper nests. She had been ready, finally, to meet the Furies. What was she to do with objects that lay so quietly in their places? She unpacked them onto the rug, feeling the small weight of each one as she lifted it, feeling the lightness of her hand each time after she set one down. Why had she brought so little?

Judith stared at the array for a long moment before she picked up the Santa mug, took it to the bedroom, and set it on her bedside table to replace the plastic water tumbler. She went back for the wine-coloured glove, which she draped over the edge of the basket of rolled washcloths in the bathroom. One by one she distributed the other articles throughout the apartment until she had achieved a modest clutter. She stood the card of mounted buttons on the ledge above the fireplace, and the Westclox alarm on the kitchen counter, close to the stove. She set the *Life* magazine on the coffee table, retrieved *A Shropshire Lad* from her bag, took the tintype and the envelopes full of photos and postcards from the pile of unrulies and put them all beside the magazine. The blue wind-up cat was still operable; she wound it and set it to run its brief course on the hearth. (Her mother's voice, the soft voice, from when Judith was small: *See how it purrs along the floor. Listen!*) She placed the tatting shuttles in a cluster in the fruit bowl and the porcelain rabbit on the shelf below the television. (*Look what Grandma sent for Easter.*) She scattered the crochet hooks on her bedroom dresser, like pick-up sticks. (*Aunt Eleanor gave me the first three as a start when I was a girl. I don't much use them these days, do I?*)

JUDITH BOUGHT the Saturday paper in the gift shop at the Bessborough and went to wait in the restaurant for her aunt. The hostess seated her where she had a view of the indoor pool one floor below.

"Coffee?" the waitress asked, and started to pour before Judith answered.

"Sure."

Judith was early. She waited five minutes, turned away from the view of the swimmers, checked her watch, and opened the paper to the obituaries. They read like variations on a theme, as if someone had taken a single form and customized the details.

Aunt Pauline came in and stood beside her chair. "Hello, dear. How are you managing?"

"I'm doing all right." Judith got up to give her a squeeze around the shoulders. "How about you?"

"The same."

"Did Maggie tell you she came out to Flat Hill with me last week?"

Pauline nodded. The four little lines that formed a "W" between her eyebrows when she was tired were pronounced today.

"I found some things you might want from the house, Pauline. Some postcards the relatives sent to Grandma from Ontario. And there's this." Judith passed her a studio proof of a much younger Pauline with Elsa. "It must have been taken in the forties some time. I can get a copy made for you."

"Well, look at that!" The lines between Pauline's eyebrows softened. "I remember going to have this taken. I don't think I ever had a copy."

"I hadn't ever seen it before. It was buried in her room under stacks of paper."

Pauline laid the photo down and set a hand on Judith's arm. "I feel so bad about you having to go down there and sort through everything. Why didn't she clear her things out and sell that house years ago?"

Judith looked at the table. She didn't reply for a moment. Then she said, "I guess she didn't want to face it. Everything inside it, I mean."

"Of course she didn't. I expect you didn't want to either, Judith. But you did it. And now it's done with."

Judith shrugged her shoulders and said nothing. She

still had to make at least one more run at cleaning up. She felt nowhere near done with it.

"Elsa never did learn to face up to things," Pauline said.

A rush to defend. Judith's voice sharpened. "I think she faced her share."

"I'm sorry, dear. You're right. Things couldn't have been easy."

Judith looked down at the swimmers. The pool was flanked with mirrored panels that reflected a fragmented, discontinuous view of the hotel lobby. She swallowed to smooth her voice. "Mom wrote about this hotel in her diary," she said. "About the trip she made here with your father during the war. How the carpet was so thick a regiment of soldiers could cross it and not make a noise. She wrote about the tea room and the china and the ballroom with mirrors."

Pauline took off her glasses and massaged her forehead. "Your mother was always scribbling something. Fancied herself a writer. She had to have the most expensive notebooks too. When she saw the war shortages coming, she went down to the drugstore and bought the last they had that were made with the good paper. She was always laying claim to the dining room table, fussing about her fountain pen, telling Frederick and me, even Mother, not to disturb her. Filling up those books with heaven knows what. Grand romances."

"Grand romances," Judith repeated. What her mother had written down at the age of twenty had such an optimistic ring, as if it could have been written by any normal girl. It was no easy exercise to reconcile the person in the notebooks with the resurfacing memories of the woman who'd written them – memories riveted together in a series of hard, short, episodes. Judith was beginning to think that the gap between her mother and that girl was exactly the distance between fantasy and reality. Her mother's fantasy, her mother's reality.

"As a matter of fact," Judith said to her aunt, "there is a little romance in Mom's diaries. Do you remember someone named John Jacobs? An Englishman."

"I remember him. Sure. He was a high school teacher. I wouldn't have called him English, but his mother was, way back. I remember when I was in his lit class he made a big deal about how he'd taken a trip 'back home' once to visit relatives. We all laughed at that, I remember. Made fun of his 'airs' when he left the room." Pauline put the back of her hand to her forehead and Judith pictured a class of wartime high school students doing the same.

"Evidently he was English enough for Mom," Judith said. "He's all through her notebooks. I knew she had a thing for Brits, but I never knew there was a particular Brit. Apparently she even went to the Anglican church some Sundays to catch a glimpse of him. She wrote that she found 'all the ups and downs' confusing."

"Oh dear. I knew she liked him, but I didn't realize she was so gone on him. He was much older. She couldn't have been serious."

"Must have been. She wrote about him for over two years, off and on, then stopped mentioning his name. Didn't say what happened. I thought maybe he was one of those 'good men who died in the war' she used to go on about."

Pauline laughed at this, a little laugh that was barely enough to relax her face. "No, no. The army let him go over something or other…I don't remember what. Maybe eyesight; could have been any old thing. Why resort to him when there were so many young fellows in their twenties around? At any rate, I don't expect he was interested in Elsa."

"So that was all there was to JJ," Judith said. "She always did have a sense of drama, didn't she?"

The waitress came around with refills. Pauline added sugar to her cup and stirred, round and round and round, twirling the spoon a little. "You could put it that way." She paused. "Elsa was one of those people life was never smooth for. But you knew that." Pauline stared into her coffee. "Even when she was a girl. She tried so hard to fit herself in, it made people uneasy." It was the most personal thing Judith had ever heard her aunt say.

"Of course every girl's had a crush on someone who didn't like her back," Pauline said. "Your mother was just like the rest of us that way." Judith heard the note in her aunt's voice that said she was done with that part of the conversation. Pauline took her napkin and wiped a drop of coffee from the table.

JUDITH STAYED in the coffee shop with her newspaper after Pauline left. She ordered lunch, returned to the obituaries, read one at random.

"Lillian Atkey died peacefully at her home, Sunday, June 10, in her eightieth year." Judith had never heard of Lillian Atkey. She took a pen from her purse, replaced the name with "Elsa Eriksen," and stroked out words, sentences, in an effort to make the paragraphs about Lillian Atkey apply to her mother's life. Doggedly she kept at it until she was left with "Elsa Eriksen died peace-fully…after a long struggle." It was a short sentence, tidy; it was true as far as it went. Judith began to doodle. She inked in the "D" in the word "Deaths" at the top of the column, cross-hatched the shadows on someone's photo-graph under "In Memoriam," scrolled a flowing border in ballpoint along the narrow margin of newsprint. Then she slid her coffee cup out of the way and shuffled back through the paper until she found a large block of extra white space inside the frame of an advertisement, room enough to begin composing a rambling, disorganized obituary. Now the words would come.

No words came. What came instead was a deep hol-low feeling in the place in her gut where elemental emo-tions always present themselves first. The feelings Judith had been playing tag with had caught up with her. Let them in, then, get them over with. Grief, loneliness, loss. These she could deal with. It wasn't as if she and her mother had been close.

But she knew better. This grief was not about loss, it was about helplessness, about her inability to remodel her mother's history. There once was a girl who started to write a life for herself in a couple of scribblers. That girl disappeared and showed up later as someone else. Whatever Judith might manage to compose in the space on the page in front of her, it would not be an ending to match what her mother had started out to write. She folded the newspaper and paid her bill.

Judith was on the path, walking by the river without noticing how she got there, couldn't say whether she'd left the hotel by way of the stairs or the elevator, the front door or the side. She stopped on the path, opened her purse, looked again at the picture of her mother and her aunt Pauline. Her mother's life would never change. She memorized the careful, dark curls that lay against the young woman's forehead, imagined the feel of the wool sweater draped around her shoulders, traced with her finger the outline of her face, thinner than it was in later years. She invited the girl to take a walk with her. Judith knew very little about her companion, couldn't honestly say she'd have been friendly toward her if they'd known each other way back when, but the girl had a smile that was engaging, if a little toothy.

Judith walked for hours with her imperfect imagination alongside her, walked hoping that the physical exertion itself would somehow make the young face under the dark curls indelible. She tested her memory to recall the details of the notebooks – the turns of phrase, the mix of sentimentality and tall talk. She walked north and across the railway bridge, with its wind and its smell of creosote. South along the river trail where all the green summer smells of water and growth mixed together. Further south, past blocks of three-storey houses huddled together, then down unfamiliar sidewalks, past wartime houses with their steep-sloping roofs, past rows of squat pastel bungalows where petunia beds gave off their strong late-afternoon scent. She walked until sweat soaked her blouse and made her scalp itch, until she had to blink to see clearly, until breathing was work and her leg muscles shook. Her route became a long loop that delivered her back to her apartment and the collection of unrulies, scattered through the rooms on tables and dressers and ledges and countertops.

BOILERMAKERS

For the four days she'd had to wait between doctor's appointments last week, Evelyn had checked and probed, probed and checked. At work, she'd visited the storage room at intervals, closing the door so no one would see her feeling around underneath her sweater, shuddering at the way the lump slipped about so easily under the pressure of her fingers. She convinced herself it was as large as a peach pit; she convinced herself it was only the size of a small pea. At home in the evenings she carried on with the usual things – house-cleaning, sewing, a chapter or two of a novel before bed – while her hands groped with a will of their own, repeatedly palpating her left breast, comparing what she found there against the right, re-examining the left. If the lump disappeared in one position, she shifted about until she could feel it again.

In fact, she was still having trouble controlling her hands. Today in Greenwood's, sitting across from

Candace, she'd found she could prevent involuntary movements by putting her elbows on the table and cupping them squarely with opposite hands. That was her posture when the tall oak door opened and Shirley, the last member of their threesome, came in. Bright winter sun lit Shirley's hair for a moment before the door swung shut behind her. She greeted each of them with a quick, one-armed squeeze around the shoulders, then sat down in the chair Candace pushed out for her. She parked a shopping bag at her feet, held it open and invited Candace and Evelyn to lean across the table and look inside. "I brought cookies."

Evelyn laughed. "Cookies?" Side by side in the shopping bag were two foil bundles, each topped with jaunty ringlets of green ribbon.

"You know, sweet treats often seen in people's homes at Christmas time. Go well with tea."

"And these are to nibble on while we drink our beer?" Evelyn said.

"Well, we could, but the idea was for the two of you to take them home. Christmas baking."

"Very festive," Candace said. "Thanks, Shirley. I've hardly made anything yet."

Evelyn leaned back in her chair, still clutching her elbows. "I didn't bring anything. I'll get the first round."

"Nice hair, Evelyn," Shirley said. "Red this year, good for you. Seriously though, it looks good. Me, I stick to basics."

With basics like that, why not? Fine bones, a Vogue-photo smoothness to her blunt-cut, dark brown hair, a long-legged, long-waisted frame. And Candace. Candace looked good in a different way, petite and energetic, wearing sparkly Christmas earrings that turned in the light when she moved her head. At the corners of her eyes, tiny crow's feet emphasized her smile.

"I had the dye job weeks ago," Evelyn said. "I'm used to it by now."

"So," Shirley said, looking up and down the room, "this is what your neighbourhood bar looks like, Candace."

Around them were oak-trimmed walls; under their feet, plaid carpet; halfway along the room, a low divider that was inset with an etched glass panel. Above the bar hung cardboard cut-outs of Santa and his reindeer, twirling in air currents in a way that made them look as if they were scanning their surroundings, double-checking, their surprised expressions implying they'd expected to decorate a daycare or a kindergarten classroom rather than a bar.

"Not that I've seen the inside of the place before now," Candace said. "I just thought we'd try it."

Arrangements had been made. The two husbands, Candace's and Shirley's, had taken all the kids to the movies and had been assigned Christmas errands to keep them busy afterwards. As for Evelyn, she lived alone, had no one who needed to be packed off for the afternoon. ("Single at thirty-five – who'd have thought?" Shirley sometimes said, and Evelyn would decide each time to accept the packaging of pretended envy in which Shirley always wrapped the comment. And each time, the three would quickly find a different path for their conversation. Her own performance in this exchange, Evelyn sometimes felt, was the social equivalent of signing for an unwelcome registered letter from the tax department, then wishing the postie a smiling good morning.)

They were down to only about two get-togethers a year now, these three women. They still called themselves the Boilermakers, even though the old nickname was hardly appropriate anymore. They'd thought it suited well enough six or seven years ago when each of them had a job in a store or an office downtown and they met at Bartleby's on Friday nights for drinks. Despite their jobs and their regular paychecks, they'd still thought of university as their natural state in those days, something they'd be back to after a year or so. They'd mixed the post-mortem of the workday with topics that bled in from books they'd read two or three years before: arguments about Doris Lessing's politics; speculation about whether or not the grape boycott did any good; efforts to validate Berkeley's claim that the world didn't really exist anyway. Their jobs had seemed to be some sort of intermission before the next degree, though none of them ever did go back to school.

Shirley was the one who used to drink boilermakers (some people called them depth charges), a shot glass of Scotch dropped into a glass of draft. She used to order just one to start the evening, then switch to straight beer after that. The three women had adopted their collective nickname partly in reference to Shirley's preference in drinks and partly as the result of a fiction they practised on overly friendly men who interrupted their conversations at the corner table, trollers who would send them drinks, wave across the bar, eventually wade over and try to wedge themselves in on spare chairs, sometimes leaning in to put a startling hand, sweat-moist, warm, and uninvited on a shoulder or a back or a breast. Usually, the three women would create what they referred to as a "force field" made up of cold shoulders and disparaging looks. Sometimes, though, they'd let things go as far as introductions, further even, pulling fictional names for themselves out of the air, then struggling to remember what to call each other for as long as the game went on. The masquerade spilled over into occupations, always the same field for all three. We're all typesetters, Candace had told their new acquaintances one night. To another threesome they had announced themselves as schoolteachers, and on another night they spoke only French, not very well but it hadn't seemed to matter. They struck on their favourite identity when Candace, who'd once had a summer job doing invoices for a plumbing and heating company, looked at the shot glass nestled in the bottom of Shirley's empty beer mug and told the man next to her that the three of them were station-ary steam engineers. Across the table Shirley laughed and said, "Boilermakers." Evelyn had even kept, for a few months, the bar napkin on which Candace had drawn a smudgy, ballpoint diagram of a water-tube boiler, the hot water in the inside pipe waiting to turn to steam, sur-rounded by a cylinder of hot gas. She'd tacked the napkin to her bulletin board at the insurance office where she was working at the time. A conversation piece, she'd thought, but no one had ever asked about it, no one ever wondered aloud at the scribbled words "critical point" and "change of state."

EVELYN SURVEYED the other customers in Greenwood's: three suits at a table close to the bar, shadows from the cardboard reindeer moving across their faces; not far from them a group of four women, all with hair that looked meticulously arranged but not at all stylish; three more men in the corner, younger by several years than Evelyn and her companions. Together the three younger men wore more items of black clothing than Evelyn had seen at some funerals. "Do you think we'll need a force field in here?" she said to Candace and Shirley.

"No need to worry about that," Candace said. "Those days are gone. We're not exactly babes."

"And what makes you say that?" Shirley asked.

"She's right, Shirley," said Evelyn. "I think, by definition, someone who comes into a bar with a brown paper shopping bag containing homemade cookies cannot be a babe. Nor, by extension, can the women who accept delivery of the cookies."

THEY BECKONED the waiter over, ordered beer and the biggest plate of all-dressed nachos the place had to offer, and started up a scattered conversation that ricocheted among must-see movies, Christmas lists (their own and others'), ought-to-read novels, where to get a good haircut these days, and where's a good consignment clothing store.

Though the number of their get-togethers had tapered off each year, they'd managed to coast on the intimacy they'd banked in the past. They'd held on, at least until now, to the ease with which they'd always told each other the complications, small and large, that knotted up their lives. So why, Evelyn asked herself during a lull in the conversation, after she'd been sitting with the other two for close to an hour – moving her hands from her elbows to her chin to the table and back again to keep them from wandering to her breasts, even sitting with her fingers tucked under her thighs for a short while – why was she keeping her recent scare to herself? An experience like hers should have been one of the first things to talk about. Shirley and Candace would want to know the details, in case they found themselves in the same position. The offhand manner of the radiology technician as she explained the need to flatten each breast to a fraction of its natural diameter; the sign taped to the wall in the waiting room: *We compress because we care*; the gel on Evelyn's breast before the ultrasound, cooling the skin so that one side of her body felt at odds with the other. Nothing macabre in talking about any of it now that it's done, now that everything is tickety-boo, thank you very much.

EVELYN PICKED UP the round black ashtray, turned it upside down and absent-mindedly drummed on it with her fingers.

"We need some smokes," Candace said. She took the ashtray from underneath Evelyn's fingers and spun it the way a child spins a coin. The three of them watched it clatter to a stop on the arborite table. Smoking was something that went with the occasion on these visits. All three had given up serious smoking years ago, but their grouping shared too much history associated with tobacco to be ignored. "It's okay," Candace would remind them from time to time, "we only use it for ceremonial purposes now."

"We could probably buy some singles from one of

the P-I-Bs over there," Evelyn said.

"P-I-Bs? What's that mean?" Shirley said.

"Persons-in-black," said the waiter who'd stopped at their table to pick up empties. Adjusting his stance to reach across the table, he bumped Shirley's shopping bag with his foot. "Sorry. What's in the bag? Hope I didn't hurt anything."

"Just cookies, I'm sure they're fine."

"Cookies?"

"I made them for my friends here," Shirley said. "Two dozen each. I like to make a lot all at once. Economies of scale, very practical. Simplify life."

Not so practical for me, Evelyn thought. Two dozen cookies for one woman (single at thirty-five). She fixed her eyes on her nearly empty beer glass. What made Shirley think that this buzz-cut, white-shirted young man cared about her personal philosophy of baking?

Simplify life. Economies of scale. The ideas of economy and simplicity had never sat easily with Evelyn. Life isn't simple, it's a bloody maze. And what do you end up missing when you try to make it something else?

Weren't other people, these two friends for instance, almost deafened by all the thoughts that can fit into a head at once, like a whole flock of waxwings in a single tree? All that noise and flutter. Was Shirley's mind always as uncluttered as it seemed to be, tidied away under her smooth, obedient hairstyle? Did she ever wonder what she was supposed to do next, or was it always clear as a list, large and small items all together: meet with the kids' teachers, let the birth control prescription lapse, visit Mom? And did someone like Candace, so apparently commonsensical, ever think of going back to school and taking up some new field of study on a whim? Linguistics or architecture or printmaking? Small motor repairs? Did she ever walk into the booth on election day and wish she could vote for all of the candidates at once?

For Evelyn the noise and flutter inside her mind had intensified to even a more frenzied pitch than usual during this past week, during the days of doctoring and the nights of soothsaying, when it seemed the only way to attend to all the necessary thoughts was to think six or eight of them all at once. What if this, what if that? What if something inconceivable? And what would that be anyway?

"BRING US ANOTHER ROUND," Shirley said to the waiter. "We'll leave you a cookie with your tip." He smiled.

"Better yet," Candace said, "you can have one right now if you can score us three cigarettes somewhere. We'll pay."

"Cigarette machine's in the corner," the waiter told her.

"We just want three," Shirley said to the waiter.

"What about your economies of scale?" he asked, but he delivered three Player's Light to the table when he came back with their drinks.

"How much for the smokes?" Evelyn said.

"Never mind. Merry Christmas."

Evelyn used the cocktail napkin she'd been twisting around the fingers of her left hand to wipe at a splash of salsa on her shirt. She gave up, realizing the mess was too much for the tool in hand. Never mind. She took a breath, let it out, smiled at Shirley. "What kind of cookies did you bring? Let's see them."

"Sugar cookies, gingerbread men, oat squares." Shirley leaned down and reached her long thin arm into her shopping bag to retrieve a foil-wrapped bundle. She shimmied the ribbon off one end of the package and unfolded the foil to display green-sugared trees and red-sugared bells and gingerbread men with icing for britches and silver dragées for eyes. "Sorry, Evelyn, I leave the sophisticated stuff to you. Barry and the girls won't eat anything they don't recognize."

In her own small kitchen, Evelyn made a point of experimenting. She'd left sugar cookies and oat squares behind with all the rest of adolescence; she associated even their aroma with the school bus trip to Ripley every second Friday morning when she and the other Flat Hill students trooped into someone else's school, girls to the home ec labs, boys to the shop. In Evelyn's current apartment, seventy-odd cookbooks were ranged along the black steel shelves, evidence of an addiction she found impossible to curb, especially working in a bookstore. She had hundreds of other books as well, going right back to first-year university texts for math and psychology and sociology. Couldn't part with them.

University had been something she'd gotten around to late, started a classics degree when she was five years older than everyone in the seats around her, often thought she valued the whole experience more highly than the others in her classes because she'd earned her own living all the way through school.

Life was, after all, about making yourself up as you went along. You couldn't say it was a lesson she'd learned early – in fact she'd been quite slow in that regard. When she thought about it now, it appalled her that it had taken her years of fidgeting, looking after her wheelchair-bound father in Flat Hill, to realize that she could actually leave home and the world wouldn't fall apart. Running away from home at twenty-one was one of the first real choices she'd ever made. She'd followed it with other acts of self-creation, making up a city-self from what she'd seen around her. How to ride the buses, find a job, get a better apartment; where to shop, now that there appeared to be so much choice. Gradually, she'd invented herself as a member of the middle class. Learned what to read; what to eat and drink; how to cook a catalogue of foods that required her to master new rules of pronunciation; where to get the news and how to talk about it as if her opinion mattered; how to replace four-letter words with euphemisms. How to stifle, usually, the nursery rhymes that used to run through her head in mockery of both her surroundings and herself: *sugar and spice and everything nice and that's what little girls are made of*.

And now, this past week, she'd found herself still making up Evelyn as she went along. In bed before sleep, she'd sorted through the index in her mind for a blueprint she could copy, instructions for how to deal with cancer at an early age. She remembered a movie, *Terms of Endearment*. If Debra Winger could manage cancer, why not Evelyn? In the movie, Winger's character died. Good for half a box of kleenex. Evelyn had watched it on video with a friend who worked in the lab at the Plains Hospital. "Women who are dying of cancer," Evelyn's friend had said, "don't look anything like that near the end."

Four nights in a row, Evelyn's mind had raced ahead, sized up the range of conceivable morbid outcomes, questioned whether or not she'd be equal to them. And now it all seemed so silly. Imagine becoming that alarmed over such a routine occurrence. An everyday lump, large as a peach pit or small as a pea, nestled inside her tissues. Doctors come across them all the time.

THE NEARLY EMPTY NACHO PLATE sat on the table, strewn with chip splinters, bits of black olive, crumbs of ground beef, and swirls of cheese. Beside it, open like a small boat, was the foil package holding its festive assortment of cookies. The three cigarettes, untouched as yet, threatened to roll onto the carpet each time one of the women set down her drink and rocked the unstable table. Commenting that they'd had enough of that, Candace tore a corner off the foil, crumpled it, and leaned down to wedge it underneath the shortest table leg to steady it. She passed the cigarettes around and, striking a match from the book the waiter had left, offered the others a light.

"Good thing my kids can't see me," Shirley said, exhaling. "Or my Brownie troop."

"You and Brownies," Candace said. "What do you do with a roomful of girls that age?"

"There's lots you can do," Shirley said. "Sing songs, thread popcorn, play games – there's one they like called string-along."

"Is that the game where you take turns making up a story?" Candace said.

"That's the one. The girls love it," said Shirley. "They like the way I always throw a twist into the plot."

Evelyn stared at the smoke curling off the end of her

cigarette. As a girl, she hadn't been a Brownie. There were no Brownies in Flat Hill; instead, there were Explorer and CGIT groups run by the United Church. From these, Evelyn remembered Anonymous Good Deeds, mosquito-plagued hikes along country roads, craft projects featuring salmon tins and macaroni, and one particular, rollicking song, the chorus of which still skipped through her head once in a while:

> *So high, you can't get over it,*
> *So low, you can't get under it,*
> *So wide, you can't get around it –*
> *Gotta go through the door.*

Feeling queasy, her body reacting to the invasion of smoke after only two drags, Evelyn stubbed out her cigarette. "How do you play this story game?" she asked.

"You take a ball of string that has knots tied along it at different places," Shirley said. "One person starts telling a story and unwinding the string at the same time. When they come to a knot, it's the next person's turn to take up the story."

"We could play it now." Evelyn said, and lifted her glass in a toast to her own idea.

Candace looked at her, reinforced a loose hair clip with her small hand, unhooked a tiny earring shaped like a Christmas tree, and fiddled at an irritated earlobe. "I suppose," she said.

"Come on," Evelyn said. "All clubs have games. And we're a club. We must be a club, we even have a name." She sipped her beer.

"I might still have the string," Shirley said. From

within her purse she produced a wad of white kitchen cord not much bigger than a golf ball. She freed the loose end from a comb it had tangled with. "It isn't much string," she said. "Those Brownies can't sustain a storyline for long. We'll have to be efficient." She dropped the ball in her lap. "Okay?" she said.

Candace gave a small shrug; Evelyn nodded.

"Here goes," Shirley said. She began pulling the loose end of the string slowly between her clamped thumb and forefinger.

"Once upon a time," she said, then paused. "Once upon a time there was a woman. Let's see…something about her…I'll say she was a muddled woman."

"Muddled how?" Candace asked.

"You know," Shirley said. "Off in all directions. She could never make up her mind about anything. This woman could see every side of every argument. She liked too many things, couldn't make decisions."

"For example?" Evelyn asked.

"Okay, an example," said Shirley. "Take the university question. She couldn't settle on an area. Liberal arts, or something more practical? Say, business admin, like our commerce grad here." Shirley looked over at Candace.

"A lot of good business administration did me," Candace said. "Three years selling gloves and watches and then a pink slip."

Shirley went on. "She couldn't decide, so she went back and forth, back and forth. Same with her personal life. Get married or not? Have children or not? Well, needless to say…oops, there's the first knot. Your turn, Candace."

Evelyn interrupted. "Is this supposed to be about

anyone in particular?" It didn't feel like a coincidence, Shirley inventing a person with a mind as crowded as Evelyn's own.

"God no, she's nobody. I made her up," Shirley said. "Well, actually, that's not quite true. She might be a little like I used to be. Years ago, but not any more. Let's just say she's pure fiction."

"Whatever you say," said Candace. "As long as she's made up, I can say anything I want about her. I say she's like the windsock in my back yard. Blows whichever way the wind blows." She looked at Shirley. Shirley shrugged. Evelyn held on to her elbows and stared at the table top. Candace kept pulling the string, using it up without adding anything but a long hmmmmm.

"Oh shit, no fair!" she said when a knot came up. "I never even got a chance."

Evelyn took the string. She leaned well back in her chair and the others had to sit forward to hear her. "How about I give her a name? I'll name our heroine Myriad, because there are so many sides to her." In for a dime, in for a dollar, Evelyn thought. If this person seemed like it could be herself, she might as well see where it took her. "She followed a series of…um…passions, one after another. Collected all the paraphernalia that went with each one along the way."

"Fine, fine," Candace said. "But remember how short the string is. We're using it up and nothing's actually *happened* yet. Make something happen." She tapped her small fingers on the table.

Evelyn rolled her eyes, then smiled to keep things light. She twisted the string around her finger, let go of it, twisted it again. She looked for a way to piggyback the events of the past week onto Myriad's story. "Let's give Myriad a bad dream." She hesitated. "Do you ever have wild dreams?" she asked the others.

"All the time," Candace said. "I try to forget them."

Evelyn had had a series of bizarre dreams this week. Dreams to do with being at sea, dreams to do with men she hardly knew, dreams to do with outdoor picnics on windswept knolls. She'd even had a version of the dream they use in the movies, the one where a person is lost in the mist, running and running. Evelyn had never had a mist dream before.

"Are you going anywhere with this?" Candace said.

Evelyn didn't answer immediately. She didn't want to talk about nightmares with these two after all. Finally she said, "Forget the dream, let's think of something else…. Myriad decided she would be…um…an artist. She bought canvases, big ones, and gesso and acrylics and oils and thinners and sable brushes." Evelyn dropped the string to sweep an imaginary paintbrush through the air, then retrieved it. "But then she got interested in something new. The next month – " But there was the knot.

Looking up, Evelyn saw one of the young, black-clad men making his way back to his table from the bathroom. When he saw the cookies on their table, he did a double take and started to detour.

"Incoming," Evelyn said to Candace and Shirley as he approached. "Want a cookie?" she asked him when he slowed down as he passed their table.

A friendly smile broke between his moustache and his goatee. "Sure, as long as you're offering." He looked toward his table. "What about my friends?"

"Take three," Shirley said. He started to reach out, paused to look at the assortment for a moment.

"Better take all the same kind," Candace said. "Prevent an argument over who gets what."

He made off with three gingerbread men and Evelyn pictured the three men biting off heads and arms and washing them down with Scotch. Surrendering to an impulse, she picked up one of the remaining gingerbread men, ran him, puppet-like, along the edge of table, and squealed, "Run, run, as fast as you can, you can't catch me, I'm the gingerbread man!"

The other two exchanged a look – a look that, it seemed to Evelyn, they hadn't had to pause to think about beforehand. Was this new? Had she ever seen it before? She honestly couldn't say.

"What?" she said, looking from one to the other. Shirley darted her eyes to the people at nearby tables, Candace played with the fringe of her plaid scarf.

"It just was a little loud, Evelyn," Candace said quietly, her cheeks unnaturally pink.

Looking beyond their immediate table, Evelyn saw that the bar was considerably more populated than it had been when they came in, and that, in fact, two couples at the next table were looking directly at her. But weren't you supposed to laugh about things like that, not tell someone to shush? Wasn't that what they always did? Weren't they, in the first place, sitting here playing a children's game?

"My turn," Shirley said quickly, taking the string from Evelyn's lap. "I know what's next. Myriad gave up painting and took up candy making. If she did well, she thought, she could quit her job as a…clerk at a music store. If she's good enough in the bonbon business, she can get rich selling sweets. The next month it was something else altogether, say sewing." She left the string hanging for a second, then said, "But enough of that. Candace wants some action here, I can tell by the look on her face. It's time for one of my famous plot twists. Ready?"

Shirley's voice dropped a note or two. "Myriad disappeared under mysterious circumstances one day. After her disappearance, her friend came with a detective to check the apartment.

"Too sudden?" Shirley asked the others. "Don't worry, you'll catch up.... In the spare room they found a stainless steel table, the kind with a built-in heating coil for making candy. There was a sewing machine on top of the table. And in the storage room, there was a camera and a tripod and a photo enlarger. Chemicals too, and trays, stacked on top of textbooks from Myriad's philosophy period. Behind all these was a four-foot-square canvas, half-painted."

Shirley stopped pulling the string for a moment. Then, "Okay, I know," she said, and moved the string along again. "When they slid the canvas aside, they found candles and crystals and books about women's spirituality, Gaia and that sort of thing.

"The detective looked at them and shook his head. 'Occult,' he said.

"'Naw,' the friend told him. 'It's just some reading she was into a few years ago. It's about the mother goddess, not the occult.'

"But he shook his head again and said, 'Wacky.'

"Okay – finally," Shirley said, coming to a knot. "Your turn, Candace."

"At least we're getting the beginning of a plot," Candace said. She sat up straighter and hooked an ankle around her chair leg. "Let's figure out why she disappeared. Obviously, this woman's crazy. A sane person doesn't spend her life bouncing around like that. Even you don't, Evelyn."

"Ouch. Be nice now." Evelyn knew this was supposed to be funny. She waved her hand as if to tell Candace to continue, but she couldn't help saying just a word or two more. "I've been known to commit to things. I've stuck with piano lessons for three years now. I've had the same job for five." It was as if the words, once dislodged, wouldn't stop spilling out. "All right, I didn't last long at the watercolour classes, but neither do most people. Reading is the only thing where you can accuse me of being really bad. Just because I'm always putting down one book to start another doesn't mean I can't stick to something if it's important."

"Whoah. I'm teasing," Candace said. "I didn't say *you're* crazy. I'd never say that, Evelyn. I said the story woman's crazy."

"I want to go back to why she disappeared," Shirley said.

Evelyn didn't speak, felt hot, resisted the temptation to defend her own defensiveness. It wasn't a good week for an argument.

THE DOCTOR, pressing gently on Evelyn's breast, had said to her, "Don't tell me where the lump is. Let's see if I can find it myself first." Then immediately, "There it is." In a rush of easy words, she'd told Evelyn there was no cause for concern just yet. Cysts are so common, it might be full of fluid, might be full of air. She'd felt things like this before – bigger even – that turned out to be nothing at all, disappeared within a few days.

"OKAY," SAID CANDACE. "How does someone like that drop out of sight? Let's give her a problem. Say she got fired a while ago and her unemployment money's about to run out. She needs a job. She goes –"

"Knot," said Evelyn. "My turn."

"No fair. I hardly got any air time."

Evelyn put her hand out. "That's because you move the string so fast." Evelyn pulled the string slowly between her thumb and forefinger. "So Myriad needs a job. She looks through her closet for something to wear to job interviews. Physically, she's trying on clothing, but mentally, she's trying on different jobs. It's not so different from the way she tries on ideas. She's elastic; she can stretch in any direction she chooses. Let's try receptionist. She could do that, she thinks: smile, modulate her voice, welcome people, screen calls."

Candace broke in, "How about dealing with this disappearance?" She rolled her hands like a child playing *This Old Man*. "We'll be out of string and all we'll have is your elastic person."

"Don't panic. It's very important what she's like." Evelyn smoothed the folds of her denim skirt and the others stretched to see over the table, as if there might be a picture of Myriad there on her lap. She took a deep breath. How could she put this? "She's a lot of things all

234

at the same time, like a jug with a narrow neck and a dozen flower stems in it. All the stems get hooked together at the narrowest part, so when you pull on one flower all the others come along."

Candace tapped the table. "I would like," she said, "to know what happens next. Are you sure there are knots in that string, Shirley?"

"Oh here, then. Shirley's turn," Evelyn said.

"I'll have that detective take Myriad's friend to the café," Shirley said, "where they can have coffee and chocolate-covered doughnuts. Like cops on TV. He's looking for clues, wants to know about all that stuff in the closet. The friend tells the detective that Myriad's always going off on some new thing.

"'Funny way to live,' the detective says."

Evelyn looked at Candace. Candace looked at Shirley. Shirley looked at the string as she unwound it. "So the friend said to him, 'Of course it was a funny way to live. I told Myriad once that a person has to pick something and stick with it. It got worse when she lost her job. Work was the only thing she had still tying her down to earth. When she didn't have that anymore, she lost her tether. Said she felt like a helium balloon cut loose.'

"Okay, Candace," Shirley said, offering up the string. "Give us an ending."

Candace set what was left of the ball of string in her lap. The several yards they'd already unwound trailed off her jeans and onto the floor. She didn't bother to uncoil the last bit as she spoke. "So we have the friend saying Myriad felt like a helium balloon. Light-headed, was the detective's assessment. He thought she should've sold some of that stuff in her closet when she lost her job. A person could live for a month on what she could get for the camera. Of course, the detective's offhand mention of the camera caused both him and Myriad's friend to drop their doughnuts, look meaningfully at each other, and rush back to the apartment."

Shirley sat forward. "Great!" she said. "Just like TV again. Clues in the photographs."

IN THE DOCTOR'S OFFICE, Evelyn had answered a series of clinical questions. No, she'd never breast-fed a baby, never even had a baby. The doctor made a note in her file. Family history? Yes, three of her aunts – a suddenly alarming number – had died of breast cancer, two maternal, one paternal. The doctor made another note. "And your mother?" she asked. No; years of severe arthritis, then died finally of pneumonia, in her thirties. But there had been a serious scare when Evelyn was a toddler. Evelyn could remember Auntie Lenore coming to stay while her mother went away to Regina. There'd been a biopsy, her aunt had told her years later, a nervous wait, and then a great deal of relief.

"You're in a high risk group," the doctor told Evelyn at the end of the office visit. "We'll book a mammogram." On the requisition form she wrote, "Mass in left breast." That's quite a word, Evelyn thought: Mass. On the lower half of the form, the doctor drew a cartoon map of a breast, a circle with a dot in the middle. She put an X in the upper left quadrant.

The mammogram had been inconclusive, but the

subsequent ultrasound had cleared her, for now at any rate. She'd walked out of the clinic into a bright and frosty afternoon, hadn't bothered to go to back to finish out the day at work, had chosen instead to do what she damn well pleased. Wrapped against the cold and wearing her forty-below boots, the ones that made her feel like a moonwalker, she'd made her way along the snowy paths in Wascana Park, taking in the winter landscape, struck by its sharp contrasts, by the way the bark of the trees and shrubs, red and gold and grey and near-black, stood out against the snow and the sky.

CANDACE DOWNED the last swallow of beer from her glass and said, "Let's see. When Myriad's friend got the film developed, she found pictures of Myriad in her apartment, and pictures of…a guy, a skinny guy with a long ponytail.

"'An old boyfriend from her home town,' the friend told the detective. 'He used to come out from Winnipeg to see her every few months.'"

"Now we're rolling," Shirley said. "Wrap it up."

Candace thought for a second. "Okay," she said, "here it is." Her voice sped up. "So they track down the fellow from the photographs and find out Myriad went to stay with him in Winnipeg for a few weeks to check out the job situation. You see? She's not so crazy after all, she just needs some stability." Candace stopped to draw a breath. "So in the end," she went on, "she finds a job, gets back together with the guy, and escapes a close call with insanity. End of story."

Candace sat back and looked at the other two. "Okay, so it isn't thrilling," she said. "But it does the job."

"No complaints here," Shirley said as she pulled the second foil package from her shopping bag. "At least it's an ending, and I have to get going."

"One more week to finish the Christmas shopping," Candace said as she redistributed cookies to top up the diminished contents of the package they'd opened. "Be glad you don't have to figure kids' toys into the budget this time of year, Evelyn. Are you at the bookstore tomorrow?"

"I'll be there. Overtime every night 'til the twenty-fourth." Such a normal conversation they were having. Should she break ranks with them, respond somehow to what had gone before? *Since you asked,* she might say, *I like who I am just fine. Do I scare you,* she might say, *do I make you jealous, or do I just embarrass you? Or is it simply that we have absolutely nothing in common anymore?* But no, she wasn't going to lose it in front of them. She reached for her jacket, then stopped. Looking from Shirley's face to Candace's, she said, "I need to tell you how I would have finished the story."

"Go ahead," Shirley said. "As long you're quick about it. I still have to make a run to the grocery store on the way home."

Evelyn sat awkwardly with her coat in her arms. "So the skinny guy comes to visit," she said, "and they're taking pictures of each other, he and Myriad, and Myriad starts to float up off the floor. In each new picture her feet are a few inches higher until finally, in the last picture, she's floating out the window. Like a helium balloon. Smiling. Nothing holding her."

Shirley leaned back in her chair and looked at Evelyn. "I can't see why she'd smile," she said. "She ought to be hollering. You know, shouting 'Help! Hold something up to me, a mop handle, anything! Pull me back down.' That's what I'd do. Clever ending, though. Put up your hand, everybody who thinks Evelyn's smart."

Evelyn refused to laugh at that. "But she's perfectly *happy* about flying out the window," she said.

Shirley folded her empty shopping bag and slid into her jacket. "Whatever," she said, smiling. She gathered her things. "I have to run." She leaned in to give each of them an awkward, across-the-table hug. "Don't be strangers."

The door closed behind Shirley. Candace got up to leave as well, but Evelyn said, "One second, I just need to visit the can."

"I'll wait."

Evelyn threaded her way among the crowded tables, wondering whether she should ask Candace to stay for a few minutes more. It might be easier to talk about doctors and mammograms and vulnerable breasts if there were just herself and one other person.

In the bathroom, none of the open stalls had a functioning lock. Not prepared to wait, she made do, sat on the toilet with one arm extended to ward off intrusions. After a moment someone came in and worked her way along the row, pushing at the doors of the stalls. Evelyn's door swung in and her thumb, absorbing the momentum, twisted at an unnatural angle.

"Ouch!" It hurt more than it should have, she could feel a burn in the tendons at her wrist.

"Oops, sorry, didn't know."

Evelyn took a long time washing her hands, running the water ice-cold, holding her sore wrist under the stream for as long as she could stand. She confronted her mirror image: had she always been the different one? When she was a girl in Flat Hill, had her girlfriends always thought of her as the odd one out, the brown-nose who did her homework faithfully, the girl without a mother, the girl who didn't slide into an early marriage as most of the other Flat Hill girls had?

Nonsense. Not so different then, not so different now. Shirley and Candace had been her friends for years. Maybe she had just been imagining that their three-way relationship had changed its shape. Maybe she was just insecure, stripped, her protective coverings unwrapped, layer by layer, during the recent days and nights of uncertainty.

She rubbed her hands together under the vent of the air dryer. It didn't matter, did it, where the change had happened, whether it had happened inside herself or inside the relationship? It didn't matter because, either way, the difference felt permanent, irreversible. She wouldn't go back and attempt a new conversation with Candace.

Turning the dryer vent upward, she moved her face in over the air current and fluffed her bangs, trying to force some body into them. She still wasn't sure about the auburn dye job. But then, neither had she been sure about the deep brown that had preceded it. Never mind, she was sure of other things. She punched the silver button on the dryer once more and moved her face this way and that in the warm air current, feeling the lightness of the warm air, imagining it could send her floating like the woman in the story. She felt an urgent need to be out of the bathroom, out of the bar, alone somewhere.

Back at the table she opened her backpack, a big, frayed bundle with a drawstring, and stowed her packet of cookies inside. "Thanks for waiting," she said to Candace.

"This thing's seen better days," Candace said fingering the frayed fabric at the base of Evelyn's pack.

"I know. I was thinking of ripping it apart and using it as a pattern to make myself a new one. They can't be too hard to make."

"Next thing you know you'll quit at the bookstore and go into business manufacturing backpacks," Candace said. Then she said, "Joke."

"Laughing," said Evelyn, following their traditional call and response pattern.

Outside they marvelled that it could be so dark so early, only five o'clock. The streetlights were on, the standards along this stretch of the block tricked out with green garlands that were wound around them like glittering feather boas. Evelyn and Candace hugged, patted each other's shoulders, wished each other happy holidays. Evelyn found herself holding on a second longer than necessary, patting Candace's back an extra time, looking for reassurance, in herself, in Candace, in the embrace, but feeling only a sad sharing, a sense of sliding from one stage of affection to another.

Stepping along the snowy, blue-shadowed sidewalk on the way to her bus stop, Evelyn rolled her shoulders as if she could physically shrug off the afternoon's gathering of anxieties. She ran a few steps, then slowed her pace, relaxed her mind and let it fill up with designs for homemade backpacks and shoulder bags. Something new, something new. She might stick with the idea and she might not, but that wasn't the thing to think about right now. The thing to think about right now was all the possibilities for creation: how she could find sturdy old draperies and sofa throws at the Salvation Army store and recycle the fabric; how she could stitch outside pockets in contrasting patterns onto the bags, how she could weight the ends of the drawstrings with chunky yellow beads from the necklace she broke last week and knew she'd never get around to putting back together.

WHAT WE ARE LEFT WITH

Two things stay with Lillian from the robbery the night before last. One is the stitch that fear has left in her stomach. The other is the purple pressure mark on the skin below her temple. She had pressed her cheek hard into the kitchen floor almost from the moment they ordered her to lie down until they left. She had borrowed steadiness from the floor, had used it to link herself to Howard who lay a few feet away from her.

The pressure mark has faded a little by now. Lillian leans toward the mirror and spreads makeup over the bruise. The purple turns grey.

Her daughter Joanie's reflection appears behind her in the bathroom mirror. "Don't wear black, Mom," she says. "Wear something cheerful. Yellow or green."

As soon as Lillian called yesterday morning, Joanie had closed Crystal Health Foods, left little Matthew with her roommate Carol, and driven over from Ripley.

Howard doesn't want her here. Told Lillian he could do without her quackery, her New Age hocus-pocus. Today, at Joanie's insistence, they will have a ceremony for the dog the robbers killed. She wants to free his soul, she says.

THE LINOLEUM, cool and steady against Lillian's cheek the night before last. The smell of Mr. Clean because she'd mopped up before they drove into town for Norm and Jean's anniversary party. Old linoleum, laid in 1965 when Joanie was learning to walk. Little baby shoes stepping over its printed roses and branches, scuffed patches on her white toes from all the early missteps.

Now a big black shoe, almost a boot – with yellow stitches all around where the upper meets the sole – is planted by the table leg. The girl wearing the boots half-sits on the table, half leans against it. Her other foot swings back and forth above the floor. Lillian cannot guess at what makes this girl with long brown hair and freckles like spilled cinnamon take to carrying a tire wrench. Or what makes this boy listen to her orders. These two are from some foreign world. You can't get there from here.

They are little more than children, really, these two who now tramp through the house and who have told them to lie down facing in different directions. Lillian cannot see Howard. She tries to send the memory of Joanie's white baby shoes to him through the floor. Wants to give him something to fill his mind and replace what is happening this moment. She raises her head to turn towards him.

"Don't move," the girl says. Barks. The way Pepper does when a stranger drives into the yard. There was no greeting from Pepper when Lillian and Howard drove up tonight. No damp nose breathing clouds onto the black vinyl of her purse, no front paws snagging her slacks. The farmyard so oddly quiet, the light from the living room windows throwing rectangles on the snow-dusted dogwoods and peonies. Howard and Lillian made for the house without a thought about danger because, even in their imaginations and even though there was no sign of Pepper, there would never be someone in their house who had no right to be there.

Lillian obeys the girl's command, presses her cheekbone down again. It is better after all not to meet Howard's eyes. If this is the end, then some things are better left unsaid. If not, there will be plenty of time to talk. Plenty of reason as well. Howard had no right to stand in front of a dozen people at the party for Norman and Jean's fortieth and declare that his daughter makes her living by stealing from people who don't know any better. Tricking them into paying good money in exchange for oily-looking pills and flavourless crackers.

But there may never be a chance to talk about that. Whatever this young girl and young boy plan to do to them, they will do. Lillian only hopes it won't hurt too much or too long. She's ready enough for the end, but she isn't ready for it to hurt.

"God damn, you're slow!" the girl shouts up the stairs to her partner. "Get down here."

A series of muffled bumps and curses and the boy stumbles down the stairs, through the hall, into the kitchen dragging a green garbage bag.

"So. What you got?" the girl asks him. Accuses him.

"Got a loonie collection," the boy says. His voice is

surprisingly deep for someone so young, but it cuts in and out like a radio with a loose wire. "And some stamps. Quite a few. Some necklaces and earrings and stuff."

"Stamps! What am I supposed to do with stamps? Not worth the space they take up in the bag. And a bunch of junk jewelry. This place doesn't have shit worth stealing. You don't have *shit* worth stealing!" she yells at the floor, at Howard, at Lillian.

So they have emptied Lillian's trinket box. The girl is right; they won't find anything they can get money for. Howard has never bought jewelry for her, isn't good at gift giving at all for that matter, doesn't know how to buy pretty presents, women's comforts, sweet smelling soaps and oils. Mostly he doesn't try. Sticks to kitchen gadgets. One Christmas, years ago, he'd gone out on a limb and bought her talcum powder. A big red shaker full of Old Spice. Didn't appear to know Old Spice was for men.

"That's the right stuff, isn't it? I got a feeling from the store lady I maybe bought the wrong thing."

"It's fine, Howard. It's fine."

Joanie, a teenager at the time, shifted beside Lillian on the sofa, shook her head, snatched the wrapping paper, squashed it into a ball. Threw it down and stomped off and shut herself in the bathroom.

"For after your bath, right?" Howard said to Lillian. "For your skin?"

"For after my bath."

SUPPOSE these robber children just leave them alone now, run away with their garbage bags full of worthless loot. Suppose she and Howard do not die here on the floor without ever looking at each other again. Suppose they go on for years? Housecleaning on Mondays, card game in town on Wednesdays, pub on Fridays, church on Sundays. Joanie checking in by phone every weekend. Howard waving away the receiver in Lillian's hand. Then surely they will have to finish the argument they were in the middle of when they drove up and saw the light shining from the windows and felt the quiet in the yard.

"Christ! The old man's up and croaked on us, Gertie!" The boy's radio voice cuts in and out. "He's kicked it!"

Oh Jesus, Oh Jesus. Lillian feels a rush of terror and soaks her slacks.

"No, he didn't," the girl says, calm as can be. "He's fainted, stupid. Seen it before."

"How do you know, Gertie? How do you know?"

"I said I seen it before," the girl says and her voice gets louder. "Seen it lots."

The girl walks over to where Howard lies. Her tread depresses the floor slightly, easing the pressure against Lillian's cheekbone for an instant with each step.

Maybe the girl wants to see for herself if Howard is dead. Maybe she will hold her finger under his nose to feel for breath. Maybe she just wants to pick up the wallet she told Howard to pull out of his pocket before he lay down, the wallet Lillian made for him on successive Thursday afternoons at Sixty Plus, stitching leather to leather, first punching a row of holes in each piece because of the way the hide resisted the needle. Lillian thinks of the tire wrench on the table and doesn't try to look at Howard or the girl.

After a moment the steps come closer to where Lillian lies. "Old lady's pissed her pants," the girl says. Lillian feels her muscles give again, feels her pants soak a little more. She clenches down there the way she used to for exercises after Joanie was born. Holds tight to steady every part of her insides. The muscles aren't as strong as she wants them to be.

The big black shoes walk over to the stove. Soon Lillian feels a tiny breeze and something flimsy settles over her backside. It's the tea towel she keeps tucked through the oven door handle.

"You don't like something, cover it up," the girl says. Lillian is glad of the towel. "Go get the VCR," the girl tells her partner.

"Now," she says, and her voice comes close to Lillian's ear. "Where the fuck's the good stuff?"

Joanie used to swear too. Went through a swearing phase that lasted years.

"There is none," Lillian says to the black shoe in front of her face. How does she know the shoe won't swing in and hit her nose any second?

JOANIE HAD OPENED her own present that Christmas, the talcum powder Christmas, and said, "I'm supposed to wear something you bought in Ripley at Wilson's f-ing *dime* store to school?" Lillian cannot even think the swear word inside her head. "It isn't enough that my parents are *ancient*," Joanie had said. "That they look like the fortrel *twins*, for Christ's sake. Now I'm supposed to wear a Wilson's f-ing *sweater?*"

But Joanie cleaned her mouth up somewhere along

248

the line. Joanie never went around terrorizing seniors. Joanie grew up and learned how to support herself properly – after the first few missteps. Joanie does just fine, in spite of what Howard says.

She has always been one surprise after another, Joanie has, starting with her appearance when Howard and Lillian were both almost thirty and thought children weren't going to come at all since they hadn't come yet. Then turning out to be smart as a whip but ignoring school in favour of boys by the time she was ten, and in favour of beer by the time she was fifteen. Running away in the middle of grade eleven to live with her wild cousins in Regina. Suddenly settling down five years ago over in Ripley and having her own child. Refusing to say who the father is.

"USELESS," the girl says to her partner. "Let's get the hell out of here."

Lillian is relieved and afraid. Relieved this will be over soon. Afraid they will hurt her. Afraid she will find out Howard is dead. Her ears hurt, as they often do. The ears are the children of the kidneys, Joanie has told her. The emotion associated with the kidneys is fear. Lillian has given in and agreed to let Joanie put her on a regime of special tea and tiny green pills for her ears.

Lillian closes her eyes. The floor shudders as the girl and the boy run outside and down the steps and away without closing the door. Cold air rushes in and settles around her. She hears a vehicle start behind the house. It sounds like a half-ton truck. She doesn't move until the sound is well out of the yard.

Howard doesn't stir, and Lillian crawls over to where he lies. When she nudges him, he comes to. Soon he is up, crossing the kitchen, closing the door, wiping his forehead, asking how long was he out and what did they do when he wasn't awake to know about it. His head shakes slowly and his eyes blink repeatedly. He moves toward the phone, but as Lillian stands and puts a hand on the table to support herself, he comes to her instead, takes her by the shoulders and says, "It's cold in here. Let's get you some dry clothes."

LILLIAN finishes her makeup and changes into a green dress for Joanie. She descends the stairs and the three of them sit and wait a few minutes in the living room. They look at their laps. They look out the window toward the shed. They look at each other. Howard's eyes are swollen, the way they have been for months. Lillian sees the grit in them each morning, as if the sandman has stayed all night.

Joanie tried, during a visit a few weeks ago, to convince Howard to forgo his habitual trip to the bar on Friday night. "The eyes are the children of the liver," she warned him. "If you harm your liver, you harm your eyes."

Howard silently folded the farm paper he'd been reading, set it on top of a stack of papers on the kitchen table, and walked toward the door without acknowledging that Joanie had spoken. He took his cap from its hook and prepared to leave.

"There's a kind of tea I can get for you," Joanie told him. "It would clean you from the inside out. You'd see better." Joanie doesn't know that Howard has a few beer on Tuesday nights too, sometimes on Wednesdays as well, and there's a bottle of whisky in the cupboard beside the television for when there's a game worth watching.

At the door, cap in hand, neck flushed, Howard turned. "You should be embarrassed!" he said, his voice louder with every word. "The crap you spout sometimes! I won't be drinking your goddamn magic tea."

Joanie remained where she was sitting, looked away from her father, moved the papers about on the table.

"Do you know what a fool you're making of yourself?" he yelled. "Do you know what people ask me at the pub? 'Has she met Shirley MacLaine yet?' they ask me! They know all about that stuff, they read magazines. They know wacky when they see it. They laugh at you. At me. They ask me if you're going to find yourself a husband in a bottle of magic pills."

"The emotion associated with the liver is anger," Joanie blurted out.

Matthew came into the kitchen spinning the propeller on a noisy toy helicopter. He held the toy up to his mother, who accepted it, held it in her left hand, and used her right hand to spin the blades for Matthew.

Howard slammed out the door.

TODAY HOWARD WEARS his coveralls and his frayed work jacket. He is only there to do the heavy work, to do what's required, he says. Not to be part of no funeral for no damn animal spirit. Very well, he has every right to be there on his own terms. As has Joanie, Lillian will remind him when the opportunity presents itself.

Lillian will wait until after Joanie leaves to talk to him about Tuesday night. It isn't the robbery that she wants to talk about, they've been all through that with the Mounties. Those two won't get far, the Mounties say. Amateurs. They've hit three houses and everyone knows what they look like.

No, Lillian wants to finish the argument the robbery interrupted.

She knows nothing is about to change between Howard and Joanie, even though they have been almost civil for the better part of two days. And nothing is about to change between herself and Howard, in spite of the fright that is still with them. They will argue this latest thing through, as they always do. When they are finished arguing their life will be the same mix of irritation and anger and public embarrassment it has been for years. The same mix of certainty and shared small rituals and the little ripple she still feels inside when he comes up behind her at the sink and lifts her hair as if they are still new together. Lays his cheek against her neck the way he did at the Legion Hall in 1954 when she was a bridesmaid in marigold tulle and he was the best man.

SNOW CRUNCHES UNDERFOOT as the three of them walk across the farmyard. Howard has dug the hole behind the old machinery shed. He had to keep a bonfire going for two hours yesterday to thaw the ground enough to dig. Now he drags the bulky tarp, with the rigid weight inside it, around the corner of the shed.

Joanie bends to pull the tarp away, but Howard stops her.

"Leave it," he says. "No need to look. We'll bury him like this."

Joanie steps back, looks steadily at the tarp, as if she can see Pepper's body by staring through the oiled canvas.

Howard uses his foot to nudge the body in its makeshift shroud gently into the hole. It is an awkward fit, the corpse frozen, the tarp stiff. He uses the shovel as a lever against the rim of the short grave to adjust first one end of the rigid bundle of bone and flesh, then the other.

Standing between the two of them, Lillian watches Joanie, who fixes her father now with the same hard stare she directed toward the tarp a moment ago. What, Lillian wants to know, does she see when she looks so hard? A man who will do what's required and nothing more? A man who helped his wife upstairs and into dry slacks two nights ago, both of them with hands that wouldn't be steadied? Joanie's gaze turns toward Lillian's own face, the right side, the side with the bruise. Lillian turns to meet her daughter's look straight on. What do you see? Two people who have nothing worth stuffing into a plastic bag and throwing into the back of a pickup truck?

Lillian sets her mouth against the cold and the sore at the corner of her lip burns. Joanie has supplied her with two-tone red capsules to treat the sore. The mouth is the child of the heart. The capsules taste like plastic on Lillian's tongue, but she takes one every day because who knows, maybe it will help. As she waits for Howard to fill the grave, she thinks of the hot tea she will make when they go back to the house. Real tea, orange pekoe, for Howard and Lillian; something else for Joanie if she insists. Cold fingers wrapped around warm cups to feel the heat.

MEMORABLE ACTS

Every plant in the back yard knows just where it wants to be this spring. The bachelor buttons have seeded themselves amongst the vegetables; volunteer tomatoes are pushing up between the peas; quack grass has stolen underneath the charred remains of the fence and now, with an enviable sense of direction, it's marching across the yard in the patches where the lawn grass is burned out.

Someone set fire to the garbage bin one night a couple of weeks ago. The grass wasn't the only thing in the way. The blaze jumped to the garage, then to the house, where it damaged the roof, scorched everything in the kitchen, burned a hole in the corner of the back bedroom I use as a studio. I'm staying with Harriet two doors down until the carpenters and painters finish. I come back here to my own place every day – to the garden, not the house. I yank out stray plants, hoe between rows, inspect tomatoes, demonstrate to myself that here, if nowhere else, I have some control over things. Some control.

The day after the fire, twelve-year-old Jason from down the block collected ninety-three dollars from people who drove by to look at the aftermath. Barely an adolescent, and already he has a sense of how to overturn misfortune, which is more than I can say for myself. The one-paragraph report in the newspaper gave the name of the street, so I suppose that's how people who like to see such things knew where to come looking. Jason stood at the curb under the leafy canopy of elm branches holding a felt-pen-and-cardboard sign: SEE THE BURNED OUT REMAINS, *Donations accepted*. He gave me the money, minus ten per cent for his time.

"I could've raised more, Kate," he said, "if you'd had a better fire." He pointed out to me that it didn't look like much from the street, and not everyone wanted to park and walk around the back to see the messiest part, the hole in the studio wall, the scorched shred of curtain trailing from the rod, the unfinished canvas on the easel, dirty with smoke.

"Too bad for them," I told him. "They miss out on the smell too." Does that smell, that sharpness of wet ash, ever go away?

I'll have to go through the kitchen, throw out all the food, start over with basics, buy flour and sugar, soup and cereal. I've already stuffed every stitch of clothing into my little car and delivered it to the cleaners, following the instructions of the insurance woman. I told them not to rush, I haven't got a house to bring my things back to. It's just luck that I didn't lose any finished canvases. Every piece I'm willing to expose to public view is either in the group show or in the back room at the gallery downtown waiting like an orphan to stand out from the rest and be taken home. I worked all winter, the hardest I've worked since my BFA show. Lived according to an erratic rhythm that drew comments from my neighbours, awake for days at a time, forgetting the hour on a couple of occasions and playing Elvis Costello too loud after midnight.

I approach the canvas as a puzzle to be solved, work with the space for its own sake, with no intent to imitate recognizable objects. I invent shapes, look at them long enough to guess what hues, what intensities they ought to have. Do they want to come forward or recede? Repeat themselves? Argue with each other? What colours do they want to sit alongside?

At least, I should say, that's been my approach until recently. It's the manner of working I was most attracted to in art school two decades ago. After I finished my bachelor's, I turned down a scholarship that would have gotten me started on a master's. Ran away to library school – afraid of art, of not being good enough, whatever that means. Afraid of starving too.

I made a late return to painting, bought a leave of absence away from my library job in order to convince myself I'm serious. Told the personnel office I'd be back in a year, told myself I wouldn't, fantasized I'd spend the rest of my life making art. Now I fear I've mortgaged my middle-aged life and my credit's unworthy. The big push for the show left me empty; there's nothing left to put on canvas. Even before the show, I'd lost feeling for the work, couldn't locate the energy on the canvas anymore, finished the last two pieces by force of will, without being fair to them. Pastiche with my own style as the referent. Utter dishonesty.

The real fright set in the day we hung the group show. There was Gerald, halfway up a stepladder in front of a canvas that was already in place, a wet brush in his hand, making last changes. He had that excitement, that force that seems to come from outside yourself and propel you forward in the race with the deadline. At home the next day, I walked from window to window inside my little house, staring out, feeling restless, unfinished. Gerald and the others would be crashing, I knew – they might not stand up to the easel for weeks or months – but I couldn't fall off a cliff that I'd never reached the edge of.

I tried to begin a new piece, started with cadmium red (medium) on my favourite wide brush and didn't know what to do next. Against my better judgement, against everything I knew about my own way of working, I wanted to see the whole piece in my mind before I could begin; I wanted to be the boss. And so I was; I was the boss of nothing.

IN THE BEGINNING, when I was a girl, I drew horses and fashion models, the way girls do. I copied eye-pleasing landscapes from the insurance company calendar, made pencil sketches of my own hands, drew portraits of my family and my best friend. Face-on, just the heads. Then I went to university. We trekked across campus one morning in a September drizzle, I and the other students in Drawing 101, to the gallery to view a retrospective of the work of David Kitts, professor emeritus. I remember the walk, the rain varnishing the yellow elm leaves, the smell of wet bark, the grass a soaking sponge. Inside, first the dark hallway, then the bright white room hung with rectangles of fighting colour fenced in by simple frames. Colours that struck and shouted and slapped at each other and tricked my retinas into projecting bleeding afterimages when I looked away. They made me uneasy.

I walked the circuit of the gallery, followed the artist right back to his beginnings. Once I'd seen it all, I wanted to go outside and paint whatever was in front of me, the water-shine on the yellow autumn leaves, the stone fence leading up to the gallery, the solid presence of buildings against the grey clouds. Real things. Standing near the door with the instructor, waiting for the others, I said, "I like his earlier work, the figures in charcoal, the landscapes."

The instructor was a graduate student, full of secret, elevated knowledge. "I'm not surprised you would say that," she said, looking at the art and not at me. "But it's the observation of a person who has no artistic vision."

When I think about that incident now, I pronounce her both right and wrong in my mind. Right about the fact that at that stage I hadn't the first sniff of what making art was about. Wrong about how to talk to students. We were both young.

I've thought about this at length, have concluded that, no, I didn't choose the style I adopted over the next few years simply out of a wish to meet the standards I thought the arbiters of taste demanded. I came to it with honest excitement, found in it a way to unlatch myself from the temptation to draw pretty pictures and have people admire my fine rendering of the world. And

I did feel a real energy in the whole process, in my attempts to find new ways of seeing, in my efforts to exert the power of art to take a person to an unfamiliar place. Always though, glinting at the periphery, if I'd just been willing to turn and look at it, was the question of whether the choice I'd made and the way I so strictly held myself to it, meant I'd too hastily closed myself off from other ways to make art.

Now that I've tried to begin again, I see I'm not as good at organizing statements out of form and colour as I used to tell myself I was. Even the fact that there's a modest abstract revival going on (I'm so old I'm back in style), even that doesn't help. These days, when I close my eyes, there is only dark. When I open them, I find myself staring and staring. Staring mostly at blank spaces on walls, trying without success to conjure up colour, pattern, vibration. What I see instead is detail. A crack, a nail hole, an irregular shadow thrown by something as puny as a rough patch in the paint.

I phoned downtown last week; the gallery's been quiet. I've considered registering with an office temp service or asking if they need help at the coffee shop on Avenue H. Can't go back to the library. New ways of seeing. Power of art. Who the hell did I think I was, anyway?

I HAVE A COTTAGE-STYLE bungalow on a short, angled street lined with houses similar to mine. Some are solid; some look to be slowly caving in on themselves. I know little about my neighbours' lives, can't guess how closely the look of each house matches the people who live inside, the way my fire-damaged walls mimic my own spent state of imagination. Harriet's the neighbour I know best, a poet who supports herself working banquets at the Park Town. She keeps hours that sometimes overlap with mine.

My fire was part of a pattern in Saskatoon this spring. Kids torching plastic neighbourhood garbage bins, creating blazes that melt the bins and catch any back fence within range before the hoses are trained on them. Houses are usually safe, but mine's built far enough back on the lot that the flames jumped to the roof of the ramshackle garage and made the short leap from there to the house.

The night of the fire, I woke to orange light bathing the wall of my room like a watercolour wash. Fantastic dreams are so common with me that it took a few minutes to convince myself I was awake. The certainty of the smell, the hot sting in my eyes, brought it home. A fire in the back alley, judging by the direction from which the orange light and the crackle came. I wasn't out the door yet before I heard the sirens. Someone who wakes more readily in an emergency than I do had called the fire department. I opened the door to flashing lights, saw smoke swelling around the side of the house. Yes, the fire must be in the alley. There went the yellow trucks, down to the corner and back toward the lane. Harriet ran toward me across the lawn, legs bare below her giant T-shirt, sleepy hair standing out around her head. "Get out of there! Get OUT!" she shouted.

I didn't see what was really happening until Harriet and I were on the main sidewalk. "My house, my house is on fire!" I said, talking to no one or anyone. Harriet took my hand and held it securely, without pressure, the way a parent holds a child's to cross a street.

The commotion had woken the neighbours. A group of them stood on the sidewalk across the street. The slight, nighttime breeze flapped the skirts of their robes, ruffled their nightgowns, played in the hair of children lifted in their parents' arms.

A cinder landed in front of our bare feet, Harriet's and mine, and we backed away. A firefighter in his over-large yellow pantsuit guided us across the street. I looked at my front door, still open the way I'd left it. There should be things I could rescue. What would be the most important? Photographs, sketches, paints, blank canvases, clothes, shoes, framed reproductions in the living room and hallway.

"You can stay with me," Harriet said.

TODAY Harriet comes by while I'm puttering in the garden. "Enough of this," she says. "The weeds can wait." She takes me back to her house, pours me wine even though it isn't noon yet. I don't object.

"I used to start little fires when I was a kid," I tell Harriet. "My friends and I did. In the pasture at the edge of town. We used to say there were little people in the grass. We burned their houses and undid their lives, sent them looking for new homes."

"I like fire too," Harriet says. "I've been thinking about it steadily since that night. I'm going to write about it. Fire poems. D'you mind?"

I shrug. "If life delivers a fire, you might as well use it." I take a drink, look into the lights inside my wine. I wish the fire could make me paint, the way it's giving Harriet new poems. I'm tempted, in fact, to blame my empty palette on the fire, to play the incineration metaphor as a handy excuse. Nothing doing, though. My brush and paint tubes and I had already finished what we were up to. The blaze was no more than a fiery punctuation that cauterized for good and all any remaining impulse to paint in the manner I'd been trying to paint.

"We'd make little piles of dry grass," I tell Harriet, going back to my childhood fires. "We burned out patches of pasture about the size of your coffee table and then stamped them out." I can still see the dry yellow stalks flaring up in blue-edged orange, then dying back to silvery black charcoal; can still smell the delicious, forbidden aroma of smoking straw. I swirl my wine so it slides up the sides of the glass, take a sniff, then drink.

IT'S A THREE-HOUR DRIVE to Flat Hill, but it seemed to go quickly this morning. I'm making the trip for the first time since my stepfather, Ginger, died ten years ago. My recent physical displacement has nudged me into my little green Chev and onto Number 16 East. The fire's disrupted my life the way the pyro experiments of my girlhood disrupted the lives of the imaginary people in the pasture grass. I suppose I'm looking for some solid, unchanging thing, some sense of stability.

There's the Department of Highways sign, white on green: Flat Hill. Then the painted billboard the town's put up, navy blue on white: "Welcome to Flat Hill, population 523." The number is significant – pass the five hundred mark and your village becomes, officially, a town. From the highway I see familiar landmarks, the first landmarks of my world: grain elevators – three now, not the five there used to be; the two-storey, beige brick schoolhouse; the infamous water tower, built to serve the railway but out of use for years now. The summer I finished grade eight, Stephen Parker drowned up in that tower. July 1, 1968, Canada's hundred-and-first birthday; the junior high boys were celebrating with a swim in a forbidden place. The other boys said they didn't even notice he was missing 'til they all climbed out and down the wooden ladder and Stephen's things were left over once everyone else got his clothes on. I can picture that shucked heap of fabric, obscure in the blue darkness, underwear on top of the pile, the last thing taken off.

What the boys said – that they didn't miss him until that moment – was hardly surprising. He was the quietest of the lot, kept a low profile. That fall when he should have started grade nine with me and the others, he was simply gone. There was no remarkable void, he just wasn't there, his absence noticed to the same extent, probably, that my departure was noticed when I left Flat Hill after high school. Simply gone. I was never one to commit memorable acts, never had a quick enough sense of what was called for in a given situation; instead I followed along after people who did appear to have such wisdom.

I'm still not one to perform memorable deeds; I'm still the one looking around, trying to hold events and actions and moving objects in check long enough for someone like me to have time to think things through.

If staring at things is what I do best, well then I should go with my strength, shouldn't I? Make it my job to pay attention to shadows and light, to texture and size and how things rub up against each other, and then make something as a result of all that staring.

Right. If I could just make it work, that is.

Not far from the water tower is the flat hill itself – the gentle rise with the shaved-off top that's responsible for the town's contrary name. The first hamlet of farmers and storekeepers near the site christened their settlement after this hummock. When the railway came through, the company tried to change the official name to Foster, but that name never took hold with the people who lived here at the time. They were used to what they were used to.

People love to make jokes about the place names in this province. There was a movie once, where Bob Hope or Bing Crosby – it was one of the two – got into a scrape and needed to come up with a string of nonsense words to fool people into thinking he was casting a spell. He twisted his lips for effect and said, "Saskatoon, Saskatchewan." It worked. It happens on TV too. If someone wants to name a ridiculous place she'll say, "Moose Jaw," and then laugh at her own cleverness. Moose Jaw, Smuts, Climax, Flat Hill. When I first moved to Saskatoon, I hated to say where I was from when I met someone new. I used to brace myself for the snicker. Even Keith, the man I lived with for two years a long time ago, even he laughed out loud when I said Flat Hill. He was from out of province, from Hamilton. He'd never heard the name before; we're not as well known as Moose Jaw.

Ginger, my stepfather, hated the name Flat Hill. A synonym for disappointment. A promise that wasn't necessarily broken, he said, just never kept. Like a person, I could say to him now if he were here, a person who says she'll do something, makes a few gestures in that direction, and then can't find the wherewithal to see it through.

Ginger was part of an aborted move in the early seventies to have the town officially adopt the name Foster, the name the railway had preferred. He took out a map during a town meeting, stood with it at the front of the Legion Hall, the print far too small for people to see, took his flat, white carpenter's pencil from behind his ear and circled the names that pleased him: Goodsoil, Success, Fortune, Pleasantdale. Those places were christened by people who knew what they were doing, he said. Mom, who backed Ginger on most things, didn't support him on this. She'd grown up calling the place Flat Hill and wasn't about to give it up. It was two ideas at once, she said, opposites together. "I can't say why," she told us, "but I like that." She raised her generous brown eyebrows in the way she had that seemed to pull up the corners of her mouth.

My opinion? I think you'd have to be an exaggerated optimist to call that hummock a hill. Barely enough height and slope for a good toboggan ride in the winter and, it seems from my grown-up-and-moved-away height, even more gentle a grade than it used to be. It must have been deposited, then leveled off by some vagary of glacial activity. Nature playing a prank. My sister Pen says we should all just lighten up and have a sense of humour about it. At the end of the day, I'm with the camp that says the name doesn't matter as long as it's a good place to live. And I'm not qualified to comment on whether it is or isn't. You'd have to ask the people who live here now.

I TURN INTO TOWN and pass the pasture where we practised small-time arson, pass the church, the school with its maple trees, the yellow bungalow with the clipped lawn where my first boyfriend lived. I need a cold drink, so I drive to Main Street and park. When I was a kid I rode my bike around town as if I owned the place. Now the town belongs to other kids. Three of them cycle by, turn their heads as they pass, give me and my car the once over. I'm parked in front of the grocery store and the hardware. These stores used to be Nichol's Red and White and Tredwell's Hardware. Now I see the grocery is an IGA and the hardware's allied with a new chain. Underneath the signs, though, they look much the same as they did years ago. Tall, wide windows, wooden siding, false fronts. I can't imagine being small enough to fit into the cranny between the two stores and eat a bag of jawbreakers, but we did it often enough when we were kids, Pen and I and our friend Lorie.

I slip out of the car and make directly for the lath of shadow between the stores. I can squeeze in, barely. Once in, I can hardly move. This slim space used to contain a whole world, a world where Lorie and Pen and I spent time with bags of candy, where we caught our breath after ditching someone we didn't want to be with, where we looked for and sometimes found stray dimes and nickels. Out of habit, my eyes sweep the ground for coins. No luck.

I emerge from between the stores and walk into the IGA. The woman behind the counter recognizes me. She's at least ten years younger than I am and her last name when she introduces herself is familiar, but not her face. She says I used to babysit her. She mentions what's happened to my family's former house as if I must already know: the couple who own it loaded it onto a flatbed last fall and hauled it out to the country. I'm rattled, strangely embarrassed not to know this; I ask questions. It's to be a bed and breakfast, part of an eco-tourism project at Little Brine Lake. The new owners – the people who bought it from the family Pen and I sold it to – spent the winter stripping woodwork and fitting the piano window and the front door with stained glass. A beautiful heritage house, the woman in the store says. They're hoping to open for July first.

When I leave the store, I turn left at the end of the block and drive to where the house should be. There's a messy, empty lot, a gaping, busted-up basement. Just that. No rooms, no doors, no closets, no nook under the stairs. I realize now that if the house were there, I'd knock on the door and ask to look around.

I KNOW WHERE TO GO. Grandma Mueller was a bird-watcher; she used to take me to Little Brine Lake every June. I follow the grid west of town a few miles, then slow the car and turn down a newly graded lane. The brush on either side dwindles and I see the house. It's on a rise some distance from the small lake, placed so the living room window will frame the view, placed to take advantage of the sunset. The directions are all wrong; that window faced north when the house was in town.

I park in the graveled lot, the only vehicle. I drove out here thinking I wanted to see the house, but it's almost unrecognizable. No longer slate grey, it's now pale yellow with white trim and lacy woodwork under the gables. I was asking too much of my house, wanting it to look the way it used to. Pen and I sorted and disposed of all the family things after Ginger died and before we sold the place. I can hardly remember what we did with it all. There's no white-painted iron bedstead in there for me now, no green arborite kitchen table, no familiar books on shelves where they've always lived, no chance of finding in the back of some closet a forgotten cache of drawings, or bubble gum cards worth ridiculous amounts of money in today's collectors' market, or third-place ribbons from a field meet. I suppose the old light fixture in the kitchen wouldn't have survived the renovation. I've never seen a similar one; it was a circular, fluorescent tube. Mom called it the family halo, the way it floated above us at mealtimes. I expect the new owners have replaced it with something more old-fashioned, something more fitting for a "heritage house."

Leaving the car, I take the path through the poplars and chokecherry bushes to the beach, where I slip off my sandals and walk across the sand. The beach is decorated with fragile deposits of dried salt, wandering lines and lacy patterns that break under my bare feet. Tiny, exoskeletal creatures crawl along the shore; I hear a trill but can't identify it; a yellowlegs rises off the beach; a sandpiper runs for a few yards and lifts off. Grandma would have known what type of sandpiper. These are the special birds we used to come to see – birds that migrate the length of two continents to nest in the high Arctic, stopping at saltwater bodies along the way to look for brine shrimp eggs and other familiar food.

There is a smell of wet sand and the marshy smell of grasses in shallow water; I can barely detect the salt that seemed so noticeable in the air when I was small. Grandma grew up in Maine; she was familiar with oceans. I asked her once if this was how the ocean smelled. She laughed and shook her head, *No Dear, not at all*. She leaned down then, tasted a handful of water, shook her head again. *No*.

This is Little Brine Lake and no amount of wishful thinking can make it the ocean, but the shorebirds find what they need here. I envy their automatic compasses, the magnetic maps in their brains that tell them where to go next, envy also the stamina that takes them from Patagonia to the Far North. I take a last deep breath and return to the car, stepping around milky-grey bird droppings. Tufts of dried grass poke out of the ground, salt bristling from them like hoarfrost. Back on the grid road, I meet a half-ton, probably the owners of the house. I could go back and ask to see it, but I don't.

I turn onto the highway and make for Saskatoon without driving through town again. Nothing here is the same as I remember, and why should it be? When I was small the place seemed sealed all around, a contained place. People from Flat Hill rarely traveled anywhere. When Jimmy Craig's grandpa died in Scotland and Jimmy's dad flew overseas to the funeral, his trip was the talk of the town; he showed slides at the Legion Hall after he came back. These days, miners and mechanics and storekeepers fly to Hawaii and Nashville and Las Vegas. Or to England or Norway or Ukraine, depending on their roots. Farmers make specially arranged trips to Egypt to learn about ancient grains and talk about dryland farming. The world is wider again, the way it was during the war; the way it was three or four generations ago when people funneled in here from all over Europe. And now there's ecotourism. People from who-knows-where will stoop under the sloping ceiling of my old room at the top of the house as they look out at the lake and the birds and the hot orange sunset.

I HEAD BACK to the short, angled street in Saskatoon that is home to me now. I didn't go to Flat Hill to gather a collection of images, but that's what the result has been. Afterimages of quite a different sort from the kind that appear when you turn your eyes away after gazing at a field of colour on a flat canvas. What did I go looking for? I wanted, I think, to fix myself. Not "fix" in the sense of "repair," not entirely. I wanted to be fixed in the sense of attaching myself to some permanent place. But there is no fixed place, there are only points of departure. All those visual ciphers that have moved into view – birds gliding above the lake, grass burning in a pasture, the sorry bundle of clothes in the dark at the foot of the water tower, the halo floating above my family – they are nothing more and nothing less than places from which to begin. What I need to know is where I'll end up – for a moment at least – if I follow one. Pick one, any one, I tell myself.

Find within it some emotion, some idea, some energy waiting to rattle a picture frame.

THE REPAIRS to my house won't be complete for a couple of days. I make a trip downtown and buy supplies because it's something to do. When I return to Harriet's, I spread my new things across the hardwood floor in her living room. I pick up heavy drawing paper, reach for instruments you'd find on any high school art supply list: HB pencils, oil sticks, conté crayons; a limited spectrum. I intend to start over with the basics, to begin simply.

I want to make a drawing about Little Brine Lake, want to draw the way a child would draw, hoping that artlessness will help me know what the important parts of the picture are. What things want to be large or small, which objects place themselves in the lower third and which in the upper left hand corner where a person begins on a page when learning to read. I think of the lake as a yellowlegs would see it from above – a living, blue magnet. I picture the tiny, exoskeletal creatures on the beach, the grasses around the lake, the trails of salt on the sand. I stare hard into the texture of the unreceptive drawing paper, halted by the puzzle of where in the space to locate the elements of the piece. Slow down, I try to tell myself, it isn't as if I can't rearrange it all later, cut it apart, recombine it, make it into something entirely different. Begin anywhere.

Ignoring my own advice, I go for an extended, late-afternoon walk, make a detour into my garden to pick a handful of parsley (the only thing I've grown that's ready to be consumed), then make a stop at the grocery store.

I arrive back at Harriet's with a load of leeks, carrots, zucchini, beans, tomatoes, and herbs. For an hour I scrub and peel, chop and slice, taking a momentary transfusion from the fresh, raw aromas. My mind fastens itself to the task, step by step; my hands delight in their purposefulness. By the time Harriet arrives at nine-thirty, a pot of minestrone simmers on the front burner.

TWO DAYS LATER I leave Harriet with a hug and a bottle of wine, and move back home to newly painted walls and a pristine studio. The barest reminder of smoke hangs in the air. My nose accustoms itself in seconds and I cease to notice the smell, can't find a hint of it moments later when I take a quick, deep inhalation to test for it.

I have yet to lay pastel or charcoal to paper. Gazing at the blank studio wall, I imagine the lacy deposits of dried salt on the sand at Little Brine Lake. The patterns echo the shape of the crocheted antimacassar that used to rest on the back of Grandma Mueller's armchair. I've no idea what happened to it after she died, but it seems to need to go on existing somewhere.

Still staring at the wall, I picture a sandpiper drawn in red-brown conté. It appears as a stylized compass, the sort you find on illuminated maps. Its needle-like beak points north, its wings spread east and west, its long legs trail behind, pointing south. I make several attempts on sketch paper, but dislike both the doing and the results. This isn't working. Perhaps it's the wrong idea altogether. I want this to be easy, want to see where to go and what to do next, the way a sandpiper finds the horizon by lifting itself into the air, or the way a twelve-year-old

sees immediately how to earn a few dollars from a neighbour's fire. But I've neither the instincts of a bird nor the
boldness of the boy who lives down the block. Better to
understand myself as a relative of those tiny, displaced
people I used to imagine in the burned-out grass.
Moving in circles through a jungle, seeing no further
than the next step, but trusting that somehow they will
find their way to the next place. Walking and walking
through the dense green blades.

ACKNOWLEDGEMENTS

HEARTFELT THANKS to my editor, Edna Alford, for her patience, her support, and her skill. Special thanks to Sandra Birdsell for her insight, support, and encouragement. Thanks are due also to the following mentors and teachers who've been important to my development as a writer over the past several years: Dave Margoshes, Judith Krause, Guy Vanderhaeghe, Janice Kulyk Keefer, and Elizabeth Harvor.

For reading drafts of several of these stories and providing helpful discussion and comment, thanks to Bev Brenna and Brenda Baker. Thanks also to Murray Fulton for his encouragement and support, and for being a good reader.

I acknowledge with thanks the support of the Canada Council. I am grateful to the Sagehill Writing Experience, the writer-in-residence program at the Saskatoon Public Library, and the University of Saskatchewan for creating opportunities for writers to develop their craft.

Some of these stories have been previously published. "Homemade Maps" aired on *Ambience*, CBC Saskatchewan. "Hard Frost" appeared in *The Fiddlehead*. An earlier version of "Edges" was published in *NeWest Review*. "What We Are Left With" appeared in *Prairie Fire*, where it won first prize in the short fiction competition. "Memorable Acts," (previously titled "Roadside Attractions") appeared in *Grain*, and was a finalist in The Writers' Union of Canada short prose competition for developing writers. Three stories, "What We Are Left With," "Air Masses," and "Passing On" appeared in *Coming Attractions* 98 from Oberon Press. "The Unrulies" received a Saskatchewan Writers Guild literary award.

LEONA THEIS was one of three writers featured in the 1998 edition of *Coming Attractions*, and has been cited in a number of award programs, including The Writers' Union of Canada short prose and *Prairie Fire* competitions.

Born in Bredenbury, Saskatchewan, Leona has lived in Saskatoon since 1973, with sabbaticals in Vancouver, Copenhagen, Perth, and Canberra. She obtained degrees in sociology and continuing education from the University of Saskatchewan, and has worked as a freelance editor, librarian, and adult education program developer.